'Oh...'

Something in Justi[n] beat faster. She sta[red] on a sigh.

'You...are kind, sir.'

'Kind?' Justin laughed, the devilment leaping up in his eyes. She was an innocent. How little she knew of men! 'No, mistress, do not deceive yourself. Had you been other than you are, I might have done my best to lie with you this very day.'

Annelise lowered her gaze, her heart racing. His words ought to make her angry. He had no right to say them to her...but, somehow, she did not mind.

Anne Herries lives in Cambridge but spends part of the winter in Spain, where she and her husband stay in a pretty resort nestled amid the hills that run from Malaga to Gibraltar. Miraflores means *see the flowers*, and there are lots of beautiful flowers to see. Gazing over a sparkling blue ocean, watching the sunbeams dance like silver confetti on the restless waves, Anne loves to dream up her stories of laughter, tears and romantic lovers. She is the author of over thirty published novels, thirteen of them for Harlequin Mills & Boon®.

SATAN'S MARK

Anne Herries

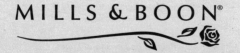

MILLS & BOON®

First published in Great Britain 2000
Harlequin Mills & Boon Limited,
Eton House, 18-24 Paradise Road, Richmond, Surrey TW9 1SR

© Anne Herries 2000

ISBN 0 263 82294 X

Set in Times Roman 10½ on 11½ pt.
04-0003-87406

Printed and bound in Spain
by Litografia Rosés S.A., Barcelona

Chapter One

Annelise paused to glance over her shoulder as she heard a burst of raucous laughter. Three men had come staggering out of the inn behind her, their arms about each other's shoulders; they were obviously in high good humour, seemingly the worse for strong drink as they laughed and shouted at some jest of their own.

Such behaviour was frowned on by her uncle and his friends—but these men were surely strangers?

Her heart raced wildly, nerves fluttering in sudden apprehension. They were Royalists! Cavaliers, soldiers, newly returned from wherever their wanderings had taken them these past years. She knew them by their extravagant manner of dressing, so different from her own much plainer garb, which was the simple gown and cap favoured by those of the Puritan persuasion.

The men were indulging in friendly horseplay, pushing each other as though they would fight a mock battle and creating a great deal of noise. They were obviously intoxicated, she thought, her face freezing into an expression of distaste as the tallest of them swept his hat off, making her an elegant bow; his action brought another burst of merriment from his companions.

'Have at it, Justin—the wench is worth the bedding, I'll vow.'

Annelise turned away, her cheeks flushed with annoyance as she realised the laughter concerned her this time. If this was how the new King's supporters meant to behave after their long exile, her uncle was right—England would soon return to the bad old ways!

Sir Hugh Featherstone had been a close friend of Oliver Cromwell long before he had become the Lord Protector. Sir Hugh and Cromwell had fought together in the wicked Civil War, which, her uncle maintained, King Charles I had inflicted on his people, and the great man's death had been truly mourned in the Featherstone house.

In her heart, Annelise had not really liked the Lord Protector, though she had respected him as she ought. She had found him a solemn, stern man, despite his kindness to her whenever they had met, and...

'Mistress Woodward.' The woman's cry brought her from her reverie. 'Pray wait a moment. I would have you carry a message to Lady Prudence.'

Annelise stopped at once, waiting for the woman to come up to her. She could hear the men laughing loudly just behind her, but refrained from looking back, suspecting that yet again some of their merriment might be on her account. She would not let them guess she had heard their wicked remarks about her person. Shame on them for their immodesty!

'Goodwife Hale,' she said with a smile as the woman arrived, puffing slightly from the effort. 'What may I do for you?'

Mistress Hale was the wife of the village parson, a good, devout woman, though somewhat dour and stout of person. Beneath her plain black gown, with its collar of white linen, her more than adequate figure bulged and struggled for freedom, so that she resembled nothing so much as a bag of turnips tied up in the middle.

'I wondered if…' Mistress Hale halted as the three men passed by on their way from the inn, one of them brushing his arm carelessly against her basket. 'Have a care, sir,' she cried, glaring at him. She crossed herself fearfully. 'Your kind are not welcome here. The mark of Satan is upon you.'

The Cavalier she had addressed could not hide his astonishment, for his carelessness had surely not warranted such a tirade. His brow creased, and for a moment Annelise thought he might strike the parson's wife, such anger was in his face.

He was a large man, with a florid complexion and narrow-set eyes. Annelise felt a shiver run down her spine. Mistress Hale was surely unwise to speak so harshly to such a man? He and his kind were in command now, and no one could yet be sure how King Charles II would behave towards the followers of the men who had so cruelly killed his father. Better to tread carefully, to avoid confrontation.

'Hell's bells!' the man muttered. 'May a man not walk in the street now without being accosted by a shrew? A sorry place these Puritans have made of our merry England. I've a mind to teach you better manners, witch!'

'Mistress Hale meant no harm,' Annelise said quickly as she saw the older woman's expression of indignation and feared a further outburst. 'She was but startled, sir.'

The man's dark eyes came to rest on her. Despite the plainness of her gown and headdress, nothing could deny the girl's beauty. Only a few wisps of golden hair showed beneath her linen cap, but her eyes were wide and clear, more grey than blue, her complexion so delicate and perfect that the man's jaw dropped.

'Come, Ralph,' another voice commanded. 'We have business, remember?'

It was the tall man, who had made Annelise a mocking bow. His words had a powerful effect on the man called Ralph. He nodded, some of the anger fading from his face.

'You are right as always, Justin,' he said. He bowed his

head to Annelise, a rueful twist to his lips. 'You are fair of
tongue and face, mistress—'tis a pity you wear the colours
of a crow.'

'Forgive him,' the second man said, causing Annelise to
look at him more closely.

She caught her breath. How attractive he was! He had
taken off his hat once more and his long dark hair shone
like the wing of a raven as it hung on his shoulders. His
eyes were very blue and at that moment seemed to be
laughing at some private jest all his own. She did not think
she had ever seen such a well-favoured man in her life, and
her heart had begun to beat very oddly.

How foolish! Annelise scolded herself mentally for her
thoughts. She had been taught to disregard the vanities of
life, and, though she had often rebelled inwardly at the
strictness of her uncle's rules, was accustomed to accepting
his word as law. She went to church every Sunday, morning
and night, listening to the long, dull sermons without complaint—and if she did smuggle a book of poems into her
bedchamber, to read by the light of her candle, there was
no harm in it. At least as long as her uncle did not discover
her fall from grace.

'I fear Ralph's manners have not been what they ought,'
the man went on, bringing her wandering thoughts back to
him. 'He was clumsy. But, though we have broken our
journey at yonder inn, we are not drunk on wine, only the
pleasure of being home again. Nor does poor Ralph carry
the mark of the devil, despite his looks, which, God knows,
do not favour him!'

Annelise sucked in her breath. Her eyes opened wide.
Was he insulting his companion? What would the man he
called Ralph say now? Her heart raced with a mixture of
apprehension and something else…something she was far
from understanding.

'Damn you, Justin!' Ralph said, glaring at him. His hand
rested on the hilt of his sword. 'I should call you out, knave

that you are—and I would if I did not know it to be use-less.'

Justin Rochefort laughed, his white teeth gleaming in the sunlight. He had the alertness and vitality of a man used to living by his wits—the look of a battle-hardened soldier. But when he laughed, his eyes crinkling at the corners, Annelise glimpsed another, very different character. There was a charm about him then that made her heart skip a beat.

'No, no, my friend, I beg you,' he said. 'Why should I kill the best companion I have ever known over a mere trifle? I do not mind your ugly face—but I fear you have distressed this lady.'

Suddenly both the other men laughed. 'Ralph is a clumsy bear as always,' the third and youngest said. He swept off his hat and made the ladies an elegant bow. 'Forgive us, ma'am, mistress. We have been remiss. I am Sir Robert Harris, the son of the late Sir Richard of Longton Hall, come to reclaim my inheritance—and my friends Colonel Ralph Saunders and—'

'Nay, nay, Rob,' Justin put in, cutting off his flow. 'We tarry overlong. Pray let us be on our way without more ado. Forgive us, ladies, we are already late.' He bowed to Annelise once more.

His will seemed to be the other two men's law. He turned away and they followed, laughing at some private jest as they mounted their horses and rode off.

'Well!' exclaimed Mistress Hale with a sour look after them. 'So that is Sir Richard's son. He was no more than a youth when his mother took him to France to join his father, after the estate was sequestered at the end of the war. I had heard his father had died, and that the estate had been restored to Sir Robert by the King. Much good may it do him!'

'It has stood empty for two years now, has it not?'

'Since Matthew Clarke died. God rest his soul!' Mistress

Hale crossed herself piously. 'He was a good man and kept the estate well...but after his wife and son died of a fever he had no will to live.'

Annelise nodded. Matthew Clarke had been her uncle's friend and a constant visitor to the house: she had liked him and his wife very well—indeed, there had once been a suggestion that the two families should be united by marriage, joining their estates as one. If David Clarke had not died, she might have been his wife even now—and waiting in fear to be cast out of her home! For no one could be sure what would happen now that the King had come back and the old order had been turned upside down.

Matthew Clarke had bought the estate fairly after it had been sequestered by Parliament, and perhaps it was best that he had died, leaving no heir, before all the wrangling began.

King Charles II had returned to England in May of that year, making a glorious entry into London and welcomed by people who had grown tired of the rigid rules laid down by Parliament and the Puritan faction, who had forbidden so many of the pleasures enjoyed by simple folk. Now that Charles was restored to the throne, there were many who lay abed at night and trembled. Some were in possession of estates taken from their rightful owners by dubious means, and could only wait to discover if they would be turned out by returning exiles. Others had paid good money for their land and were prepared to fight for their right of ownership.

Despite the outward rejoicing, England was still an uneasy land, with many still holding a grudge in their hearts and old hatreds simmering just beneath the surface. People spoke in whispers of godly men dragged out of their homes to face a beating or violent death, for many of those who had returned with His Majesty had come with a lust for vengeance against those who had caused their downfall.

Annelise was thoughtful as she left the village and began

to walk towards her home. The Woodward estate, since it had belonged to her father, was, she supposed, hers by right. Lord Henry Woodward had fought for the King, leaving his beloved wife and only child alone in the huge house the Woodwards had owned since the days of the Tudors, to be cared for by their faithful women and a few men who had been too weak to march to war.

Annelise had been little more than a babe when the war began. She vaguely recalled a man's laughing face as he kissed her and told her to mind her mother until he came home again, but though she'd wept when she had learned of his death at Naseby, she had not truly mourned him. How could she mourn a man she'd hardly known?

In truth, what she'd truly mourned, had she but known it, had been the absence of laughter in the house. Where there had been joy, music and happy faces, there was now only duty and solemn words. She had once been a merry child, a little naughty sometimes, but blessed with a sunny nature that made her truly loved. Over the years Annelise had come to accept the teachings of her uncle and aunt, but somehow in her heart she retained the core of joy that had been her birthright. Sometimes she rebelled against the doctrines forced on her and longed for that other life. Yet she could not but be grateful for her uncle's care of her.

When at last the war had ended, her father's estate might have gone the way of many others had her uncle not stepped in to help his sister. He had claimed his right to be Lady Woodward's protector—and, because he was a close friend of Oliver Cromwell, had been granted the stewardship of her husband's estate. He and his wife had come to live at Woodward House, and when Annelise's mother had gradually died of a broken heart had assumed the guardianship of his niece.

Annelise had never had reason to complain of her uncle's behaviour towards her. He was a stern man, but honest and fair in his judgements. Nothing had ever been said of her inheritance, but she supposed that would happen when negotiations for her marriage were begun. She knew her uncle had recently started to consider the idea again—indeed, had it not been for the Lord Protector's death in 1658, it would probably have been arranged long before this. She was almost twenty years of age, and more than old enough to be married.

Sir Hugh had been greatly affected by the Protector's death, which had followed that of Matthew Clarke by a few months, and was spending more and more time alone, reading from the Bible and neglecting the affairs of the estate. Annelise knew her aunt was worried about him, but there was nothing they could do—Sir Hugh had never been a man to take kindly to helpful suggestions from his wife.

Annelise frowned. She had not given much thought to marriage before this, but now found herself wondering what kind of a man her uncle would choose to be her husband. She hoped it would be someone she could like and trust.

For a moment the picture of a man's laughing eyes flashed into her mind, but she dismissed it at once. It was unlikely that her uncle would choose a follower of the King he despised. Besides, she could not wish for such an alliance. She had been taught to think ill of such men, though now and then she rebelled in her heart. Her own father had been one of them, and her dear mother had died of love for him, so they could not all be as evil as her uncle claimed, could they?

How wicked she was! No, no, she would not consider the idea for a moment; it could only bring unhappiness. A good, sober man of her uncle's choosing would surely make a comfortable companion and she would be a fool to ask more.

Indeed, she did not expect to meet the stranger again. She thrust the memory of his handsome face from her mind and hurried into the house to give Aunt Prudence the message from Mistress Hale.

* * *

'My God, Justin,' Ralph muttered as he threw himself down on an oak settle and took up the tankard of ale Robert's man had poured for him. 'This is a sorry homecoming for that young scamp. 'Pon my word, I never expected to find the estate so neglected.'

The two of them were alone in the parlour, the only comfortable room in the house, their host having gone off for a walk to cool his temper. Which, considering the neglect they had found, was perhaps the best thing Robert could have done.

'I dare say it is as well,' Justin remarked wryly. 'Had it been flourishing, Rob would have found himself fighting through the courts for possession.'

'As you must,' Ralph said, nodding. 'It is fortunate that you have not been idle these past years, my friend. At least you do not need to be a burden to your companions.'

Ralph Saunders had lost everything he had left behind. A devoted supporter of Charles I from the first, he had beggared himself by giving away his plate and gold in the King's cause. His house was in ruins after a fiercely resisted siege, and the land had been neglected so long it had gone wild. Due to the generosity of Justin he was not a pauper, but it irked him to live on another's charity.

'We may be able to do something about your house,' Justin said, frowning as he saw the flicker of anger in the other man's eyes. 'No, no, don't poker up like that, Ralph. I have more than enough for my needs. If your house can be restored, I shall lend you the money—and you may repay me at your leisure.'

'Damned good of you, but I don't like it,' Ralph muttered. 'The Black Boy has promised to give me a pension, but God knows when I shall get it—you know he is surrounded by petitioners on all sides.'

Justin smiled at the irreverent description of the King; those who had shared Charles's exile during his years of wandering had many a name for him.

'And it does not suit your pride to join them?' Justin mocked, the light of battle in his eyes. 'Well, my finicky friend, we must find you a rich heiress to marry.'

'Now don't start that again,' Ralph protested, throwing up his hands. 'No woman of fortune would take me—why should she? I'm damned near forty, too heavy, and set in my ways—and I never was a catch, even as a young man.'

'You wrong yourself,' Justin said, smiling at his companion of many years. 'You are no beauty, but you have a good heart. I am sure we can find you an honest widow, who will be willing to share both her fortune and her bed with you of a cold night.'

It was now that the character Annelise had glimpsed won through. To strangers, Justin might at times appear stern, distant, but to his friends he gave generously of both his money and his self.

Ralph scowled at him. 'Mock me if you will, wretch! If you were not such a damned fine swordsman I would call you out—speaking of which, what did you think of the Puritan wench? Now if she would glance my way, I might consider marriage. I have seldom seen such a beauty, even at the court of France.'

'You would compare her to Mademoiselle Dubonnet?' Justin asked with raised brows. 'Or the Comtesse Migonet? I thought her a pretty little sparrow but she cannot compare to Mirabelle Varennes.'

'Your *chère aimée*?' Ralph lifted an eyebrow. 'Few women can compare with her, Justin. She will be missing you. I dare swear she expected a proposal of marriage from you now that her period of mourning is over.'

Justin frowned, his eyes narrowing in thought. 'Yes, I imagine you are right. Mirabelle's temper will not have improved since we left Paris. I am not sure that I want to marry her, Ralph. She is beautiful, charming, sophisticated—everything a man could desire in a wife—and yet I hesitate. It was in my mind to ask her, but I was reminded that I had a duty here and I decided to settle that first.'

Ralph looked at him curiously. 'What are you going to do about that—the girl, I mean? Her father's will makes you her guardian and custodian of his estate, but it was meant to be your father who stood guardian, Justin. Woodward could not have known that the date he wrote out the document was two weeks after your father was killed—that he was in fact making you his daughter's guardian. You were not much more than a lad at the time.'

'If he had written down the third Marquis Saintjohn, the will would have become void,' Justin said, his brow furrowing. 'He must have written it in a desperate state, knowing he was dying, forgetting that my father was the third Marquis Saintjohn and that I would be the fourth. If he had made his wishes plain, I should not be in this awkward position. All reports of Featherstone say that he is an honest man—and was a true friend of Cromwell, who you know I admired, despite his misguided actions in regard to His Majesty's father.

'Had the will been clear, I should not have sought to interfere—but I feel obliged to at least make sure she is being properly cared for. The estate is hers by right. Her mother's brother has no claim to it, despite the stewardship granted by Parliament. If I chose to fight him through the courts, I should undoubtedly win.'

'But you are not sure you want to do that—is that not so?'

Justin took a turn about the room, glancing out of the window at the neglected drive. He had promised Robert help with restoring his estate. It would take weeks of hard work to bring this place back to its former state, and that time would give him an opportunity to look about him, to make discreet enquiries and discover what he could of Mistress Annelise Woodward and her guardian.

'I am thirty-four,' Justin said at last with a wry smile.

'Half my life has been spent abroad. I have made a fortune from a trade some would call piracy—though I sailed under the French flag and had a licence from the Crown—and now I am back in England I must fight to gain my rightful lands. If I am to have an heir I must marry soon. I have little time to dance attendance on a young girl. She has no husband. Her guardian has been remiss in this: he could surely have found someone to take her with an estate of that size?'

'She must be nineteen or twenty by now,' Ralph said. 'Not so very young. You could do worse than wed her yourself, especially if you seek an heir. At least you could be certain the child was yours, for she's hardly likely to have had a lover; these Puritans keep their women close.'

'She is probably as plain as a pikestaff,' Justin said, his sense of the ridiculous coming to his rescue. He chuckled deep in his throat. 'Indeed, she must be, or Featherstone would have matched her long ago. No, no, Ralph. Spare me that sorry fate, I beg you. If I marry, it will be to a lady of the court—a woman in her twenties, a widow, perhaps— who will understand my ways and give me a son without expecting me to love her. I have no time for courtship and pretty words.'

'You are asking much,' Ralph said, lifting his brows. 'Most women desire at least a show of tenderness. Even I know that!'

'Tenderness?' Justin arched his brows mockingly. 'I am not sure I know how to love, my friend. I have been too busy staying alive these last years to have time for tenderness. What do I know but fighting? I have been a mercenary and a privateer, taking comfort from a willing woman where I found it. Besides, what is love? My mother took lovers even before the war, while my father lived. Most women I have known are as inconstant as the moon.'

'Oh, ye foolish one!' It was Ralph's turn to mock now. 'I'll take a wager with you, Justin—one day you will find a woman who will show you what love is, and then you will fall hard. Believe me, you will suffer then. She will twist you round her dainty finger!'

'A hundred gold guineas says you're wrong,' Justin replied, mouth twitching at the corners. 'If I marry, it will be for a son and no more.'

'Where have you been?' Lady Featherstone asked as Annelise entered the parlour. 'I have been looking for you this past age.'

'What is the matter?' Annelise asked. She could see her aunt was really upset. 'What has happened to trouble you so, Aunt?'

'Your uncle has locked himself in his private room and will not come out,' Lady Featherstone replied. 'I have called to him, but he will not answer me and I know he is not well.'

'How do you know?'

'Master Blackwell told me he turned pale after reading a letter come this morning from London. Apparently, he cried out that the mark of Satan was come upon this house and rushed away to his sanctum, locking the door after him. He has since been heard to moan and cry out strange things.'

'What could have been in the letter?'

'I do not know, nor even who sent it,' Lady Featherstone said, shaking her head. 'Your uncle has never discussed his affairs with me. When I have tried to question him about…about his recent neglect of things, he has turned from me.' There was a catch in her voice. 'I do not know what is happening to him, Annelise. He seems…' Her eyes filled with tears. 'I worry about him. Sometimes I think he might be losing his mind.'

'Oh, no!' Annelise cried. 'Never say it, Aunt. It cannot be so. Let me go to him, let me talk to him…he may be recovered from his distress by now.'

'Yes, please do so,' Lady Featherstone said, looking relieved. 'He will sometimes listen to you.'

Her uncle had always been a cold, distant man, with strong views, but clear in his thinking and fair in his treatment of others. Annelise thought it unlikely her uncle really listened to her, though sometimes if he was in a good humour he would permit her to give him her opinion. He did not relish interference from either her or her aunt. Yet she must try to help him if he was ill.

What could have upset him so much?

She paused outside her uncle's door, knocking softly. 'May I come in, sir?'

There was silence for a moment, but just as she was about to knock again the door opened. Her uncle stood there, looking much as always. His thin lips parted in a smile.

'Yes, child—what may I do for you?'

'Are you well, sir? I heard that you had been unwell earlier.'

'Unwell?' He seemed surprised. 'Who told you such a tale? I am perfectly well. I have been busy working at my accounts and did not wish to be disturbed, that is all.' He stood back, indicating that she might enter.

'I am so relieved.' Annelise followed him into the rather dark room with its crowded shelves and heavy oaken table, at the end of which was a chair with a high back. It was here that her uncle had been working. She could see the rolls of parchment, his quills and the pewter inkwell. 'Is there anything I can do to help you, sir?'

'No, thank you, Niece. I have finished now. I believe everything is in order.' He hesitated, staring at her oddly. 'I have not taken as much care of your estate recently as I ought. I beg you will forgive me, Annelise.'

His apology surprised her. 'I am sure there is nothing to forgive,' she replied. 'You have been a good and faithful guardian to me.'

'And you would say as much to anyone?'

'Yes, indeed, sir.'

He smiled at her, reached out and patted her cheek. 'What a good child you are: the daughter your aunt was never able to have. You will always care for her, I hope?'

'Yes, of course, Uncle—and you.'

'Then perhaps all will be well,' he said, and turned away. 'Leave me now. I have much to think about.'

'Will you not come to the parlour for your dinner, sir?'

'No, I am not hungry—but your aunt may send in a warm posset when it suits her. I shall sit quietly by the fire and think… Yes, I must think of what is best to do for the future. Satan's mark must not fall on you or your aunt…'

'Satan's mark, sir?' Annelise felt a cold chill at the base of her neck. 'What can you mean?'

Something was different. It had happened in the space of a heartbeat. She sensed it and felt chilled. For a moment her uncle's eyes seemed to hold a strange glitter. He *was* ill! If not in body, in mind.

'There is evil all around us,' Sir Hugh said, a new wildness about him. 'When *he* died I felt it strike here.' He beat at his breast in anguish. 'There is no one to do God's work, no one to intercede for us. The evil has come back to this land—and the mark of Satan is upon us all. But I shall not let it fall on you. No, not if it costs me my life.'

Her uncle's eyes were looking far beyond her, searching for something. She saw him start, as if he saw what he feared, and then he began to shiver, his whole body shaking as with an ague.

'You are ill,' Annelise cried. She saw him clutch at himself, clearly in pain. 'Pray, let me help you…'

She tried to take hold of his arm, to lead him to the settle, but he threw her off, his eyes wild. She was frightened by his strange manner. What could be wrong with him?

'You are in danger,' he cried. 'Do not trust him, Annelise—the man who comes to claim you. He is the devil in disguise. Beware...beware the mark of Satan...'

Even as Annelise cried out for help, Sir Hugh's eyes rolled upwards and he fell forward against her. She could not hold him, and must have let him fall had his steward not come rushing into the room at that moment.

'Let me take him, mistress,' he said. 'I thought this would happen...I have seen it coming on, feared it.'

Annelise helped him to assist her uncle to the settle. It was clear that he had lost consciousness, though she could see that he still lived. She believed his illness was of the mind, brought on by grief and fear for the future.

'What do you mean?' she asked the steward. 'Has this happened before?'

'It was not so bad the last time,' he replied, looking grave and sad. 'But I see the hand of God in this, mistress. It is a warning. Unless Sir Hugh consents to seeing a physician, the next seizure may be the finish of him.'

Annelise moved away when her aunt came to take her place; servants were summoned and Sir Hugh was carried up to his chamber and laid on his bed.

What had he been trying to tell her? She was sure that he had been frightened for her sake—that he had been trying to warn her.

But of what?

Annelise snatched off her cap, allowing her long hair to flow freely on her shoulders; her silken tresses caught the sunlight through the trees. It felt so good, but she knew it was wrong. Both her aunt and uncle would have disapproved of her removing the headdress, because it was immodest for a woman to flaunt her beauty; it tempted men to sin and was frowned upon by the church.

She breathed deeply, lifting her face to the sky as she ran helter-skelter, heedless for once of propriety. How sweet the air was here in the woods, full of the scents of summer, and how glad she was to have escaped from the house at last.

For the past five days she had felt like a prisoner. Her uncle had been pronounced gravely ill, though he had come back to his senses a few hours after his seizure. It was then it had been discovered that his right arm and leg had been affected, leaving him partially paralysed. He was confined to bed, ordered to rest by the physician.

Annelise had naturally helped her aunt to nurse him, and she had been distressed by the change in Sir Hugh. He seemed to have aged overnight and was prone to fits of weeping. Worst of all had been the way he had clung to Annelise's hand and begged for forgiveness. She had tried to reassure him that he had done nothing that needed to be forgiven, but his mind was no longer as clear as it had been and he would not be comforted.

The sun was so warm, but beneath the canopy of leaves Annelise felt cool and refreshed. She began to sing as she danced, abandoning all restraint in the knowledge that she was alone. Her song was one of those she had learned at her mother's knee, a song of love and betrayal, a song that she would never have dared to sing in her uncle's hearing.

> *And so, my love, come lie with*
> *me…*
> *There beneath the apple tree…*
> *Give me, sweet, your own true*
> *lips,*
> *And I'll not press for…*

Hearing a sound behind her, Annelise swung round, conscious that she was being watched. Her song ceased abruptly as she saw the man. It was the Cavalier she had met in the village—the one with the mocking eyes! The one who had made her heart behave so oddly.

'Forgive me if I startled you, mistress. Your singing was

sweet. It is long since I listened to a maid singing in the woods.'

'You startled me, sir. I had not thought to see anyone here…' She blushed as she realised she was in fact trespassing: these woods belonged to Longton Hall. 'Master Clarke allowed me to come here and I had forgotten there was a new owner…' She faltered as his eyes narrowed. He was angry. What had she said to make him look like that?

'Say rather the rightful owner has come home. And none too soon, it seems, by what we have found here.'

'Master Clarke was a good steward for some years,' Annelise replied, eyes sparking at the criticism. 'He was a good man, a godly man—the neglect began only after his wife and David died of the fever. And he died soon after, so cannot be blamed for what you have found.'

'You are staunch in their defence,' Justin said, his eyes intent on her face. 'They were perhaps your friends, mistress?'

'They were neighbours and friends,' she replied, still on her mettle, her face proud, back stiff. 'Had David lived only a year or so longer, I might have been his wife.'

'Ah…I see why you defend Master Clarke.'

Justin nodded his understanding. At first he had not been sure that this enchanting creature was the little Puritan wench from the village. Without her cap to hide that hair she was indeed beautiful. Ralph had been right; she was well worth the bedding. A smile touched his mouth as he imagined her beneath him, her body naked as nature intended, her mouth soft, inviting his kiss. Her drab clothes belied the true nature of the wench. Beneath that veneer of modesty lay passion. He'd dare swear there was fire in her, though she no doubt did her best to quench it—perhaps not with her sweetheart, though.

'Master Clarke's son was your sweetheart, then. That is why you come here, to remember him and the delights of love he taught you here in some secret glade.' He moved towards her, feeling the desire stir in him. A surprising thing, since his tastes usually ran to more sophisticated ladies of the Court. She looked up, eyes wide and, to his mind, inviting. He reached out, touching her cheek, his thumb brushing over her mouth, tempted to kiss her. 'Perhaps you came looking for a lover today?'

'No, indeed you are wrong!' Annelise was horrified. Why was he looking at her so strangely? She stepped back hastily, her heart racing like the wind. How could he say such lewd, wicked things to her? 'You mistake the matter, sir. My uncle spoke of arranging a match—to unite our families and lands, that is all.'

'To unite…' Justin frowned as he was struck by a sudden thought. Robert's lands marched with those of Lord Woodward. Of course, why had he not realised at once? 'Are you by chance the niece of Sir Hugh Featherstone?'

'Yes.' She was puzzled by the immediate change in his expression; the hot, intense look had gone from his eyes and he seemed stunned. 'I am Annelise Woodward—do you know my uncle, sir?'

'I know of him,' Justin replied, his gaze narrowing. He was aware of frustration, of an unreasoning anger. 'I had not thought him a man to allow his niece to run wild. It is hardly proper for you to be wandering about in this manner, Mistress Woodward. You could be mistaken for…' He recollected himself. His own behaviour had been less than correct, but he had thought her a village girl. 'I should have expected a girl of your station to be more closely watched.'

How dared he suggest that she was a hoyden—or worse? Annelise glared at him, her wrath simmering.

'I have always been safe in these woods until today,' she said, temper suddenly flaring. 'Indeed, there were only godly people here—until you came with your friends, sir. My uncle knew me to be safe.'

'Indeed, mistress, I will bow to your uncle's superior knowledge.'

Justin smiled inwardly as he recovered from the shock. Damn it! He had come close to seducing his own ward; the knowledge that he had been on the verge of kissing her...of far more if she had been willing...shook him to the core. It was his duty to protect her, to challenge any who would dishonour or harm her—and to see her safely wed to a decent man.

Now that Justin had seen her, seen the beauty and the passion that lay beneath the surface, he knew that her marriage was a matter of urgency. Perhaps she had been safe in this place, but life in England was bound to change now that the old inhibitions had been swept away. The people had been repressed for so long that some were bound to fall into bad ways—he knew only too well the nature of men. He had taken his women where he'd found them, often on the ground, sheltered only by the warmth of a velvet night and a shared blanket. He was not the only soldier to have forgotten that a lady should be treated with tenderness and chivalry. And England would be awash with men who had lost their youth, lost all the finer feelings they had once had, together with their land and houses.

His next thought surprised him. This girl was too beautiful to be left to wither away in a tiny Cambridgeshire village. She should have the chance to live, to shine in the right surroundings—and it was his responsibility, his duty, to see that she had that chance.

She was turning away, her face reflecting the troubled nature of her thoughts. He had frightened her, distressed her. He did not want her to leave with harsh words unresolved between them.

'Stay a moment, mistress,' he said, catching at her sleeve. 'I meant no disrespect, nor did I intend to imply your uncle was at fault. I have been a soldier too long, and my manners leave much to be desired. If I have upset you, I apologise.'

Annelise hesitated. There was something about him that

attracted her, even when he made her angry. She sensed
the power of the man—a man who had seen too much of
war and killing. Yet there was a softer nature, an inner self
he kept hidden but which she had glimpsed when he'd
teased his friends. She thought she might like that other
man very well.

'There is no need for apology,' she said. 'It was my fault
for taking off my cap. You thought me something I was
not. It is only…that I needed some release. My uncle has
been confined to his sick bed these past five days and I
have been anxious. It was good to run wild for a moment,
to feel free…but it was not proper and I should not have
done it.'

The stubborn pride had gone from her lovely face, re-
placed by a look of shame. Justin felt a surge of anger at
himself and those who had trodden down her spirit, making
her believe that to live for pleasure was sin. He had scolded
her, but in truth why should she not enjoy her innocent
pleasures?

'You were not at fault, Mistress Woodward,' he said, and
now the softness in his voice sent little tremors down her
spine. 'But perhaps you ought not to come here alone in
future—for your own sake. There are men who might be
tempted beyond bearing by such loveliness as yours, men
who could not be trusted to behave as they ought.'

Annelise bent her head, her cheeks flaming. 'I have been
told…'

'Nay, I do not mean that you should hide your beauty,'
Justin said. 'I am not one of those who think beauty a sin,
indeed I revere and treasure it. I meant only that these are
dangerous times. For your safety I would have you bring a
servant with you, to protect you from those who might
harm you.'

'Oh…' Something in his look made her heart beat faster.
She stared up at him, her lips parting on a sigh. 'You…are
kind, sir.'

'Kind?' Justin laughed, the devilment leaping up in his eyes. She was an innocent. How little she knew of men! 'No, mistress, do not deceive yourself. Had you been other than you are, I might have done my best to lie with you this very day.'

Annelise lowered her gaze, her heart racing. His words ought to make her angry. He had no right to say them to her…but somehow she did not mind.

'I…I think you mock me, sir.'

'Oh, no, not you,' he replied, his lips twisting in a wry smile. 'Myself, perhaps—but not you.'

She looked up at him, the beginnings of confidence in her eyes. Justin drew in his breath. By God, she could be a charmer if she chose. She had been kept close, indoctrinated with a creed he found abhorrent—but what if she were shown another way to live?

His mind began to draw pictures. He saw her at Court, dressed in a gown more fitting to her beauty and station. He saw her beginning to emerge from her chrysalis, developing into the woman she could become—and he felt the laughter begin to bubble inside him.

How amusing it would be to turn this little Puritan into a lady of the Court. She was innocent, malleable—he could make of her what he wished. He imagined himself as her guardian, watching over her education. She could be anything he desired…the mistress of the King!

That was an idea to play with, Justin decided. It would put Barbara's nose out, and he had never cared for the shrewish temper of Mistress Palmer—or Lady Castlemaine as she was now known. She might think herself invincible and flaunt the honours her husband had received from His Majesty, but Charles was not a fool; soon he must see how avaricious his mistress was—and then he would surely look about him for a replacement. And why not Mistress Woodward?

Justin found the notion amusing. He would not make up

his mind just yet, but if this little beauty managed to catch Charles's interest, it could bring him favour at Court—and yet she surely deserved more.

It was his duty to see her well married. After that the game was all to play. Only a fool would expect fidelity from his wife—and most would be flattered if she were chosen to grace the King's bed.

'I should like to call on Sir Hugh soon,' Justin said, bowing his head to her. 'When will it be convenient for me to call?'

Annelise was uncertain. She did not quite like the way he was looking at her.

'I am not sure, sir. I could send word to Longton Hall if my uncle would like to see you—what name should I give him?'

'Justin Rochefort,' he replied. 'It is important that I speak to your uncle, mistress. Please ask him if he will see me as a matter of some urgency.'

'As you wish.'

Annelise hesitated. He had let go of her sleeve; she was free to go, but somehow she lingered. Though at times he seemed stern, there was a charm about him—something that made her want to know more of him, something that made her foolish heart leap like lambs in the spring.

'How long will you be staying here, sir?'

'Until my business is finished,' he said. 'After that, I shall be returning to London.' He looked at her again, taking her breath away. 'Have you ever been there, Mistress Woodward?'

'No…no, I have not. A visit was planned, but cancelled after the Lord Protector died.'

'Should you like to visit there?'

'Yes…I think so, but my uncle is too ill to travel and my aunt could not take me without him.'

'I have a house in London,' Justin said, surprising her.

'My mother lives there for the moment. Perhaps she would invite you to stay.'

'Why should she? She does not know me.'

'No,' Justin replied, a puzzling look in his eyes. 'But she knew your parents well. One day you will meet her. I am sure she would like to meet the daughter of old friends.'

'Your mother knew my father…my mother?' Annelise was filled with a sudden longing. 'Oh, if only I could meet her! I should like so much to hear what she remembers of my father. I was a small child when he was killed.'

'Then I shall do my best to arrange it,' Justin said, and his smile was so sweet that it reached out to her, seeming almost to embrace her. 'I shall walk with you to the grounds of your home, mistress—and then I must say farewell. But do not forget to mention me to your uncle.'

'No…' Annelise lifted her eyes to his. 'No, sir. I shall speak to him as soon as I feel he is well enough to listen…'

Chapter Two

'I am glad to see you so much better, sir,' Annelise said as she carried in the tray for her uncle's breakfast. He was sitting up in bed, looking brighter than he had for several days. 'My aunt told me you wished to see me. Is there anything I can do for you?'

'Put that tray down and come here, Niece.' Sir Hugh beckoned to her. His grey hair had been neatly combed that day and his man had shaved him. 'I have neglected your affairs, Annelise. I should have arranged a marriage for you long since. It was remiss of me—but I am resolved to put things right. I shall this day have my steward send a letter to a cousin of your aunt's. Mr Broughton is a good man, not yet forty, sober and clean in his habits. I believe we can trust him to take care of things when I am gone.'

'You are getting better,' Annelise said, gripped by a sudden fear she could not explain. 'There is no need for haste. I should not wish to marry while you are ill.'

'If it is God's wish, I shall be spared to see you safely wed,' he replied, giving her a compelling look. 'Have I ever treated you ill, Annelise? Have I ever forced you to something that gave you pain?'

She hesitated, then lowered her gaze. There had been

many times when her heart had rebelled, but that was because she was a woman and therefore sinful. Her uncle had sometimes been strict with her, disciplining her for the good of her soul. She knew she owed a duty both to him and to God.

'No, sir, you have not,' she said, 'but I would meet with this man first. If…if I am unable to respect him…'

'Then I would not force you to marry,' Sir Hugh said, gazing at her with reproach. 'How can you think I would marry you to an unworthy man? All I ask is that you will behave with modesty and keep an open mind. It is for your own good, Annelise. I shall not always be here to protect you. Besides, you are of an age to marry. You would not want to live alone? It would not be fitting. You need a good man to be your husband—and who better than a kinsman of your aunt?'

Annelise was silent. All that her uncle said made perfect sense. Indeed, she had expected this, even hoped for it. Her life had sometimes seemed dull. A husband and children would fill the hours that were occasionally empty…so why this reluctance to wed the unknown Mr Broughton?

It could not be because she had been unable to rid her mind these past days of the picture of a man's laughing eyes, could it? She would be foolish indeed to put her faith in his vague promises.

'I shall try to do my duty, Uncle—but I beg you not to make your decision before I have met Mr Broughton.'

'You are a sensible young woman,' he replied. 'I have no doubt that you will accept your duty, as we all must.'

'Yes, sir.' Annelise hesitated. She had not so far mentioned Master Rochefort's request to speak to her uncle for fear of upsetting him, but he was so much better. Surely it could do no harm? 'I told you that Sir Robert Harris had come back, did I not?'

'I dare say he has a right to claim the land,' Sir Hugh

said, frowning. 'We must hope he is a godly man—but his presence here makes your marriage all the more urgent.'

Annelise did not ask why. She knew his opinion of the King's followers all too well; he thought them disciples of the devil, sinful, lewd men. She had accepted his doctrine, but now she had begun to doubt. He was a good man, and she had been taught to obey, but she was an intelligent girl and her mind still questioned.

'There is a gentleman staying with Sir Robert, Uncle. He begs you will grant him an interview.'

'An interview?' Sir Hugh started up, clearly alarmed. 'Who is this man, Niece? When did he speak to you?'

Annelise glanced at her uncle's servant, who had been discreetly moving about the room all the time she was present; he ceased his tidying and looked at his master in concern.

'His name is Rochefort, sir,' Annelise said. 'I met him by chance three days since.'

'Met him? Where?'

Annelise was disturbed by the expression in his eyes. It was not the wild, unbalanced look she had seen there before his seizure but one of fear.

'In the wood,' she replied, dropping her gaze. 'I went for a walk and we met by chance. I knew him because he was in the village with Sir Robert the day I spoke with Goodwife Hale.'

'This man…' Sir Hugh's hand clutched at the bedcovers. 'Did he attempt to harm you…to say anything untoward… anything that disturbed you?'

'Do not distress yourself, master.' The servant came forward, glaring at Annelise. 'You will be ill again.'

'Be quiet, sirrah! I am speaking to my niece.'

'Indeed, Uncle, there is no need to distress yourself,' Annelise said hastily. This was not like her uncle, who was always courteous to his servants. 'He…said only that he wished to see you on some private matter. I told him you were unwell and that I would mention his request when you were better.'

It was not quite the truth, but to reveal everything that had been said would rouse Sir Hugh's temper and cause untold harm.

'Rochefort…it may not be him, and if it is, I may yet prevent him…' Sir Hugh muttered as though he were feverish. His fingers plucked at the sheets, showing the extent of his disturbance. 'I must act without delay.' He stared at Annelise, the pupils of his eyes seeming to narrow to black dots. 'I shall save you, child. Fear not. Satan's hand shall not fall upon you if I can prevent it.'

'You are ill, sir,' she said, his expression frightening her. She looked at the servant. 'Call my aunt, please, John.'

'No!' Sir Hugh caught at her wrist. 'John will tend me. I forbid you to worry your aunt. Go now, and send my steward to me. I have much to do and so little time…so little time…'

'As you wish, Uncle.'

Annelise left him to the ministrations of his body servant and hurried away to do his bidding. She was anxious as she sought out Master Blackwell, and sorry that she had mentioned the stranger to her uncle. It had seemed to bring on another disorder of his mind.

What was it that her uncle feared so? It obviously concerned her. Why was he in haste to see her wed all of a sudden?

She wished she understood.

It was the following morning, and Annelise was sitting in the parlour alone, concentrating on the letter she had been composing. She finished sanding the wet ink and read anxiously through the fine script once more. Would it do?

Was it wrong of her to have written without telling anyone? Ought she to throw it away and forget the idea altogether?

Earlier that morning, Mr Blackwell had told her that her uncle had so far dictated only the letter to Mr Broughton. Clearly he had no intention of seeing Master Rochefort, and, after his adverse reaction to her message from that gentleman, she had decided never to distress him over the matter again. Instead, she had written to Master Rochefort herself, telling him that her uncle was too ill to see him.

She sealed her letter with wax and used her father's crest to mark it, then sat staring at it for a moment. Should she send the note with a servant or deliver it herself? It would be more proper to send it, of course, but if she did so her uncle might learn of it—since the servants would no doubt feel it their duty to inform her aunt, as they always did. She was sure both her aunt and uncle would consider it immodest for her to write to a man she scarcely knew— and one, moreover, who was not of their persuasion.

Could she, dared she, take it herself? Taught to behave with modesty, to listen and reserve her opinions as befitted a woman, she hesitated. Yet Master Rochefort had asked her to enquire whether her uncle was well enough to see him…

She would take it herself! It was but an hour's walk there and back. She could pick wild flowers and herbs on her way home. Aunt Prudence was in need of certain ingredients for her simples, so the time would not be wasted.

Glancing from the parlour window, Annelise saw that the sky was cloudless. The weather was still very warm; she would have no need of a cloak.

Some half an hour later, Annelise was at the door of Longton Hall. She frowned over the neglected gardens. Only two years earlier they had been flourishing; now they had gone wild. She noticed some attempt had been made to clear a patch of brambles, and the paths nearer the house had been picked clean of weeds. At the back of the house, she could hear the voices of men working on the thatch. Clearly the new owner meant to restore the place to its former graciousness.

Annelise lifted the heavy front door knocker. A servant came to answer her. She was relieved that he was a stranger to her; servants tended to gossip, but this man did not know who she was. Perhaps her family would never discover her indiscretion.

'I pray you, sir, tell me—has your master guests staying?'

'Yes, mistress.' The servant stared at her suspiciously. From his dress, he was not of the Puritan persuasion, and he distrusted all those who were. 'What be your business here?'

'Would you give this letter to Master Rochefort, please?'

'Be no one of that name here.'

Annelise was taken aback. 'But he was visiting—a tall man with black hair and blue eyes.'

'That be His Lordship,' the man replied with a superior air. He looked down his long nose at Annelise. 'Don't know as I can rightly give him this, being as it's wrongly addressed.'

'But I have walked here on purpose to deliver it!'

'Might offend him…'

Annelise sighed. She ought never to have come here. She was about to turn away when she heard the crunch of boots on stones and turned to discover the man she sought was striding towards her.

He was wearing stained breeches and was naked from the waist up, his shirt slung carelessly over his shoulder; obviously he had been working and had taken it off. His hair was wet, as if he had put his head under the pump in the stableyard, and his skin gleamed like gold satin, bronzed, she imagined, by frequent exposure to the sun.

'Good day, Mistress Woodward.' Justin stared at her in astonishment. 'Forgive my appearance. I had not expected to find a lady at the door.'

Annelise blushed, turning aside as he pulled on his shirt. But not before she had seen his powerful shoulders, and several scars on his back that looked as if they must have been made by the blade of a sword. When she looked again he was dressed, and regarding her through narrowed eyes, his expression one of disapproval if not censure.

'I came to deliver a letter, sir. I have spoken to my uncle but he begs your pardon. He is too ill to see you.'

'Could you not have sent your message with a servant? There was surely no need for you to come yourself.'

Annelise stiffened. His criticism stung all the more because she knew her behaviour to be unseemly.

'I should not have come…'

She flung away, walking swiftly, her head bent. How foolish she was! It was very wrong of her to have been so forward. In her heart, she knew her reasons for delivering the letter had been more than a natural concern for Sir Hugh's health. She had hoped to see this man again—but he thought her immodest! He was angry with her.

'Mistress Woodward, wait!' Justin caught up with her. He grabbed her arm roughly, swinging her round to face him. 'Do not leave in anger. I meant not to hurt you. I was surprised to see you. Stay a moment, I beg you.'

'I was wrong to come,' she said. 'It is just that…' Her eyes misted with tears. 'My uncle is so strange. When I asked him if he would see you, he talked so wildly. I think his mind has begun to fail. His steward has not written to you?' Justin shook his head. 'No, I did not think so. He dictated only the one letter…' She swallowed hard, stifling the tears that threatened. 'I thought it only right that you should be aware…' Her breath caught on a sob.

Justin's forehead creased as he sensed her acute distress. There was more here than she had told him. He offered her his kerchief, touched by her tears despite himself.

'I am grateful for the intention,' he said, his voice becoming soft, almost caressing. 'If I seemed to censure you, it was only out of concern for your safety. We have spoken of this matter before, if you recall?'

'Yes.' She smiled through her tears, comforted by his tone. 'It was foolish of me to walk here myself—but I was afraid my uncle might learn I had written to you and…' She hung her head then, unable to meet his gaze. 'I fear it was forward of me, sir.'

'I understand.' Justin looked at her thoughtfully. 'If Sir Hugh will not see me… But you mentioned a letter. To whom was it addressed? Could it have been the Marquis Saintjohn?'

'Oh, no,' she replied, a little surprised. 'It was to my aunt's kinsman—a Mr Broughton.' A flush stained her cheeks. 'My uncle intends…to arrange a marriage…'

Now why had she told him that? Annelise looked away. She was embarrassed by her own indelicacy. This man was a stranger to her. She could not discuss matters of such intimacy with him.

'Does the idea please you?'

Annelise looked up, her heart racing. Something in his expression made her blurt out the truth.

'No! No, it does not. I have never met Mr Broughton.' Her cheeks were flaming. 'My duty is to obey my uncle, but…I do not wish to marry unless I truly like my husband.'

'Will your uncle force you to the match?'

'I am not sure. He will expect me to do my duty.'

'I see.' Justin's mouth drew into a tight line. Featherstone

had no right to choose her husband. His haste to arrange
the match was clearly an attempt to forestall anything that
the Marquis Saintjohn might be planning for his niece. 'But
he will not force you?'

'Not at once,' Annelise said on a sigh. 'I shall not be
locked in my room or beaten, but there are other ways of
commanding my obedience. I should not like to be the
cause of distress to either my aunt or uncle, especially
now.'

Justin was thoughtful. The girl had been taught to obey.
These damned Puritans had almost succeeded in making
her something nature had never intended. She might resist
in her heart, but she was a dutiful girl who would accept
her uncle's dictates in the end. The idea of her being tied
to the kind of man Sir Hugh had no doubt chosen filled
Justin with revulsion. It must not be allowed to happen!
Yet he must tread carefully here.

'Thank you for your visit, Mistress Woodward,' he said.
'Shall I send a servant to escort you home?'

Annelise felt as if he had thrown cold water over her.
She was not sure what she had expected, or if she had
expected anything. In the woods, he had spoken of a visit
to his mother, but now he was dismissing her—his manner
one of indifference. She had foolishly placed too much re-
liance on what had obviously been a careless promise.

Why should he care for her problems? She hardly knew
him. It had been wrong of her to discuss her uncle's affairs
with a stranger. She raised her head, her expression one of
pride.

'I shall be perfectly safe, sir. You need not trouble yourself on my account.'

But that was exactly what he must do, thought Justin.
He should have insisted on seeing Featherstone weeks ago,
but he had allowed the matter to drift. Now he must act.

'Since you are determined to be independent, I shall al-

low you to have your way.' Justin smiled inwardly as he
saw the spark in her eyes. For all their mealy-mouthed
ways, the Featherstones had not succeeded in crushing her
spirit. 'At least in this. I must beg to take leave of you,
mistress. I have urgent business…' An air of disappointment about her stopped him as he started to leave. He
reached out, taking a fine strand of hair that had escaped
from beneath her cap between his fingers, then let it fall.
'Do not fear, Mistress Woodward. I have your interests in
hand. Do not give your word to Mr Broughton or your
uncle on this matter and all will be well.'

Annelise stared after him as he strode away. What could
he have meant by that? Her heart took a dizzying leap. She
was suddenly glad she had come here, no matter what her
aunt or uncle might say.

She was drawn to this man of conflicting moods. When
he was stern, she was a little afraid of him…but when he
smiled and spoke to her with kindness she liked him.

She liked him more than any other man she had ever
met.

Annelise heard the shouting coming from her uncle's
room the next morning. Her heart caught with fear. Was
Sir Hugh ill again?

'What is wrong?' she asked as she reached the landing
and saw her aunt emerging from Sir Hugh's room. 'Is my
uncle worse?'

'Send someone for the physician,' Lady Featherstone
said. 'Your uncle has had another fit, Annelise. He was
reading a letter that upset him terribly and he tried to get
out of bed; he fell and hit his head on the oak hutch…'
She gave a little sob of distress. 'He is unconscious, Annelise. I think he may be dying.'

'Oh, no!' Annelise looked at her in concern. Despite her
uncle's stern manner, he was a good man at heart and did

not deserve this. 'I will send for the physician immediately, Aunt.'

She ran down the stairs, calling for Master Blackwell. He came almost at once, shaking his head at the news.

'It was the same hand that wrote the other letter,' he said, looking sorrowful. 'It was my duty to give it to him, but I fear I have killed him.'

'Not you,' Annelise replied, shaking her head. 'I do not know what has been distressing my uncle these past weeks, but it was not your fault.'

'May God forgive whoever has caused this,' the steward replied, crossing himself. 'He has done for a good man. I see the work of Satan in this, Mistress Woodward.'

Annelise was silent as he hurried away to send for the physician. What could be in the letters that had disturbed her uncle so? A cold chill went down her spine as she recalled her uncle's wild talk of the devil's mark falling upon them. Something had frightened him—frightened him so much that he had lost his senses.

She looked back towards the stairs she had just descended. She was not needed in her uncle's chamber for the moment. Instead, she would busy herself with the tasks her aunt normally performed; it was all she could do to help.

The next few days were anxious ones for Sir Hugh's family. The physician came when sent for, and shook his head over the sick man, who still clung precariously to life but seemed incapable of speech or thought, staring blankly at the ceiling and taking no notice of anything around him.

'I fear I can do nothing,' the physician told Sir Hugh's anxious wife. 'He is in the hands of God, madam. All you can do is watch over him and pray.'

'He was always a good man,' said Lady Prudence. 'We

must not question the Lord's work, but I do not think he deserved this.' Her mouth settled into a line of bitterness.

Annelise could do nothing but agree. She sat by her uncle's side reading aloud from the Bible for half an hour every evening, hoping that it would somehow bring him comfort, but she was not sure he understood. He gave no sign of knowing her.

The letter which had upset him seemed to have disappeared. She did venture to mention it to his servant, asking if he had put it away, but he shook his head and gave her a dour look, as if he blamed her for her uncle's illness.

It was five days after the seizure that had robbed her uncle of his senses that Annelise's aunt called her into her parlour. She smiled at her, patting the oak settle beside her.

'I have something to tell you, my dear.'

Annelise's heart caught. She knew instinctively what Lady Prudence was about to say.

'I believe your uncle spoke to you about a match he had thought to arrange for you, Annelise?'

'Yes, Aunt.' Annelise raised her head. 'But I do not think we should speak of this at such a time.'

'Your uncle was most particular,' her aunt replied. 'He told me that the marriage should go ahead even if he...' She dabbed a kerchief to her lips. 'It is his ardent wish that you should be married, my dear. And it is not as if he were dead, so there is nothing improper in our thinking of your happiness.'

Sir Hugh was not yet dead, and strictly speaking they were not in mourning. Annelise avoided her aunt's earnest look.

'I am not sure I wish to marry Mr Broughton, Aunt.'

'Annelise!' Lady Prudence exclaimed, her mouth tight with disapproval. 'It is unlike you to set yourself against your uncle's will—and at such a time.'

'I am sorry, but...'

'Mr Broughton has travelled all the way from Huntingdon to see you,' her aunt said, looking severe. 'You will at least do him the courtesy of seeing him?'

'Yes, Aunt,' Annelise said. 'I cannot refuse to do that—but I beg you will not place your hopes on this marriage.'

'May I know the reason why?' Lady Prudence looked up, a frown of annoyance on her face as a servant came in. 'Yes, Ruth—what is it? I told you I did not wish to be disturbed.'

'There is a visitor come, my lady.'

'I know. Mr Broughton…'

'No, my lady…' The servant stopped speaking abruptly as a lady swept into the room. She was clearly a person of some importance, in her middle years and dressed very finely in green silk, with a huge black hat that sported a curling feather. Her long dark hair was curled in ringlets on her shoulder, and her strong perfume wafted ahead of her, imposing her personality on the small room. 'The Dowager Marchioness Saintjohn…'

'I prefer to be called Lady Emily,' said the visitor, 'but that is indeed my title.' Her eyes swept dismissively over Lady Prudence and came to rest on Annelise. She seemed to approve of what she saw, and smiled. 'Ah, you must be Mistress Woodward, the daughter of Lady Mary Woodward. I was a great friend of your mother, my dear—and your father—which is, I suppose, why he made you my ward in his will. I should perhaps more properly say the ward of the fourth Marquis. However, the Marquis Saintjohn is a very busy man, so he has arranged for you to be placed in my care. I have come here today to take you back to London with me. We should leave as soon as possible, since I am expected at Court next week and there is no time to be lost.'

Her statement was met by a stunned silence. How could this be? Annelise wondered. She had heard nothing of a will—nothing of a guardian other than her uncle. Glancing at her aunt now, Annelise saw that she was apprehensive, but not surprised.

Surely she could not have known of this? And yet she had; Annelise could see it in her eyes.

'Is this true, Aunt? Did my father's will make me the ward of...?' She turned to the fashionable lady, who was watching closely, clearly very much in command of the situation. 'Forgive me, I did not quite understand whose ward I am.'

'The Marquis Saintjohn,' repeated Lady Emily. 'There is no need to be apprehensive, my dear. Nothing in this world will give me greater pleasure than to undertake your education. I dare say it has been neglected, for it is not the country way to teach Court manners to young ladies—but I shall see that no attention is lacking in this matter. The Marquis wishes you to be properly provided for until you marry, and, having seen you, I am certain a match worthy of your status can be arranged.' Her manner was so confident, so certain, that she seemed to sweep everything before her, taking it for granted that everyone would jump to her bidding.

Lady Prudence recovered her tongue. 'Sir Hugh...my husband...has already arranged a match for our niece,' she said. 'The gentleman is here, waiting to speak to her even now.'

'Then I am come in time, thank goodness!' Lady Emily waved her arm towards the servant who was hovering, her mouth hanging open. 'Pray tell that gentleman...if he is the one I saw in the lobby...that he has wasted his journey. He is certainly not of the station or consequence I expect for my ward.'

'He is my kinsman, madam!' Lady Prudence was indignant. She stared at the visitor as if she could not believe her ears. 'And a good, godly man.'

Lady Emily's eyes moved to inspect the other woman, her expression one of disdain. 'Indeed? Your kinsman? A very worthy man, I dare say—but not an aristocrat, not a gentleman of distinction. Lord Woodward would not have approved of such a match for his only daughter, nor would his dear wife. No, no, we can do better than that for Annelise.' Her eyes flicked back to Annelise. 'You would not object to a visit with me, my dear?'

'No, I should not, ma'am,' Annelise said. Her amazement was turning to a sense of relief. 'I have never met Mr Broughton and I would rather not marry him.'

'It is your uncle's wish,' Lady Prudence reminded her. Her mouth thinned in disapproval as she looked at Annelise. 'You would not wish to disobey him? You would not want to show disrespect now that he is close to death?'

'I owe both you and my uncle a debt of gratitude I can never repay,' Annelise replied, her cheeks flushed. She was conscious of her heart beating very fast. 'I do not wish to disoblige you, Aunt, truly I do not—but if my father's will made the Marquis Saintjohn my guardian, am I not obliged by law to obey him?'

'The will was made when your father was in great distress,' argued her aunt. 'He was close to death and could not have known what he did. Your uncle has stood guardian these many years—and none has come forward to dispute it. I believe the law would uphold his right.' She glared at Lady Emily. 'How do I know you are who you say you are—or that the Marquis has given you the care of my niece?'

Lady Emily smiled and took a rolled parchment from beneath her falling sleeve. 'This is a letter from His Majesty King Charles II,' she said, presenting it with a flourish to display the impressive seal. 'It is addressed to your husband, madam, but since he is perhaps too ill to read it, I suggest you do so yourself. It confirms all I have told you, and requests that you relinquish Mistress Woodward into my care at once.'

'I...cannot read it,' Lady Prudence confessed, her cheeks flushed with shame. 'I can sign my name, but I never learned to read more than a few words.'

'Then summon your steward, madam.'

'No.' Lady Prudence was suddenly angry. She looked at Annelise. 'This can be settled between us. We have been good to you, niece. Would you have us turned out of house and home now that your uncle is ill?'

'No, aunt, of course not!'

'That is what they will do if you allow them to have their way. It is what your uncle has feared since...since the letters came.'

'The letters...' Annelise felt chilled. She stared at her aunt uncertainly. 'The letters that brought on my uncle's illness?'

'It is these people who have killed him,' Lady Prudence cried with an accusing look at the other woman. 'They are the devil's disciples; they stand for all your uncle hated. You are not like them, Annelise. If you go with this woman, they will destroy you. They will make you like them...they will destroy your soul.'

'That is nonsense,' said Lady Emily. 'The Marquis has no wish to turn you out, Lady Prudence. He may send someone to take charge of the estate, but you and your husband are at liberty to stay here as custodians of the house...providing, of course, that you do not deny his right to take charge of his ward.'

'You are threatening us...' Lady Prudence drew back, fear in her eyes. She waved a hand towards Annelise. 'Take her, then. Take the ungrateful girl. She is a serpent, and her cruelty has struck me to the heart. I do not wish to set eyes on her again.'

'Aunt…' Annelise looked at her unhappily. 'Pray do not let us part in anger. I do not wish to quarrel with you.'

'Go with her,' replied Lady Prudence, her eyes hard, cold. 'You are no longer any affair of mine.'

Annelise felt as if she had been struck a blow in the face. How could her aunt speak so to her?

'I did not mean to hurt you…'

Lady Prudence got up and walked from the room without another word. Annelise stood staring after her, her back towards Lady Emily. She turned as she felt a gentle touch on her shoulder.

'She will think better of her words another day,' Lady Emily said. 'Are you ready to leave, Annelise? I hope I may call you that—since we are to be companions for the time being?'

'My clothes…'

'You will not need them.' Lady Emily laughed at her expression of surprise. 'You cannot want to wear such drab gowns, Annelise? Your mother was a beautiful woman and she liked pretty things. She would not be happy to see you wearing such a plain gown. I shall provide you with something more suitable to your station. You need bring only any personal items you wish to keep…such as a gift from your dear mother or father.'

Annelise nodded. Her memories of her mother had faded, but she did seem to recall her wearing silk gowns in attractive colours, at least until she had been widowed. Annelise too had worn colours when she was a small child; it had only been after her mother died that she had begun wearing black or grey all the time.

'I do not have anything but this cross and chain I wear beneath my gown,' Annelise said, showing it to her: it was silver and very plain. 'If my mother had jewels, I have not seen them. My uncle believes jewellery to be sinful.'

Lady Emily raised her brows but said nothing. Why had

the girl not been given her own property? It was possible
that the jewellery had been sold during the war, but she
doubted it. Lord Woodward had been a wealthy man, and
would not have sold his wife's jewels unless desperate; to
her knowledge, he had never been so. It seemed likely they
had been sold later or were hidden away somewhere.

'Well, we shall leave such matters to the Marquis's dis-
cretion,' she said. 'Go and put on your cloak, Annelise, and
we shall be on our way—unless there is anyone you wish
to bid farewell?'

'No...' Annelise felt a choking sensation inside. 'My
uncle would not know if I went to him, and...'

Lady Emily took her hand. 'Try to forget your aunt's
unkindness. She has obviously been under a great strain of
late. She will change her mind in time—and, if she does
not, you have a new family to take care of you now.'

'Thank you, ma'am. I am grateful...'

'Come, let us go,' Lady Emily said. 'I see no reason to
stay another moment. I shall come to your bedchamber with
you. If anyone has something to say to you, they may say
it to me. I will not have you made unhappy by these people.'

Annelise did not reply. She was relieved to have been
saved from her aunt's attempt to force her into a marriage
she did not want, but she was not ungrateful or unmindful
of the care her uncle and aunt had given her. She would
have preferred to take a fond leave of them, and was distressed by the tone of Lady Emily's voice.

Clearly she despised the Featherstones. She was a
woman of some influence, and was determined to have her
way: Lady Prudence had never stood a chance against her.

Lady Emily had a letter from His Majesty that gave her
authority to take Annelise with her, but it might have been
more kindly done, in a way that would not have distressed
Lady Prudence.

There was nothing to do but to go with Lady Emily. Annelise was distressed that the parting with her aunt had been so harsh, but perhaps Lady Prudence would relent towards her when she had had leisure to consider.

Besides, this lady must know Master Rochefort…but, no, that was not his name. The servant at Longton Hall had called him His Lordship. And he himself had mentioned the Marquis Saintjohn. Yes, they must know each other— and that meant she might see him when she was in London. Lord Rochefort. That must be his title. If he was a friend of her guardian, he would perhaps call on the Marquis's mother.

Annelise's heart beat a little faster as she remembered the smile he had given her when he'd told her not to worry. He must have gone to see the Marquis, spoken to him on her behalf. It made Annelise feel warm inside. He wouldn't have done that unless he liked her, would he?

It was suddenly very important to her that he should like her, though she did not quite know why.

Her thoughts were in chaos, her pulses racing as she collected the few possessions she wanted, then followed Lady Emily downstairs and out to the waiting carriage.

There was no sign of either her aunt or Mr Broughton, but she had not really expected to see them. Her aunt's kinsman must be mightily offended. Once again, Annelise felt regret for the harsh words that had passed between her and Lady Prudence, but she put them from her mind.

As she was helped into the carriage, with its coat of arms emblazoned on the panels, she could not help feeling a spurt of excitement. She was going to London, to a new life…

'So, this is my home,' Lady Emily said as the carriage stopped outside a very large and imposing house on the Strand. 'The property belongs to my son, of course, but there is sufficient space for us to avoid each other if we choose. He has only recently returned to England and is too busy to bother with my affairs for the moment.' She led Annelise inside, taking off her hat and handing it to a hovering footman without even glancing his way. 'I hope you will be happy here, my dear.'

Annelise looked about her. They were in a huge, airy hall, which was bigger than the main parlour at her home, and the floors were made of grey marble tiles with a gold and black border. In the middle of the room was a round table with strange twisted legs, and there were several paintings hanging on the oak-panelled walls, side tables and chairs with padded seats covered in embroidered brocade. She had an impression of luxury, even opulence, and thought that the Marquis Saintjohn must be very rich.

'I am sure I shall…' Annelise began. Whatever else she had meant to say died unspoken on her lips as she saw the man walking down the grand stairway towards her. It was Lord Rochefort!

She had never seen him dressed so splendidly; his coat and breeches were fashioned of a pale grey velvet, and in the latest petticoat style favoured by the King, his cuffs were of the finest Brussels lace, as was his falling band. He looked as if he were on his way to Court, but he had not adopted the fashion for wigs and wore his natural hair curled into a lovelock on his shoulder and tied with a scarlet ribbon. She gasped, her heart beginning to race wildly as she stared in wonder.

'Oh…'

'Ah, Justin,' Lady Emily said. 'I was not sure you would be here when we arrived. You know my son, of course, Annelise.'

'You are the Marquis Saintjohn?' Annelise stared up into his brilliant blue eyes, which seemed to mock her slightly.

She trembled, her knees seeming to go weak. 'But I thought…you said your name was Rochefort?'

'I am Justin Rochefort, the fourth Marquis Saintjohn,' Justin said with a slight bow. 'I am delighted to welcome you to my house, Mistress Woodward. Both my mother and I will do our best to see that you are happy here.'

How could she have been so blind? Of course, it had to be him! Why had she not guessed at once? She had thought him a friend of the Marquis, but she had allowed herself to be deceived. Perhaps because she had wanted it so.

'You are my guardian, sir?' Annelise felt a coldness at the base of her neck. Her guardian! This changed everything. A crushing disappointment swept over her. 'You wrote to my uncle—it was your letters which so distressed him.'

She remembered Sir Hugh's ramblings, when he had spoken of a man who would come to claim her—a man he feared so much it had sent him out of his senses.

'The mark of Satan is upon us all. But I shall not let it fall on you. No, not if it costs me my life.'

Annelise felt a deep unease as she stared at the Marquis. What did she know of him, or this house to which she had been brought? Why had he not told her he was her guardian before this? He could have done so when she had given him her name that day in the woods—or when she had gone to Longton Hall with the letter. Instead, he had let her believe him plain Master Rochefort—why?

He had been flirting with her in the woods, and then his manner had changed suddenly once her true identity was revealed. Of course he could not seduce his own ward! It would be most improper. As improper as her own thoughts of him had been.

'I am very sorry if your uncle was distressed by the letters,' Justin said, his gaze narrowing. Now what was going on in that head of hers? 'I wished only to discuss your affairs with him, to make certain you were in good health and properly settled. Had he been well enough to continue looking after your estate, I should not have interfered—unless you asked it of me.'

As she had, of course. Annelise was silent. In her heart she knew that it was she who had precipitated the visit from Lady Emily. The Marquis had done what was necessary to prevent her from being persuaded or pushed into a marriage against her will, because she had made him aware of her situation—and yet she was angry with him. She felt guilt because of her uncle's illness, and some apprehension.

Why had the Marquis's letters made her uncle so afraid? Why had Sir Hugh talked so wildly of Satan's mark having fallen upon them?

'What are you thinking?' Justin asked. 'Why do you look at me that way? As if I were some kind of a monster! I thought you wanted this visit with my mother?'

'Oh, yes,' Annelise cried, stung by remorse. The journey to London had taken some days, and in that time she had come to like Lady Emily. 'I am most grateful to you for inviting me, sir—and to Lady Emily, of course.'

'For goodness' sake, Justin,' his mother said. 'Will you keep Annelise talking for ever in the hall? I dare swear she is exhausted by the journey, as I am, and can do well without one of your scolds. I find them exceedingly wearisome myself, and poor Annelise has been scolded enough already. I mean to see it does not happen now that she is my ward.'

'Your ward, Mama?' Justin raised his brows, a faint air of mockery in his manner. 'Can I have heard you correctly?'

'Indeed, I think it would be best if you were to give Annelise's well-being into my hands,' Lady Emily replied. She smiled affectionately at the girl. 'We are already friends, and, since you are unmarried, it is more fitting that

I should have charge of her. Besides, you are too busy to bother with all our little fancies, are you not? You may safely leave the matter of her wardrobe and education with me.'

'It is fitting that you should chaperon Miss Woodward,' Justin replied. 'But you will defer to me in all matters of business, if you please, Mama.'

'But of course.' Lady Emily breezed past him, propelling Annelise before her. 'As head of the family, you must always be consulted in any matter of importance, but I shall not trouble you with inconsequential trifles.'

Annelise saw Justin's frown of disapproval as she was driven upstairs by his mother. It was clear that Lady Emily was accustomed to having her own way—and that she meant to take Annelise under her wing.

'You must not let my son intimidate you,' Lady Emily said, giving her a look of pure mischief as they walked along the upper gallery. 'You have been taught to obey without question, Annelise, but now you must learn to assert yourself. You must learn the power of your sex, the art of getting your own way with the least fuss. Men are after all but simple creatures—but they like to imagine themselves our masters. The secret of a good marriage is to let your husband believe you agree with his every word, while going your own merry way.'

Annelise stared at her. For a moment she was so shocked that she did not know whether or not her hostess spoke in jest, then she realised that beneath the teasing manner lay a will of iron.

'My aunt would think it sinful to deceive her husband, ma'am.'

'Your aunt is no doubt a worthy woman, but she is also a fool,' replied Lady Emily. 'She would be lost at Court. You are a beauty, Annelise. You have intelligence and an inheritance, which, though perhaps not huge, is still of some significance. If you would make the most of yourself, of your life, you must learn how to use your womanly arts to your own advantage. After all, why should you not? It is merely a game. You have a right to happiness. I can teach you how to play the game—unless the idea offends you?'

'No, it does not offend me.' Annelise laughed suddenly, a warm, husky laugh that surprised the older woman. She gave Lady Emily a naughty, enchanting look that only her mother might have recognised—a look first seen in her crib that had been missing for many a year. 'No, ma'am, I think I should like to learn all you have to teach me.'

Lady Emily nodded, a speculative expression in her eyes. It was as she had thought when she first saw Annelise. Beneath the veneer of modesty lay a very different personality—a warmth and charm that might win the coldest heart.

She believed this young woman might just be the answer to her prayers.

Chapter Three

'La, what a pretty thing she is!' Lady Emily clapped her hands in delight as Annelise pirouetted for her benefit. 'You will be the most beautiful lady at Court this evening, my dear.'

Annelise's gown was fashioned in the elaborate French style which had become popular since His Majesty's return, with a close-fitting laced bodice and a *décolletage* that skimmed her breasts and shoulders; the sleeves reached to her elbows, were full and banded with lace and ribbons; the trained overskirt was hitched back to reveal a heavily embroidered panel at the front. Her hair had been parted in the centre, caught in a chignon at the back and allowed to fall in bunches of ringlets to either side. Small knots of ribbon threaded with pearls had been pinned above the curls.

Annelise glanced at herself in the mirror, which was Venetian and fabulously expensive, just like her clothes. A part of her—the modest, unassuming lady that she still was by nature—was shocked by what she saw. That woman in the elegant silk gown could not possibly be her! And yet it was pleasing to be dressed so fine. She was aware of excitement, of a sense of expectation.

A knock at the door caused both Annelise and Lady Emily to turn their heads. They were standing in the small chamber which led through to Annelise's bedroom; it was furnished with a writing table, a handsome cabinet, stools and a settle so that guests might be received privately, something Annelise had found strange at first, but had now discovered was favoured by many of the fine ladies she had met since coming to town. After the French fashion, friends, privileged tradesmen, wig-makers and suitors were all invited to a lady's boudoir to watch and admire as the finishing touches were put to her toilette. The practice had astounded Annelise, who had found it shocking at first, but after four weeks, during which she had been taken to meet many of Lady Emily's friends, she had lost many of her former inhibitions.

'Enter,' she called, unsurprised when the Marquis walked in. It was not the first time he had come to her boudoir, though she had not seen a great deal of him these past few weeks, because his time was much occupied by constant visits to the courtroom in which he was suing for the return of his father's estate. 'You are home, then, sir. I vow we had begun to think you had forgotten this evening is to be my debut at Court. Is that not so, ma'am?'

She tipped back her head, her eyes bright with mischief as she gave him what could only be called a provocative smile, then sank into a very deep and reverent curtsey, her head bent as if she curtsied to the King himself.

'Did you think I would break my promise?' Justin's brows rose as he saw her and was struck by the change, not only in her appearance but her manner. She was enchanting! His mother had worked a miracle. He could hardly believe that this confident lady of fashion was the little Puritan maid he had seen singing in the woods only a few weeks earlier. 'You look very well, Mistress Woodward.'

'She looks well! Fie on you, Justin,' his mother cried, tapping his arm with her fan. 'Have you no better compliments for Annelise? She is ravishingly lovely in that gown—and, I dare swear, will cause quite a stir this evening.'

'Annelise has always been beautiful,' Justin replied, frowning slightly. His frown was for himself. For some unaccountable reason he was uneasy. Who was this beautiful young woman? Where had she come from? 'I am sure Mistress Woodward will acquit herself with the proper modesty due to her unmarried status.' He handed Annelise a velvet-covered box. 'You need some kind of ornament. I hope this will be to your taste.'

Annelise gave a little cry of pleasure as she opened the box and discovered a necklace of pearls with a large emerald pendant set in gold. She had never seen anything quite as lovely.

'Oh, this is wonderful,' she cried, her face lighting up as she looked at him. 'May I really wear this?'

'It is for you,' he said, and his mouth softened into a smile as he saw her delight in the necklace. For a moment he had thought her the sophisticated lady of fashion she looked, but underneath she was still the innocent girl who had been dancing in the woods when he had come upon her all unawares. 'My gift to mark this special evening.'

'Thank you…' Annelise hesitated as she saw the way he was looking at her. What did it mean, and why had her heart started to race? 'You and Lady Emily have been so kind to me.'

'Nonsense, my dear,' her hostess said. 'You have been a delight to teach.' Lady Emily gave her son a sly glance, noticing his intense gaze, which was all for Annelise. 'Are you not pleased with my efforts, Justin? Do you not think she has learned her lessons well?'

'I did not doubt she would,' he replied. 'Come, Miss Woodward, let me fasten the necklace for you.'

Annelise stood where she was as he came towards her, then gave him the necklace and turned her back so that he could fasten the clasp at the nape of her neck. His hand brushed her bare shoulder, sending a shiver down her spine. She glanced round at him, fluttering her lashes in the way Lady Emily had taught her, and smiled.

She was a minx! His mother had taught her too well, Justin thought as he saw that look. What a charmer she was. No French courtesan could have done better!

'We should go,' he said, refusing to respond to the invitation in her eyes. Damn it! He hadn't expected such a change so quickly; he wasn't sure how it had come about. One moment she had been the nervous, slightly reserved girl he had first met; the next she appeared to have turned into an accomplished flirt. What had been going on while he was tied up at the Court of Appeals?

He saw his frown had brought a look of dismay to her face, and remembered that this transformation was only on the surface. His mother had taught her to flirt prettily, but the girl herself was not changed. Yet something stopped him reassuring her at once. He must remember always that she was under his protection and keep a distance between them.

'I do not want to be late. The hearing seems to drag on for ever. I must speak to His Majesty this evening, see what can be done to hurry things along.' He spoke more harshly than he knew, his mind too wrapped up in his own concerns to realise that his words might be taken amiss.

Annelise heard the coldness in his voice and felt hurt. She had tried so hard to be what he wanted. Lady Emily had told her about the beautiful ladies he had known in France, his mistresses who were amongst the cream of the courtiers and much envied him by other men—and she so wanted to be like them, because then he might find her attractive. His manner told her that he was indifferent to her. Despite all her efforts to ape the manners of Lady Emily's friends, she was still only a country girl at heart.

If she wanted to make the Marquis look at her with interest, she would just have to become like the sophisticated ladies his mother said he admired.

'Take no notice of him,' Lady Emily whispered at her shoulder as they followed Justin outside to where two sedan chairs were waiting to carry them to the palace. 'He has been in a mood of late. I do not know what ails him. It hardly matters whether he regains his father's estates, he has money enough—but it is always so with him. He will have his way, no matter the cost.'

Annelise made no reply. She waited until Lady Emily was settled in her chair, then gave her hand to Justin. He nodded to her, then carried her hand to his lips, kissing it briefly.

'My mother is right,' he said softly, relenting because of the hurt in her eyes. 'I have no doubt that you will cause a stir this evening—but choose your victims wisely, Annelise. His Majesty frowns on duels amongst his courtiers. If you must break hearts, make sure the gentlemen are first your friends.'

'Are you my friend, sir?' Annelise glanced up at him wickedly.

'I am your guardian. You will gain nothing by flirting with me. You should look for a suitable husband.' Once again he was conscious of the need to keep his distance— for her sake.

'Yes, my lord, I shall do as you bid me,' she said, a glint in her eyes. 'But you would not wish me to marry in haste? You would not seek to force me into taking a husband I could not like?'

'Of course not.' What was wrong with him that evening?

Justin wondered at his own harshness. The girl was entitled to her pleasures. 'I meant only that this is your first time at Court. No doubt my mother has warned you of the dangers. I need not say more.'

'No, sir, you need not.'

Annelise drew the curtain on her chair, shutting herself in as the chairmen began to carry her through the streets. The Marquis was walking beside her and there was a footman following behind, armed with a stout cudgel. It was necessary to be on one's guard, for there were beggars and vagrants waiting in dark corners to spring on the unwary and rob them of their valuables.

London could be a dangerous place, both on the streets and at Court. Some of the men who had judged King Charles I had already been seized and tried for their crimes, and others less guilty of treason had also been punished for the part they had played after the war. In the country there were murmurs of dissent, and at the Court itself the various factions were at each other's throats.

Annelise's uncle had spoken of the Court as a wicked, licentious place, where the King set a bad example to his followers by his immoral behaviour. He had his mistresses, amongst them the beautiful Barbara Villiers, whose husband, Lord Castlemaine, was forced to accept the horns of a cuckold in return for favours given by his Sovereign.

Annelise was well aware that she must be careful of her reputation if she wished for a good marriage.

'Once you are married, you may do as you wish,' Lady Emily had told her with a wicked look. 'Providing you know how to manage your husband, of course. Naturally, you will not take lovers until you have given him an heir…though at Court, I dare swear, there are a good many husbands who hardly know whether their sons are their own or another's.' She had laughed, as if much amused at the idea. 'And it serves some of them right!'

If the ladies of the Court could flirt as they pleased, then so could she, Annelise decided. The Marquis was her guardian, but there was surely no need for him to be so strict with her—he was almost as bad as her uncle had been. She would ignore him, as Lady Emily had told her. This was to be a special evening, and she meant to enjoy herself, despite the little ache in her heart his harsh manner had caused.

Annelise was nervous as she went forward with Lady Emily to be presented to His Majesty. At first sight he looked ugly, with his long face, dark complexion and sad spaniel eyes, but as she rose from her curtsey and looked up into his eyes she saw they were not really melancholy at all. He smiled at her, a hint of mischief in his manner as he welcomed her to Court.

'So this is Mistress Woodward,' he said. 'I had heard you were become a Puritan, mistress—but it seems rumour hath lied yet again. In all the country, I dare swear, it would be hard to find a man who had not wished for my return most heartily, and the ladies cannot be brought to having wished for my banishment at all. But politics are ever thus, what say you?'

'My uncle Sir Hugh Featherstone is of the Puritan persuasion,' she replied. 'But my father died fighting for your cause, Sire—and my mother of a broken heart. For myself, I am happy simply to be at Court this evening, and know nothing of politics.'

'Well said, Mistress Woodward. You are as intelligent as you are lovely, and will be welcome to us whenever you choose to give us the pleasure of your company—which we hope will be often.' Charles looked over her head at her guardian. 'Sir, why do you frown so? This is meant to be a happy night, is it not?'

'I beg your pardon, Sire,' Justin replied. He was shocked

to discover that he did not care for the look the King bestowed on Annelise. It was far too avaricious. 'Perhaps you
will grant me a moment of your time later?'

'Yet another request for justice, I suppose?' Charles
waved his scented kerchief, looking bored and slightly out
of temper. 'Later, perhaps. Take your ward into the ballroom, sir. Dance with her. I would have her be merry. She
is a lovely child, and a credit to you, Lady Emily.'

'Thank you, Sire.' Lady Emily curtsied before him. 'You
are generous to say so.'

'Bring her often, madam. I would see her always at
Court. Such beauty is not to be hidden away. And that is
a command.'

Justin placed his hand under Annelise's elbow, steering
her away. In the next room they were already forming sets
for the first dance of the evening and he took up his place
with her. It was a courtly, gentle dance that allowed for
conversation, but for the first few minutes Justin said nothing to her.

'Are you angry with me?' she ventured at last. 'Have I
offended you, sir?'

'Angry? No. Why should I be?' He looked down at her.
'I apologise if I have seemed so.'

In truth he did not know what was wrong with him. The
King had shown interest in her, nothing more. Was it not
what he had planned—an amusing game to put Madam
Barbara's nose out a little? Yet as he looked down at Annelise's face he felt something very akin to jealousy stir-
ring.

What nonsense! She was a pretty little minx, but hardly
likely to be a serious rival to His Majesty's favourite.

Annelise knew nothing of his thoughts, only that he
looked stern, as if she had made him angry. She turned her
mind to the dance and curtsied; he bowed, and they parted
to take a turn about the room with the next person in the

line. A tiny nerve was twitching at the corner of his mouth when they came back together.

'You seem annoyed...'

'If I am, it is not with you.'

Annelise digested this in silence. He was angry, and if not with her—then who? With himself, his mother—or the King? Surely not His Majesty, unless he was displeased that his request for an interview had not been granted immediately? Of course, that must be it.

They made stately progress down the line.

'You must be careful, Annelise,' he said. 'I have warned you before. There are those who would take advantage of your innocence. You are new come to Court and cannot know how to behave.'

She had spoken to no one but the King, and then only modestly, in answer to his questions. Surely her guardian could not have objected to that? He was being unfair to her!

She lifted her head, hurt by his odd manner and determined not to let it spoil her evening. Why was he being so stern with her? She had done nothing to bring his censure on her—and she was tired of being treated like a child. Lady Emily had spent hours teaching her how to curtsey, how to hold her fan, how to catch the eye of a gentleman across the room.

She saw a man looking in her direction. He was tall, attractive in a rather harsh way, and clearly interested in her. His approval was balm to her wounded spirit. She dropped her gaze in the manner Lady Emily had shown her, but let her mouth curve just a little at the corners to signal that she was not entirely displeased with his attention.

The music had come to an end. Justin took hold of her arm once more, steering her to the side of the room. It was his intention to restore her to his mother's care, but they

were waylaid by the man who had been staring so particularly at Annelise.

'Good evening, Saintjohn,' the man said, his dark eyes
giving Annelise such a hot look that she was overcome with
confusion. 'Will you not introduce me to your beautiful
companion? Madam, I am overwhelmed. They told me
there was new star in the heavens but I did not believe
them…until I saw you.'

'God damn it!' Justin said, firing up immediately. 'No, I
shall not introduce you, Rathbone. This lady wishes to have
nothing to do with you or your kind. Lay a finger on her
and I shall kill you.'

A sneer curled the other man's lips. He bowed mockingly towards Annelise. 'Forgive me, I did not know he
had put his mark on you—but should you tire of his clumsy
attentions I am Earl Rathbone, always at your service.'

He walked away before either she or Justin could answer.
Annelise was the first to recover from the shock. She tipped
her head to one side, gazing naughtily up at her guardian.

'Was he one of the gentlemen you meant when you
warned me earlier, sir? He seemed to imagine I was your
mistress—I wonder why? How could he have made such a
mistake?'

'No doubt my mother has kept you informed of my mis-
demeanours,' Justin said, amused despite himself. He gave
her a look meant to quell her impertinence. That look in
her eye was too challenging to be innocent. She was at-
tempting to flirt with him, but he would not be drawn. 'I
do not pretend to have led a blameless life, Mistress Woodward—but I am a man. You are a woman and as yet unmarried. If you do not wish to be thought spoilt goods, you
will stay well clear of Rathbone and his kind.'

'And when I am married?' Annelise was beginning to
enjoy herself. If he was angry with her, so much the better.
He might be her guardian, but Lady Emily had told her she

had a right to her own opinions and she was determined
not to be crushed by his disapproval. Especially as she had
done nothing to deserve it! Besides, if he was angry, he
was not indifferent. 'May I choose my own friends, then,
sir?'

'You would be a fool to choose Rathbone even then,'
Justin said, glaring at her. He was no longer amused. Had
she not a grain of sense in her head? 'There are men who
make women happy—and those who care only for themselves. I would not like to see you at the mercy of such a
monster.'

'You need not be concerned,' Annelise said, a husky
laugh escaping her as she discovered how easy it was to
provoke him. 'I do not particularly care for the Earl.'

'We must be thankful you have sense enough for that,'
he said, and would have continued in the same vein had
not two men come up to them at that very moment.
'Ralph...Robert,' he said, and suddenly he was smiling as
he turned to Annelise. 'I believe you know these gentlemen? My friends—I would like to introduce you to my
ward, Mistress Woodward.'

'Oddsfish!' Ralph exclaimed as he took a second look at
her. 'I'll be damned if it isn't the little Puritan wench...'
Seeing Justin's quick frown, he amended his tone, becoming instantly respectful. 'I beg your pardon, Mistress Woodward. Your beauty has robbed me of what little wits I had,
and Justin will tell you they were never of the best order.'

Annelise liked the way he turned the jest against himself.
Nothing could deny the fact that he was ill-favoured, and
at their first meeting she had not liked him, but now she
sensed the warmth of his nature and that he was her guardian's true friend.

'I shall forgive you,' she said, giving him a smile that
would have melted harder hearts than poor Ralph's. He fell
instantly in love with her, knew his cause was hopeless,

and vowed then and there to serve her as a friend. 'Providing you will dance with me. This is my first time at Court, sir—and I would make the most of it.'

'Mistress, I would die for you.' Ralph swept her a reverent bow. 'But dance I cannot—unless you wish me to crush your toes?' He turned to Sir Robert Harris. 'I dare say Rob here would be glad to serve where I cannot?'

'Gladly,' Sir Robert said at once. Like Ralph, he had fallen immediately under Annelise's spell, but, unlike his wiser friend, he did not know his cause was hopeless. 'You could not wish to dance with a clumsy bear when I am here to do your bidding.'

'Then Ralph shall bring me some wine when we have done,' Annelise said, her smile embracing them both. She laid her hand on the younger man's arm. 'Come, sir. I would have news of Cambridgeshire. Tell me, how do you go on with the restoration of your estates?'

Ralph stood with Justin as the two went off, clearly in harmony with one another. He saw the way his friend clenched his jaw and guessed at at least a part of his thoughts. Justin was attracted to the wench himself, though perhaps he was not yet fully aware of his feelings towards her.

'Surprising, isn't it? One would not have thought it from our first sight of her—but she is a heartbreaker, a born courtesan,' he remarked. 'I am not sure if she realises her power just now—but give her time and she will have us all her slaves.'

'My mother says Lady Woodward was much the same in her youth,' replied Justin, a nerve flicking in his throat. 'I was concerned that her spirit might have been broken—but now I fear she will need a tight rein if she is not to bring herself to grief.'

'Surely not?' Ralph said mildly. 'She is merely trying

her legs, like a newborn foal. She could be gentled to the bridle, Justin.'

'All women are faithless,' he replied with a wry look at his friend. 'It would be a wasted effort to try. No, I desire only that she should have a care for her reputation until she is safely wed—after that she may go to hell in her own way.'

Ralph stared as Justin walked off, leaving the ballroom without a backward glance. He had sometimes wondered what drove his friend of late. What was he looking for— why so bitter? He had always been quick to fire up, but he had also known how to laugh at adversity and himself.

It was true that Justin had been forged in the heat of battle, that his childhood had been unhappy—but many had. Children of the aristocracy were left to the care of a nurse, and the sons of the house often spent half their life in the household of a stranger, to learn of duty and to serve. Justin was not alone in that, nor in having been forced to live as an exile for years. He had always in the past possessed a strong sense of humour; surely this anger could not merely be because he thought all women cast in the same mould as his mother?

Something had happened to Justin—but what?

Had he already begun to suffer the pangs of unrequited love? Ralph had fallen for the little Puritan wench instantly, but it was the kind of love which was as happy to serve as to possess. Justin would love very differently. He would need to own…he would demand perfection.

'And where, pray, is my ward this noon?' Justin asked of his mother. He had found her alone in the small salon overlooking the garden at the back of the house, and bent to kiss her cheek. 'I wish to speak with her.'

'Do not frown so,' Lady Emily replied, smiling inwardly as she saw his impatient look. As a child he had been quick, impatient—but so loving! Even now, there were times when he showed her a careless affection. 'There is not the least need for this stern mood, Justin. Indeed, it is not like you to take such a moral stand. Why should you deny her the pleasures you would not deny others? Annelise has done nothing that you could possibly disapprove of—and at this moment she is walking by the river, accompanied by your own friends.'

'Why did you not go with her?'

Lady Emily arched her brows in surprise. 'A servant is attending her. Surely you do not imagine her to be in danger, either moral or physical, with Ralph there? He is a gentleman, Justin—and, unless I mistake the matter, cares for her.'

'She is safe enough with him,' he agreed. He took up a quill and twisted it between his fingers. 'Robert is fool enough for anything, but I suppose I may trust Ralph as much as any man.'

'I suppose you may.' Lady Emily hid her amusement. This from a man who had hitherto shown no sign of caring for anything or anyone in particular!

Justin looked at her, his manner becoming less tense. 'Do you need anything? Have you enough money?'

'You are always generous. I want for nothing in the material sense, thank you.'

He nodded. 'Who are you writing to, Mother?'

'A friend—no one you care for.'

'A lover, I imagine.' He smiled as she did not deny it, then wandered away to stare out at the gardens, which stretched down towards the riverbank. The river itself was hidden from his view by shrubs and trees, but he could picture it in his mind. Somewhere out there, Annelise was strolling with his friends. He was amused despite himself, despite the mood that had come upon him of late. She had them both eating out of her hands as though they were puppies at her beck and call. They were both devoted to her, ready to do her bidding at the flicker of an eyelid. She had won them both completely within the space of a few days. 'Have you never loved anyone, Mother?' he asked without turning round.

'I have loved you, Justin.' He made no reply, but she saw by the way he held himself that he did not quite believe her. 'I might have come to love your father. I was fifteen when they married me to him. He took me for the dowry I brought him. He had his mistresses even then. I was the brood mare he needed to give himself an heir, no more. Once you were born he hardly bothered with me. Do you wonder that I found pleasure elsewhere?'

The quill snapped between Justin's fingers. He would not look at her as he said, 'Excuse me, Mother. I believe I see Mistress Woodward returning. I shall go to meet her.'

'Justin…'

He did not look round as she called his name. Lady Emily sighed. As a boy, Justin had adored her. He had been such a loving, loveable child—until one summer's afternoon, when he had discovered her in the garden wrapped in her lover's arms. He had turned against her from that moment, becoming prone to moods and sudden fits of temper and causing her so much trouble that she had given in to his father's demands that he should be sent away to the house of a relative, where he would complete his education.

She would never forget the look he had given her as he was taken away, a look that had spoken of betrayal and a broken heart. She had not seen him again until he had returned to join his father and fight for King Charles I—and by then he had been so changed she had not known him. The moods had gone, but there was a carelessness about him that disturbed her. He seemed to care for no one and nothing, though his manners were those of the perfect courtier—always gallant, always laughing and ready to rise to a challenge, as though his life meant nothing to him.

She often wondered what might have happened if she had kept him with her...but of course that had not been possible.

Unaware of his mother's regrets, Justin left the house and began to walk towards the little group wending their way unhurriedly through the rose garden. It would appear they were all in high good humour, he thought, experiencing a strange sensation he was unable to place. Could he be envious of his friends? Surely not! Yet they seemed to be so easy in her company, and she in theirs—while he could do nothing but quarrel with her.

He watched as Sir Robert plucked a red rose still folded in a tight bud and presented it to her with a courtly flourish. Annelise laughed, holding it to her nose to inhale its perfume, then said something that made both of her companions laugh, her head tipped to one side, eyes bright with mischief.

How lovely she was, how innocent as she teased her friends! Justin felt bereft, as though he had somehow been excluded from something very special. Then his sense of the ridiculous reasserted itself, and he allowed himself to see the humour of his situation. Like it or not, he stood guardian to this beautiful, wilful girl—a girl he had created by giving her into his mother's hands.

Annelise looked up as she became aware of him. The laughter left her face and she became apprehensive, as though she expected him to scold her.

'Were you looking for me, sir?'

'Only to tell you we are going to the theatre this evening,' he said. 'I have taken a box for us—to which you are both invited.' He glanced at his friends. 'I pray you will take supper with us, gentlemen?'

'I have a prior engagement,' Sir Robert said, looking put out. 'I suppose I could cry off—but it is with Buckingham.'

'Then you should keep it,' Justin advised. 'You know his temper. Ralph—you will come?'

'Of course. I have no engagements that could keep me away.' He turned to Annelise. 'My thanks for a pleasant walk, Mistress Woodward. I must leave you now. Rob, will you bear me company?'

'Of course. Until tomorrow, Mistress Woodward. You have not forgotten our picnic and the river trip?'

'No, sir. How could I when you have been good enough to arrange it for my sake?' She smiled at both gentlemen. 'Thank you for the rose and for keeping me company. Until we meet again, sirs.' She held the rose to her nose, her eyes bright with amusement as they kissed hands and left her.

Justin was silent, staring after the two men as they walked away. Did she guess her power over them, was she using it for advantage—or was she just playing at being a courtesan? He swung round as she addressed him.

'Do you mean to scold me, sir? Have I done something to displease you?'

Justin's eyes dwelled on her face, a faint twitch at the corner of his mouth. The little witch! He should have been warned the day he'd found her singing in the woods; she was no demure Puritan and never had been, though she had been made to follow their ways for much of her life. She had too much spirit in her, too much mischief. Yet in his heart he believed she was still innocent, still inherently modest.

That look in her eyes was meant to challenge him. Well, he would let her have sway for once.

'Do I always scold you?'

'Not quite always.' She pulled a petal from her rose, glancing at him from beneath her long lashes.

'You must forgive me if I have seemed harsh of late. I have had much to occupy my mind.'

'Does the case go well?'

'It goes slowly,' he replied, a look of frustration in his eyes. 'If the King would but intercede—but he has his own problems. He is pulled this way and that. Everyone has a favour to ask, and he cannot decide for one without offending another.'

Annelise nodded. Although a newcomer, she was aware of the undercurrents at Court. The King *was* pulled this way and that, by Parliament and courtiers, friends and enemies; she thought that only his wry sense of humour could save him from the anger he must feel at being manipulated by greedy men wishing to serve their own ends.

'Does it mean so much to you, to have your father's estates restored?'

'What is mine, is mine.' Justin's eyes glittered. His father had died on the field of battle, struck down before his eyes—and he had lived. How could he explain the guilt he felt at being left alive when so many others had died that day—the need to put right the wrong that had been done so many of his friends? 'My father died for the King, for his beliefs. I was forced to flee for my life. Why should I give up my inheritance?'

It was a thorny question. The estate had been bought in good faith by its present owner, but because it had been sequestered by Parliament at the end of the war and not sold to cover debts, Justin was entitled to compensation. He had already been offered money in lieu, but he wanted the house and land.

'You could buy another house,' Annelise offered. 'Begin again.'

'No. You do not understand. It is a matter of principle—of honour.'

'And you think me incapable of understanding that?'

Annelise turned away as the tears pricked, not wanting him to see he had hurt her, but he caught her arm and turned her to face him. He reached out, fingers gently tracing the line of her cheek. 'No, I do not think you incapable of understanding,' he said. 'But you cannot know how it feels to lose everything.'

'You think I did not lose as much as you? At least you had your freedom, sir. I was a prisoner of my uncle's doctrine for years. I lived, but was not truly alive—until Lady Emily brought me here.'

Justin was silenced, acknowledging that she was right with a brief nod of his head. In her way, she had suffered as much as anyone. He stared at her for some moments, then reached out to lift a strand of her wayward hair. How lovely she was! It was in his mind that if she had not been his ward he would have liked to kiss her—to make love to her.

'Was it very hard, Annelise?'

'It was not so very bad while my mother lived,' she said, her mouth trembling as she fought her emotions. 'After she died, I was numb for a long time. I felt so empty…so alone. My aunt was not a loving woman. She did her duty by me, and was not unkind, but I see now that she never cared for me. Lady Emily has shown me more kindness, more affection…' Seeing his expression of doubt, she stopped abruptly. 'You question her affection for me?'

'My mother likes beautiful things. You are a pleasant diversion. Why should she not be kind to you?'

'That is not worthy of you.' Annelise spoke angrily, her colour heightened. 'She does not deserve your scorn. You should not hate her. She loves you.'

'What do you know of my feelings for her or hers for me?' Justin glared at her, pricked by her criticism. He was not always as kind to his mother as he might be. His guilt made him speak harshly. 'I pray you, keep your ill-judged opinions to yourself, mistress.'

'Why should I?' Annelise flared. 'She has been good to me—and not just because I amuse her. Lady Emily is my friend. I love her!'

'Do you?' Her readiness to defend those she cared for caused him to pause, the anger draining from his eyes as swiftly as it had come. 'I am glad if it is true. It is good that she has such a friend.'

'Of course it is true!'

'Yes, of course it is. I did not mean to question it.'

A smile of such warmth and sweetness touched his mouth then that her heart caught. When he looked at her that way she could forgive him anything. She could have let herself like him all too well, yet knew it would be most improper in her to think of him as other than her guardian. She knew also that many of the ladies she had tried so hard to emulate would not have given a thought to such concerns, but despite all Lady Emily had taught her there were times when her Puritan upbringing came back to haunt her

As she hesitated, he said, 'Why do we always quarrel? Come, let us agree to tolerate each other. Shall we take a turn about the gardens—or would you prefer that I went away?'

'I should like to walk with you, sir. I did not mean to make you cross.'

'Nor have you. Take my arm,' he said, offering it to her. 'I am determined not to quarrel with you again. Let us talk of more pleasant things. I believe my mother has taken you to the theatre before this?'

'Yes, several times. We went as guests of her friends, as soon as I had clothes that were fit to be seen in public.'

Justin nodded. He refrained from asking for names, lest the answer made him lose his temper again. He would not wreck the evening he had planned so carefully before it began.

'Tonight we are to see Master Shakespeare's comedy— *The Taming of the Shrew*.'

'Oh, yes, I have read the play.' Annelise laughed as he raised his brows, giving her a quizzing stare. 'My uncle would not have approved, of course—but my mother gave me all her books just before she died. I hid them, and sometimes took a book to my room on Sunday.'

'Indeed?' Justin was amused. So she had found ways to escape the strictness of her uncle's rules even then. 'You would have been punished for that if you were caught, I dare say?'

'I was once or twice,' she admitted, her smile fading. 'My aunt did not beat me—she made me pray with her for hours. For the sake of my soul, that I might repent and see the error of my ways. She said she knew I did not mean to be wicked, that I would not willingly cause her such pain…'

'There is no sin in reading for pleasure.' Justin frowned as he glanced at her. 'I have many books that might interest you in my own library. There is a Bestiary, which has drawings of many strange and wonderful animals.'

'I should like to see that,' Annelise said, pleased by the invitation. 'But poetry is my favourite. I have a copy of a poem by Colonel Lovelace—*Lucasta*—but it is so worn that I fear it will soon fall to pieces.'

Justin nodded and began to recite.

> *Tell me not (Sweet) I am unkind,*
> *That from the nunnery*
> *Of thy chaste breast and quiet mind,*
> *To war and arms I fly.*

*True, a new mistress now I
chase,*
  The first foe in the field;
*And with a stronger faith
embrace*
  A sword, a horse a shield.

Yet this inconstancy is such,
  As you too shall adore;
*I could not love thee (Dear) so
much,*
  Lov'd I not Honour more.

'I shall lend you my own copy while I have yours re-bound,' Justin said when he had finished reciting the verse. 'As you know, *Lucasta* was written in prison and published later, but last year Lovelace's brother collected all the Colonel's poems together and I subscribed to a copy. But yours must have a sentimental value and you would no doubt like to have it restored to its former state.'

'Could that be done? I should be so grateful. Colonel Lovelace was a friend of my father—and my mother had the poem bound in his memory. I think she felt the verse stood for everything my father had believed in.'

'You told His Majesty that she died of a broken heart—was that the truth?'

'She could not bear to live after my father died, and though she lingered for several years she was but a shadow of herself. I believe she cared for me, but I could not replace the man she had adored.' Annelise's face was so sad that he was tempted to take her in his arms and kiss away the memory. He crushed the temptation ruthlessly.

'She must have been an exceptional woman,' he said, in a tone that made her stare at him.

He sounded so disbelieving, as though he did not truly

believe that any woman could die of a broken heart. Annelise was hurt, but she did not want to challenge him. For the first time they were talking without arguing. She wanted to savour the experience, to enjoy it for as long as it lasted.

Alas, Annelise's hopes of reaching an understanding with her guardian did not continue beyond that evening. Justin seemed relaxed as they left for the theatre, smiling at her as he handed her in the sedan chair, but his mood did not last long. He and Ralph walked by the chairs; both were wearing their swords, and both were forced to draw them when they came upon a disturbance not far from the theatre.

A small group of men were demonstrating about something. There was some chanting and shouts. Annelise could not quite make out what the trouble was about, but she heard Justin's voice ordering them to give way and then the sound of a scuffle.

'What is happening?' she asked, putting her head out of the curtains as Justin told the chairmen to continue a few minutes later. 'What did those men want?'

'Nothing to concern you,' he replied, looking grim. 'It is over now, forget it. You are quite safe, I promise you.'

Annelise withdrew behind her curtain, but when they arrived at the theatre a few minutes later, she asked Ralph what had been going on.

'They were protesting about some new act of Parliament's condemning the regicides,' he said. 'It seems several more are to be tried for their lives—men who were not present at the trial and did not sign the death warrant.'

'That can surely not be right?' Annelise said. 'His Majesty would not want to take such a harsh revenge?'

'You do not need to trouble yourself over such things,' Justin said, taking her elbow. 'Come, let us go in or we shall be late.'

Annelise saw the nerve flicking in his neck and wondered at it. Why should he be concerned? It surely could not matter to him if such men were brought before the courts?

She could not know that Justin suspected the demonstration had merely been a ruse, to cover a more sinister plot— that he had seen a face in the crowd he recognised, and believed he might have been done to death in the confusion had Ralph not been there to help him break up the mob.

Annelise had no time to sort out her thoughts or question his change of mood, for they were caught up in the throng of people entering the theatre.

Annelise had been slightly shocked by her first visit to a play, and not only because she had known her uncle would have considered it sinful—the press of people, the smell of heavy perfume mixing with the stench of unwashed bodies coming from the pits, and the bawdy comments of the audience during the play itself, when they lost no chance to hector or insult an actor they disliked, had all seemed overpowering at first. However, she had soon become used to it, and was looking forward to the performance that evening.

Once comfortably seated in Justin's box, she was able to look about and recognise people she had met—friends of Lady Emily and gentlemen of the Court. She saw she was being stared at by one man in particular, and blushed as she realised it was Earl Rathbone. He nodded to her and she inclined her head, before turning away to listen to what Justin was saying to his friend.

'If Charles wants peace in the country, he must make a stand against these bloodthirsty fools,' Justin was saying. 'There have been killings enough.'

'He will be more secure once he has been crowned,' Ralph said. 'But I agree with you, only those directly involved should...'

'Hush,' Lady Emily warned. 'The play is about to begin.'

The men continued to whisper in low voices, but Annelise was captured by the play, especially when Petruchio began to woo Katharina.

Their banter made her laugh aloud and clap her hands as the battle of wills began.

Katharina. Yes, keep you warm.
Petruchio. Marry, so I mean, sweet Katharine, in thy bed:
And therefore, setting all this chat aside,
Thus in plain terms: your father hath consented
That you shall be my wife; your dowry 'greed on;
And, will you, nill you, I will marry you.

Annelise laughed in delight at the look of indignation on the face of the actress who was playing Katharina, then glanced over her shoulder as she became aware of Justin watching her.

'I see the play amuses you?' He arched his brows. 'You approve of her wilfulness?'

'Why should she not choose her own husband?' Annelise replied. 'At least she need not give in to him at once.'

Justin smiled, but made no further comment until the end of the act, when the curtains were drawn and the talk became general. People were standing up, looking about to see who else was there, waving and calling to their friends.

Annelise's gaze was drawn to a woman who seemed to be looking very hard at her. She was a lady of great beauty, dressed so elegantly that she put almost everyone else in the shade, but at that moment she seemed vastly put out about something. As her green eyes narrowed to angry slits, Annelise heard Justin murmur something. He cursed softly, then stood up and bowed in the woman's direction. She nodded slightly, smiled, and fanned herself before turning away to speak to her companion.

'Excuse me,' Justin said. 'I must go and greet Madame Varennes or she will think me rude.'

Annelise said nothing as he left the box, but after he had gone she turned to Lady Emily.

'Who is she?' she asked. 'She is very beautiful.'

'I suppose so,' Justin's mother agreed, 'if you care for that style of beauty, which I must confess I do not. That striking silver-blonde hair is not her own, you know, and she wears too much jewellery. Her name is Mirabelle Varennes. She is a friend of Justin's…a close friend, I suppose. I had not heard she was in London. She must have important business here or she would not have left Paris.'

Annelise felt a chill strike deep into her heart. Madame Varennes was Justin's mistress. Of course! It was no wonder she had been looking so annoyed. She must have been displeased to see him with another woman, but she did not know Annelise was merely his ward.

Annelise could not avoid watching their meeting, though she did her best not to stare, fluttering her fan before her face as if she were over-warm. It was obvious that they knew each other well—intimately! A knot of jealousy formed in Annelise's chest as she saw Justin kiss her hand and the way Madame Varennes smiled at him so confidently.

'Take no notice,' Lady Emily said at ear. 'He will not marry her. She amuses him, but that is all.'

'It is entirely the Marquis's own affair who he marries,' Annelise replied, shutting her fan with a little snap. She raised her head proudly. 'It matters not to me!'

'Of course not,' Lady Emily replied, smiling inwardly. 'Why should you care, my dear? You have suitors aplenty to keep you happy.'

But she did care. Annelise felt the jealousy choking her as she watched Madame Varennes laughing and teasing

Justin. It was obvious she was telling him a story, one he seemed to find vastly amusing.

Annelise turned away, letting her gaze travel round the theatre. She saw Earl Rathbone staring at her again and smiled at him, her eyes meeting his boldly. He kissed his hand to her and she let him see she was amused. Why should she not? Since that first evening at Court she had deliberately tried to keep her distance from the Earl, but now she saw no reason why she should. Justin was her guardian, but the strict morality he would impose on her was not followed through in his own life. He did much as he pleased—and so would she in future.

Chapter Four

'**W**hy is Justin glowering at us, do you suppose?' asked Robert as he and Annelise strolled together to the river's sloping edge the next morning. It was a still, warm day, sunlight dancing on the water like silver stars fallen from the sky. 'He seems forever in a black mood these days. I do not know what ails him. It is not like him. He always had his moods, but not so intense—not so often.'

'No?' Annelise arched her fine brows at him. In her experience, Justin was all too often wont to frown on her. She recalled the fleeting moments when for a time she had glimpsed a very different man from the one who seemed to take his duties as her guardian so seriously. 'Perhaps he is angry because of the delay over the restoration of his estates?'

'Perhaps...' Robert had his own explanation of his friend's moods but did not voice it.

'Look at those swans,' Annelise said. 'The cygnets are almost full grown—and there! See that brilliant flash of colour? I am sure it is a kingfisher. Yes, now you can see it more clearly. Isn't it wonderful?'

Robert had eyes only for her. She looked so beautiful standing there in the sunlight. Despite her teasing and her flirting, he knew her for the honest, modest girl she was. Very few of the ladies at Court could take such pleasure in simple things. The lady who had been his own mistress until a few days earlier had only smiled like that when he'd given her a trinket of some kind, the more valuable the better. Since what money he now possessed was needed for his estate, he had grown tired of her avariciousness and they had parted acrimoniously. Perhaps in part, Robert admitted to himself, because he had not been able to hide his admiration for Annelise. He looked at her, his eyes revealing much of what he felt.

'You are still a country girl at heart, aren't you?'

Annelise's head went up, her eyes meeting his with a swift, teasing challenge. 'La, sir! Do you mean to insult me? And after all Lady Emily's work!'

'No, of course not,' he replied at once. 'I meant no insult, rather 'twas a compliment.' His look was hot, intense, betraying his desperation more than he knew to one who watched from a distance. 'For myself I weary of life at Court. It is my intention to return home soon…' He hesitated, taking a step towards her. 'My one desire is to…'

'Annelise!' Justin's voice broke in as Robert was about to declare himself. 'If you are ready, I think it's time we made our way home. You have not forgotten we are expected at Court this evening?'

'No, I had not forgotten, sir.' Annelise was grateful for the interruption. Much as she liked Sir Robert, and enjoyed his company, she was not ready for a declaration just yet. She would have to marry in time, but why should she not make the most of her freedom first? She bestowed a sparkling look on her suitor. 'We ought to be leaving, but I shall not forget this day, sir. It has been most pleasant. You were kind to arrange the picnic for my sake.'

'We shall meet again this evening, I promise you.'

Robert made her a little bow and walked off to help with

the ordering of the boats which were to row them back up river. Annelise lingered a while longer, reluctant to leave this idyllic spot.

'It is so pretty here,' she said on a faint sigh.

Justin glanced at her, a wry amusement in his eyes. She liked to play the sophisticated courtier, but at times her innocence was all too evident.

'My estates in Hampshire have a stream running through, and there are black swans on the lake.'

'Black swans?' Annelise turned to him, a look of delight on her face. 'How I should love to see them!'

'Perhaps you will one day.' A faint smile lurked in his eyes. 'Unless you marry before I have regained them, in which case you may be too busy to visit.'

'It is not my intention to marry in haste,' she said, fanning herself. Her heart was suddenly racing like the wind. How she longed to visit Justin's estate—to live there with him, away from the scandal and intrigues of the Court. No, no, her thoughts were most improper! She could not marry her own guardian. He himself had told her to look elsewhere. What was she thinking of? She turned away in confusion. 'La! It is so warm. Do you not think it warm, sir?'

'You do not wish to marry?' His voice held a hint of mockery. 'Is Robert aware of that?'

'We are friends.' She felt her cheeks flame. Had he not interrupted them, she was well aware that Robert might well have declared himself. 'You told me to practise my arts on my friends, sir.'

'But not to break Robert's heart. Ralph understands your smiles are not to be taken seriously; I am not sure poor Rob does.'

'Then perhaps I should break other hearts?'

'Now what mischief are you planning, mistress?'

There was a reluctant smile about his mouth, a gleam in his eyes that told her he was more amused than angry with her. She tipped her head to one side, giving him such a wicked, challenging look that he was forced to laughter.

'I little knew what I did when I gave my mother a free hand with you, Annelise. I doubt not I shall rue it before I am much older.'

When he laughed, when he looked at her that way, Annelise's heart wanted to dance for sheer joy. How happy they might be together if he would only cast off his dark moods and be himself with her.

'Why, sir, I seek only to please you. If you do not care to see me smile on Sir Robert, I will smile on someone else, whose heart is not so vulnerable.'

'You wish only to please me?' Justin looked disbelieving. 'Why do I think you would prefer to tease and thwart me, Annelise? Why can I not believe in this concern you profess for my peace of mind?'

'That is the fault of your own character,' she replied, dimpling. 'If you will not let yourself trust, sir, it is no fault of mine.'

Justin stared at her. Perhaps she was right; perhaps he should learn to take what she said at face value? Yet even if he believed in her smiles, it could make no difference to the outcome. He must and would see her married to a decent man.

Still, he would have an end to the conflict between them if it were possible. He would have continued the conversation, but a shout from Ralph warned them the boats were ready to row them home. It was time to leave. Annelise had turned, was walking back to join the others.

Justin watched as Ralph helped her into the first boat. He himself followed with Lady Emily in the second. Since he was facing up-river, he was able to watch his ward talking and laughing with her friends for the whole of the journey home, which did nothing for his peace of mind, and very little for his temper.

True to her word, Annelise saved her most flirtatious smiles for Ralph, which, far from easing Sir Robert's feelings, caused him to sulk and leave with no more than a curt goodbye to anyone when they were all disembarked.

'I fear Rob has fallen hard,' Ralph remarked to Justin as he lingered after the ladies and servants had gone up to the house. 'I know well she hath no love of me save as a friend, but I suspect the lad carries vain hopes of having his regard returned.'

'Why vain?' Justin asked, looking at him thoughtfully. 'She is in no haste to wed, that I know—but she would as well marry him as any man. Indeed, I think he would make her a good husband.'

'You think so?' Ralph frowned. Was Justin so blind? 'He is not the only one to have noticed her, my friend. I can name at least a dozen who would like to bed her, and three that are most willing to offer a wedding ring to gain their object.'

'You believe they have marriage in mind?'

'Breckon looks for a new wife to mother his brats,' Ralph said. 'John Marshall has no estate since it was sold by his mother to pay debts, and would no doubt be glad to take Annelise for her inheritance. Ashley Carter is better placed, but I would swear he too hath fallen hard for Mistress Woodward. There may be others, but these three have been particularly plain in their attentions.'

'Then I have no need to fear for her future.' Justin gave his friend a mocking look. 'So why do I feel uneasy, Ralph? Why do I have the feeling that I should have left her in the country, that she can only bring trouble to me? Answer me that if you can.'

'Only you can answer truly,' Ralph replied. 'Methinks you already know the truth but are too stubborn to admit it, even to yourself.'

'What mean you, sir?'

Justin frowned as Ralph shook his head, smiled mockingly and walked away.

No, it was too ridiculous to consider! Justin denied the implications of his friend's words. Love was something he had never allowed himself to feel…not since his first, very painful experience of betrayal.

Bruised and hurt by the discovery of the mother he had set up as a perfect goddess on his childish pedestal passionately responding to the embraces of a lover, Justin had reacted instinctively, hiding his pain and fear behind a child's temper. When he'd been sent away from his home he had felt betrayed, shut away from the love of the woman he had so blindly adored. At first he had been miserable, but as time had passed he had come to accept his new home—and its beautiful mistress.

Lady Isobel had had a fair loveliness that took away a man's breath. She had been charming, witty and a great courtesan, forever laughing and singing, drawing men to her as a moth to the flame. Her husband had always been at Court, spending little time at his estates.

Left to herself, Lady Isobel had done much as she'd pleased. Justin had discovered almost at once that she took lovers whenever it suited her, but she had been kind to him; she had mothered the youth who had come to her with the eyes of a wounded fawn. And, when his manhood had come upon him, she had taken him to her bed and taught him the arts of love.

'Making love is the greatest pleasure given to woman or man,' Lady Isobel had told him in her delightful husky voice as he had lain with his tender head against her breasts and wondered at this gift she had given him. 'But never give your heart, Justin—for that way lies only pain. Take your fill of pleasuring, live your life to the full, but expect no more than a fleeting satisfaction. Learn your lesson well and you will save yourself torment in the future.'

In his way, Justin had loved his mistress, but she had wearied of him in time and looked for others to take his place in her bed. He too had begun to find delight in other warm, yielding flesh. Always, he felt pleasure in giving as much as he took, for Isobel had taught him well, but he never let himself think beyond the moment of fulfilment. Romantic love was only a myth, sung of by minstrels and troubadours but of no substance, gone with the morning light as often as not, melting into nothingness as mist lapped up by the sun.

No, Ralph was wrong! It was true that Annelise haunted Justin's thoughts, waking or sleeping. Her smiles made his pulses race with excitement and his manhood burned with aching desire for her. He could hardly close his eyes without dreaming of her lying beneath him, her quivering, willing body opening to him eagerly—but she was his ward! Forbidden to him by all the laws of decency and honour.

He could not use her as he would a mistress. She was too innocent, despite the wicked, infuriating looks she cast his way.

To fall in love with her could only bring him pain.

Did the minx know what her smiles did to him? Sometimes he thought she was deliberately provoking him, and then…a wry smile came to his mouth as he thought of the punishments he would like to inflict if she were not in his care and he bound by duty to protect her.

Damn her! Damn all women! Justin swore beneath his breath. Enough of this madness. He had not lain with a woman since leaving Paris, and his restless dreams were the product of a need to relieve the demands of a passionate nature, nothing more. It was high time he called on Mira-belle Varennes!

Annelise sat soaking in the tub of perfumed water, her knees brought almost to her chest as she closed her eyes and dreamed of a man's face close to hers, his lips touching hers in such a kiss that it brought a sigh from deep within her.

She must not allow herself to think this way. It was wrong—but how could she control the prompting of her heart? When the touch of his hand sent little shivers coursing through her whole body, and his smile made her melt with longing for something she only vaguely understood.

'Is the water too hot, mistress?' The maid's voice broke into her thoughts.

'No. It is just right, thank you.'

Annelise smiled at the hovering maid. It was a delight to her that Lady Emily did not frown upon cleansing the body frequently. Annelise had seldom been allowed the luxury of a bath before she came to London. Her aunt had considered it sinful to indulge in such things merely for the sake of pleasure. Twice a year was quite enough in Lady Prudence's estimation.

Annelise had washed all over her body every day of her life since childhood, usually in cold water. It had made her shiver on winter mornings, when she had often had to break the ice on the water in her pitcher, but she needed to be clean, to smell sweet. To soak in this tub of warm water for as long as she wished was sheer bliss. And yet indulging in such pleasures had an odd effect on her, inducing thoughts she knew to be sinful.

It was only reluctantly that she got out, allowing the maid to wrap her in the bathing sheets and pat her skin dry. After she was dry, she rubbed perfumed oil into her skin, then stood patiently as the servants dressed her in layers of stiff petticoats and then the heavy overdress of embroidered silk.

That evening, she was wearing a new gown of emerald-green, its bodice encrusted with pearls and small diamonds. The neckline was rather daring, though she had threaded a filmy scarf about it so that her breasts were glimpsed

through the gauze rather than revealed too brazenly. It gave
her an air of natural modesty, of which she was totally
unaware but of which Lady Emily approved when she came
in a moment or so later.

'You look beautiful, my dear,' she said, kissing Annelise's cheek. 'But then, you always do.'

'You are very kind, ma'am.'

'Not at all; it is the truth. You must have seen that from
the way you are welcomed at Court. His Majesty has noticed you, though he is too discreet to show it—for Madam
Barbara's sake if nothing more.'

'Surely not…' Annelise blushed. Innocent she might be,
but she knew well enough what the King's interest in her
must mean. He was not a faithful man, and one mistress
would never hold him for long—even one as beautiful as
Lady Castlemaine. Nor had she any wish to oblige him.
There was only one man in whose arms she longed to lie.

'I assure you it is so, though you need do nothing for
the moment,' Lady Emily said. 'His Majesty would not
dream of making an advance to a lady of your quality until
after your marriage.' Her brows arched. 'Now, my dear,
Justin has sent his apologies. He cannot escort us to the
palace this evening, but will see us there later. However,
since dear Ralph has come to take his place, we shall not
want for protection.'

'Last night…that disturbance near the theatre,' Annelise
said, frowning as she recalled it. 'Do you know what was
wrong, ma'am? Justin seemed disturbed by it but would
not tell me why.'

'Politics,' said Lady Emily, and pulled a wry face. 'Justin
has many problems on his mind for the moment. I doubt
we shall see as much of him as before, though that is his
business, of course. It is sometimes better not to enquire
too closely, Annelise. Especially if the matter is personal…'

Annelise was thoughtful as she followed her hostess downstairs. Was Lady Emily trying to warn her that Justin's mind was now occupied elsewhere, that he was too busy to dance attendance on his ward?

Of course, it must be so. Annelise had seen the beautiful Mirabelle Varennes at the theatre. She was Justin's mistress. It was hardly likely he would bother to escort his mother and ward while she was in London.

How long would it be before she returned to Paris? Or was it her intention to live here—perhaps as Justin's wife?

The thought of Justin kissing that woman…lying with her…was too painful to be borne. Annelise remembered his warning given to her by the river that very day. He had asked her not to break Rob's heart, and she had promised to smile on someone less vulnerable—given the chance this evening, she would certainly do so!

The Earl of Rathbone was a dangerous man. Despite her inexperience and her relatively short time at Court, Annelise had no doubt as to what kind of a man he really was. A man who took lovers when he pleased and moved on to another without a backward glance. Well, she had no intention of becoming one of his discarded mistresses, but it would do no harm to flirt with him. After all, Justin could not complain. He had told her to look elsewhere—and so, if he did not like to see his ward in the company of a man he clearly disliked, it was his own fault.

'You look beautiful this evening,' Sir Robert said as he came to beg Annelise to grant him the favour of a dance. 'I swear that colour becomes you very well.'

'You are very kind to say so.'

Robert looked at her. She seemed quiet and thoughtful, even reserved. He had thought she favoured him above others who danced attendance on her, but now, sensing a withdrawal, wondered if he had done something to offend her.

'It is hot in here this evening. Do you not find it so?' Robert asked as their dance ended. 'Would you like to go out to the terraces for some air?'

Annelise hesitated. She *was* feeling very warm, but she had no doubt that Robert's desire to get her alone was for one purpose only: he wanted to propose to her. Realising he was becoming desperate, she understood for the first time how much her refusal would hurt him, and was sorry. She had thought of him as a friend, never imagining her teasing would make him fall in love with her. If only her flirting would work on the man she was increasingly drawn to, despite his apparent indifference—but, no, she must not allow herself to think of him!

'Not just yet,' she said. 'Tell me, have you…?'

She had been about to ask if he had spoken to Justin that evening, but the question was rendered unnecessary as she saw her guardian enter with Mirabelle Varennes on his arm. They were laughing together with all the ease of intimacy.

Annelise felt jealousy strike at her heart as she sensed the closeness of their mood. They had been making love shortly before they left for the palace that evening! She was sure of it as she saw the way Mirabelle looked up into his eyes, and her stomach lurched.

Why must she feel this way about a man who was forbidden her? Why did her heart behave so oddly whenever he approached?

She wanted to run away and hide her hurt, but Justin had seen her. He spoke to Mirabelle, who nodded and looked at Annelise, then smiled condescendingly towards her.

They were coming to greet her! Annelise's hand trembled on Robert's arm and he looked at her in concern.

'Are you unwell, Annelise?'

'No, I am quite well, thank you.'

She was being torn apart, but she could not let anyone see her pain.

Annelise would have avoided the meeting if she could, but that would only have postponed the moment she dreaded. She squared her shoulders, taking hold of her nerves as they approached. To save her pride she must behave as though everything were normal, as though her heart was not breaking into tiny pieces.

'Annelise.' Justin's brow furrowed as he looked at her. 'May I present Madame Varennes? Mirabelle and I are old friends.'

'La, Justin!' Mirabelle said in soft, husky voice. 'How formal you make that sound, my dearest. We are very close friends—and I am delighted to meet you, Mademoiselle Woodward. Justin's ward is naturally welcome to me and my house at any time.' She leant forward to kiss Annelise's cheek, the cloying scent of her perfume making Annelise feel sick. 'There, now we shall be friends.'

Friends! Annelise saw the falseness beneath her smiles, and knew they could never be friends.

'Madame,' she said, making her a stiff curtsey. 'As my guardian's…friend, you are as welcome to me as I am to you.'

The tone of her voice was so clipped and cold that Justin gave her a harsh look. His eyes were so accusing that she blushed and glanced away for a moment, then anger restored her and she lifted her gaze to meet his. How dared he look at her that way? He had no right, no right at all!

Justin frowned, his expression a mixture of annoyance and regret. 'You will excuse us, Annelise. Mirabelle wishes to dance.' He inclined his head towards her and Robert. 'Robert, good evening.'

'I never thought she would actually follow him here,' Robert remarked as they walked away to join the other dancers forming the sets. 'In Paris they were laying bets as to her chances of getting him to wed her. I would have taken odds against it then, but now I am not so sure.'

'Excuse me,' Annelise said, blinking back the tears that threatened to shame her. 'I must speak to someone…'

She walked away from Robert, her back stiff. Inside, she was being torn to shreds, but she must not show her feelings! She must not let anyone guess at her deep unhappiness!

It was her intention to find a quiet spot where she could be alone, but she was detained as a man laid her hand on his arm.

'Not leaving so soon?' he said. 'I was hoping you would grant me the favour of this dance, Mistress Woodward?'

Annelise had not been aware of Earl Rathbone watching her, nor had she seen his approach. She stared at him blindly, her nerves screaming in agony. Justin was going to marry that woman! How could he? Did he not know how desperately Annelise loved him?

Loved him? Yes, of course! The immodest thoughts she'd had while bathing—the way he made her pulses throb—were indications that she had been falling in love with her guardian. But she must not! Annelise struggled against her feelings. Why should she love him? He was often stern with her, bringing her to the verge of tears—but, oh! his wonderful, wonderful smile. It had captured her foolish heart from the moment she had first seen him.

But it was useless, he thought Annelise a naive country girl. It was the beautiful, sophisticated Madame Varennes he loved.

She took a deep breath, gathering her courage as she looked up at the Earl. 'Thank you, sir. I should be happy to dance with you.'

Annelise was barely conscious of what she did as she gave Rathbone her hand. The smile she bestowed on him was brilliant, brittle as glass and meaningless. What did anything matter now that her heart felt as if it were breaking into a thousand pieces?

It would have been better if she had never come to London, better if she had never met Justin at all!

'You are in a reflective mood this evening,' Rathbone observed after they had been dancing for a while. 'Would you care to share your thoughts, Mistress Woodward?'

'Forgive me, I meant not to be rude,' she said, her cheeks flushing as she met his questing look. 'It is nothing…I have a little headache this evening.'

'Then we should not be dancing,' Rathbone said, his dark eyes intent on her face, boring into her as though he would know her very soul. 'It has been hot all day and the atmosphere is stale in here. Let me take you out to the terraces for a few minutes. You are overheated and need some air.'

Annelise felt the pressure of his fingers on her arm. He had such a firm grip on her that she knew it would be difficult to break away; if she were to try it would make people stare at her. Besides, why should she? Justin had warned her against this man, told her to have a care for her reputation, but he was merely playing the part of a strict guardian. No one else would mind what she did; almost everyone she knew was engaged in some kind of intrigue with a lover. Justin was not truly interested in what happened to her, nor was he so strict where his own morals were concerned.

Despite her misery, Annelise was aware that she was taking a risk by leaving the ballroom with the Earl. Justin would be furious if he chanced to see her go.

Perhaps that was her intention? At the back of her mind, she dimly perceived the truth—that her reckless behaviour was meant to anger her guardian. He would not be jealous, of course, because he did not want her, but he hated to be thwarted. And she preferred his anger to his indifference.

'You will soon feel better, Mistress Woodward,' the Earl

said as they left the overheated rooms behind and went outside. 'It is much cooler here, is it not?'

'Yes, thank you.'

Annelise looked about her. Her mind was in such turmoil that she had scarcely noticed where they were going. Rathbone had led her to a small, secluded courtyard which led into a walled garden. A fountain was spraying water into the air, splashing into a little pool where lilies grew and jewel-coloured fish swam beneath the spreading pads.

'Oh,' she said, taking a step towards the pool. In the moonlight, the water looked dark and mysterious, and she could smell the powerful scent of lilies. She smiled in pleasure. 'How lovely. I do not think I have been here before.'

'The courtyard is seldom used,' the Earl replied. 'Especially at night. Most avoid the night air and believe it full of evils, but the dark holds no fears for me. I thought we might be private for a moment, Mistress Woodward.' His voice had taken on a husky, seductive quality that sent shivers running down her spine. 'You must be aware that I have fallen victim to your charms—that you have entrapped me in your net, sweet enchantress.'

Annelise was startled. She had not expected such a bold statement, so swiftly made it took her breath away. It made her apprehensive and she took a step back from him.

'Forgive me, sir. I think you mistake…'

He moved closer, towering over her, eyes intense, mesmerising. 'I think not, mistress. Your looks and smiles have encouraged me to believe my suit would not be unwelcome to you.'

'Your suit? Speak you of marriage, sir?'

'Alas, I cannot,' Rathbone said. 'Were I free, I would offer you my name, but I was married long ago, when I was but a child—to a woman for whom I care nothing.'

'So you would have me as your mistress, sir? What of my reputation then?'

'Marry one of those fools who hang on your every word,' the Earl said, a sneer on his thick lips. 'I am a patient man. I can wait for my prize—I might even let your husband take your maidenhead.'

Such lewd, wicked words! Annelise was shocked, despite all she had seen and heard since coming to London—but to show outrage would make her a laughing stock at Court. She could not afford to become the butt of this man's sarcasm.

'Indeed, you are generous,' she said. The eager anticipation in his eyes made her angry. He really believed he had only to lift his finger and she would fall into his arms like a ripe plum. The conceit of the man! 'But would you have me make a cuckold of my husband, sir? Am I to forget duty and honour for your sake?'

'Come, mistress,' he chided, entering into what he thought her game. 'Offer me no false modesty. I know there is fire in you. You'll make no man a complacent wife. I'll swear you take a lover before you have been wed six months. I want to lay my claim now…to taste the delights that will eventually be mine.'

'What makes you think I would choose you?' Annelise was reckless as she lifted her gaze to challenge his, her smile mocking, matching his own. 'If I wanted a lover, why should I favour you above another? What can you give me that would tempt me to be your mistress?'

'So you are as avaricious as the rest of them?' Rathbone sneered. His eyes narrowed as he studied her. 'What is your price, mistress? Name it and, within reason, it shall be yours.'

'You could not buy me with a king's ransom,' Annelise said, her eyes bright with pride and anger. 'I mean to be no man's slave—yet I would not have you for my lover or my husband.'

She turned to leave, realising that she had been foolish

to expose herself to this man's importuning. She ought to have listened to Justin's warning. None of her other admirers would have spoken so outrageously, they had too much respect for her; this man had none.

'Where do you think you are going?'

Rathbone's hand clutched at her arm, his fingers bruising the tender flesh. She glanced round at him, face proud, eyes cold.

'I pray you, let me go, sir.'

'Not so fast, mistress. I have not finished with you. I would have you willing, eager, but…'

Realising what he intended, Annelise tried to wrench away from him, but his grip tightened, hurting her so that she gasped with pain. She struggled as he reached for her, pulling her to him, imprisoning her against him, and she twisted her face aside as his greedy mouth sought hers.

'Do not!' she cried. 'Let me go! Let me go this instant!'

'You whore!' Rathbone snapped. He ripped the gauze scarf from her gown, exposing her heaving breasts, the skin so milky white and soft he was driven wild by the sight. 'Women like you who tempt a man to madness deserve all they get!'

Annelise screamed as he buried his face against her tender flesh and she felt him pushing her back against a wall, his hand fumbling at her skirts as he muttered obscenities, threatening what he would do to her in such language that she felt sick.

'Let me go, you foul beast,' she gasped as the fear flooded through her. 'Take your hands from me.'

Oh, what had she done? Why had she come here? She must have been mad! Rathbone was too strong for her, his breath hot against her neck as she struggled and knew it was useless. He could do with her as he pleased; she could not prevent him.

'Help…' she cried. 'Leave me alone, sir!' Even as she

cried for help, she knew none could come—for who would hear her in this place?

'I suggest you do as she says, Rathbone—or I'll slit your throat like the swine you are.'

Justin's harsh tone had a powerful effect on the Earl. He released Annelise, turning with an oath to meet the challenge. The moon had come out, lighting up the courtyard like some theatrical stage on which a drama was about to be played. Annelise saw the colour drain from Rathbone's face as he realised Justin had both the means and the inclination to carry out his threat.

'She was willing,' he grunted, his mouth slack with fear as he saw the deadly blade pointing towards him. 'She wanted some air, that was her excuse—the bitch was eager for it, as they all are, despite their denials and protests. All the whores beg for it in the end.'

'No…' Annelise whispered. 'No, it was not so.'

'Rape is your preference, I believe?' Justin's eyes were like splintered ice, dangerous and threatening. 'I've known your reputation, Rathbone, known what a depraved, evil creature you are, that you deserve to die in the gutter amongst the filth—but as long as you did not interfere with me, or those I care for, I let you live. You should have heeded my warning.'

'Oddsfish!' the Earl ejaculated. 'You are going to murder me in cold blood? I've hardly touched the whore. If she was a virgin before this night, she is virgin still.'

'Because I came in time?' A tiny nerve flicked in Justin's throat. 'Move away from him, Annelise!' She had already begun to do so, but at his warning gave a cry of alarm and darted to the other side of the fountain. Justin jerked his head at her, indicating that she keep her distance, his blade pointed at Rathbone's heart. 'You deserve to die as you lived, sir, without honour—but I shall give you the chance to defend yourself. My seconds will call on you this very night.'

'No!' Annelise moaned, her heart racing wildly. She looked at him, and her eyes widened in terror. 'Please, Justin—do not fight a duel for my sake. It does not matter; he did not hurt me.'

'Hold your tongue! We shall speak later,' he said, throwing a look of such disgust at her that she felt it as the sting of a whip. 'Go in before you cause more trouble—and tell my mother to take you home.'

'Justin...'

'Do as I say!' he thundered at her. 'I shall follow when this affair is settled.'

He was so angry! His eyes glittered dangerously, nostrils flaring, mouth hard. She had never seen him like this, and it frightened her. He was a stranger, a man capable of killing. Oh, why had she come here? Why had she behaved so recklessly?

'Cover yourself first! We do not want the whole Court to know you have disgraced yourself.'

Annelise flushed at the scornful words, and bent to pick up the gauze scarf Rathbone had torn away.

'I... Forgive me,' she whispered. 'I did not think...'

Justin did not look at her. His face was carved from granite, cold and unforgiving in the moonlight. 'Do as I tell you,' he said. 'I shall deal with you later, mistress!'

Annelise tucked the torn scarf across her exposed breasts as best she could. Her skin felt hot as a wave of shame washed over her. Justin believed the Earl! He believed she had encouraged Rathbone's attentions—and it was true. She had not wanted this, but she had smiled at him, she had let him think she was not averse to an approach from him.

But she had only been play-acting, copying the manners of the sophisticated ladies of the Court she believed her guardian admired. She *had* deliberately flouted Justin's wishes. Annelise admitted to her heart that she had wanted to arouse his anger…but *not* this icy coldness, her heart responded.

She wished now that she had not gone with the Earl, that she had resisted his pressure, given him no encouragement. Not for her own sake so much as Justin's. If he should be wounded—or killed!—fighting a duel, she would not be able to live with her conscience. Annelise was filled with despair at the thought. She could not bear it if Justin were to die because she had so thoughtlessly disobeyed him.

'Where is Justin?'

Mirabelle Varennes's shrill voice broke into her thoughts. Walking slowly, her head bent, Annelise had not yet reached the great hall where the dancing was being held when the Frenchwoman came rushing up to her and grabbed her arm.

'Well, have you no tongue in your head?'

Annelise was shocked into awareness by the spiteful tone of the other woman's voice. Her green eyes flashed with temper, mouth drawn into a thin, vengeful line as she stared at Annelise.

'He…is in the courtyard yonder,' Annelise said hesitantly. 'But he sent me away. He is very angry. I do not think you should…' Her bottom lip trembled and she clamped it with pearly teeth. 'He is with someone…'

'Rathbone, of course,' Mirabelle snapped. 'You little fool! Have you no sense? How could you go with that creature? He and Justin are sworn enemies and…'

'Why? Why do they hate each other?'

'Have you not been told?' Annelise shook her head and Mirabelle gave her a look of contempt. 'He raped and dishonoured a young girl from my family. There have been other incidents…whispers of black arts and cruel depravity…' A shudder ran through the Frenchwoman. 'My uncle

fought a duel with Rathbone. He was so badly wounded
that he has never left his bed since and is always in pain.'

'Oh...' Annelise gasped and turned pale. 'Justin and he
are to fight a duel. They must not!' She looked wildly at
Mirabelle. 'Please, you must stop them! He will listen to
you.'

'This is your doing, you little slut!' Mirabelle lost her
temper, slapping her across the face. 'For months I have
been at pains to prevent this very thing. Justin and my uncle
were close friends. He has long wanted to avenge him—
and by making a show of yourself you have given him the
opportunity.'

'I did not mean...' Annelise faltered as she saw the fury
in those green eyes. 'Please believe me.'

'Do not lie to me.' Mirabelle cast a scornful look at her.
'You may fool others with your innocent manners and your
pretty smiles, but I know you for the scheming slut you
are. You did this deliberately, to make him jealous—but
your plan was idle, Mistress Woodward. Justin wants only
me. All you have done is to put his life at risk. If he is
killed, I shall make you wish you had never been born.'

Annelise could not find the words to answer her. The
Frenchwoman was very angry, and she had every right.
Annelise *had* embroiled her guardian in a dangerous en-
counter, and if he was badly wounded it would be her fault.

'I have no time to waste in talking to you!'

Annelise watched as Mirabelle walked swiftly away. She
felt so helpless, so wretched. Tears burned behind her eyes.
She had not wanted this! It *was* her fault, but she had not
expected anything so terrible to happen.

'Ah, there you are, Annelise. I have been looking for
you.'

Hearing Lady Emily's voice, Annelise turned to meet
her, eyes dark with misery in a face drained of colour.

'What is wrong?' Lady Emily saw the torn scarf. 'Oh,

my poor child! Did that vile man attack you? Are you hurt?'

Her concern brought the tears Annelise had been trying so hard to contain. Lady Emily moved swiftly to embrace her, holding her gently and soothing her until the outpouring of emotion ceased.

'There, there, my sweet. It was not your fault. You could not have known he was such a brute. I should have warned you to have nothing to do with Rathbone. I have been negligent in my care of you.'

'No, ma'am.' Annelise drew back, accepting the kerchief she was offered to wipe her eyes. Honesty made her admit, 'It was my own fault. I—I was upset about something and I went with the Earl without thinking what might…'

'Did he harm you? Or was Justin in time?'

'He came before…there was only a little unpleasantness.'

'Then no real harm has been done.' Lady Emily looked relieved. 'It is a lesson well learned, my dear. There are some men it is best to stay clear of. You will not be so careless again, I think?'

'No. Never!' Annelise shuddered as she realised what might have happened if Justin had not come to rescue her. 'But you do not know what my wickedness has caused, ma'am.' The fear leapt up in her eyes as she looked at Lady Emily. 'It is terrible. Justin has challenged the Earl to a duel…'

'As I would have expected.' Lady Emily shrugged her shoulders, clearly unconcerned. 'Do not let that distress you, dearest child. My son is known for his skill with the sword. I wonder that Rathbone was so foolish as to risk it. He must have known Justin would challenge him if he attempted to dishonour you.'

Lady Emily was puzzled as to why the Earl had deliberately gone after a girl he knew to be in Justin's protection.

Annelise was indeed lovely, but there were other beautiful ladies at court…ladies with more experience in the arts of love. Rathbone's tastes were jaded, and Lady Emily could not think he would have found much satisfaction in bedding a virgin…unless he was more interested in revenge than sexual gratification?

'It is all my fault. If Justin is wounded, I shall have killed him.'

'Nonsense!' Lady Emily shook her head, touching Annelise's hand to comfort her. 'The quarrel between them is an old sore, festering and bound to burst out one day. Besides, I dare wager fifty guineas that Justin will win. You do not know all, Annelise. My son has a reputation most men fear. I have heard him spoken of as the devil himself.'

'Satan's mark…' Annelise whispered, a shiver going through her.

'Where have you heard that?'

'From my uncle. He fears the Marquis Saintjohn, but I have never understood why.'

'Nor I,' replied Lady Emily with a frown. 'Unless he has somehow misused your fortune. He might then have reason to tremble—though Justin would not do him violence but seek reparation through the courts for your sake.'

Annelise was silent as she recalled the terror she had seen in her uncle's eyes the day he had warned her against the man who would come to fetch her. She had thought him sick in both mind and body, but supposing he had heard something to make him fear for her safety?

No, no, she was being foolish and disloyal. She had received nothing but kindness from Lady Emily, and if Justin was angry with her she had only herself to blame.

'What is it, Annelise?' Lady Emily was staring at her oddly. 'What are you thinking?'

'Nothing…' Annelise could not meet her questing gaze.

'Just that…my guardian is so angry with me. He bid me ask you to take me home at once.'

'And so I shall,' said Lady Emily. 'You have been distressed enough this evening. Wait here a moment, my dear. I shall have our cloaks brought, and Ralph must summon chairs for us.' She gently pushed Annelise towards an oak settle. 'Sit down and try not to upset yourself. I shall not be long.'

Annelise watched as Lady Emily went to find a servant, then bent her head. She struggled against her desire to weep once more. No matter how kind Lady Emily was, or how often she denied it, Annelise knew that this terrible situation was all her fault.

If Justin were killed, his death would be on her conscience and her heart would break.

Annelise hardly slept that night. She tossed and turned in her bed, dozing and waking by turns, her mind so feverish that she felt unable to rest. The house was so silent— as silent as the grave! There was not a breath of air anywhere, the atmosphere heavy and oppressing. It made her head ache and she could hardly breathe.

Surely it must come to a storm before dawn? What else would morning bring? Please let it not be the news of Justin's death! Oh, God, let him not be harmed.

Annelise rose from her bed and went over to the window, which was tightly shuttered against the night air. The servants had latched it, believing as most did that the darkness held ill humours which could come upon the unwary as they slept. Some said the devil waited to snatch the souls of those foolish enough to open their window at night; it was a tale told to frighten children into good behaviour, as were the tales of goblins and trolls waiting to gobble them up.

It was so hot! Annelise could not bear it a moment

longer. She opened the window, then took away the thick wooden bar which secured the shutter, pushing one half of it back so that the air came in.

That was better. She could breathe at last. Some of the tension which had been oppressing her eased. Perhaps Lady Emily was right, perhaps Justin would…she stiffened suddenly as she heard a burst of laughter.

Two men were in the garden below her window. It was so dark, the moon obscured by heavy clouds. She could not see them properly…but surely that bulky shape was Ralph's and the other…Justin!

She was certain of it as she heard their laughter again. Relief swept over her, making her go limp so that she almost fainted. He was home! He was safe!

'Thank you, God,' she whispered, tears running silently down her cheeks. Her prayers had been answered. Justin was alive—and by the sound of it in a better humour than he had been earlier.

'Rathbone will cause the wenches no trouble for a while,' she heard Ralph say. 'You've near done for him, Justin. For your sake, I pray he does not die of his wounds. The Black Boy does not look kindly on duels at Court— and his temper hath been sorely tried of late.'

'Charles has no love of Rathbone,' Justin replied. 'Besides, the rogue deserved to die. For myself, I am only sorry my blade did not strike him to the heart.'

'As well he lives, my vengeful friend,' replied Ralph on a warning note. 'I doubt he will rise from his sickbed for many months—if indeed he ever does. And then he will be a weakling, fit only to keep to his estates in the country.'

'Then he is well served for what he did to Mirabelle's uncle.'

'She was not best pleased with you.' Ralph chuckled. 'I thought she might finish what Rathbone could not. She is a firebird, Justin—and she has the temper of a shrew.'

'Mirabelle has a vixen's tongue,' Justin replied with a harsh laugh. 'She can lash a man raw with her spite—but in bed she has more honey than salt. I can withstand her temper for the sake of...'

Their voices faded as they entered the house. Annelise sat as if turned to stone. All relief at Justin's safe return drained away from her, anger taking its place.

He had fought that duel for his mistress, to avenge her uncle! His anger at finding Annelise with the Earl was only because she had defied him—as she would again. He should find no softness in her when he came looking!

Closing and shuttering her window, Annelise thought bitterly that the tales of evil stalking the night were true enough. Had she not opened her window she would not have heard Justin discussing his mistress with Ralph.

Returning to her bed, Annelise was tortured by jealousy and hurt pride. She had been a fool to expect anything of her guardian. Perhaps her uncle was right—perhaps she ought to be wary of the Marquis Saintjohn.

It was too late! Her mind denied the painful truth, but her heart told her that she already carried Justin's mark deep inside her.

He did not want her, but she loved him. So much that she felt she might die of it. Yet she would not give him the satisfaction of knowing how much he had hurt her.

She trembled inwardly as she remembered his threats of the previous evening. He had promised a reckoning between them, and he had been so angry! Well, let him do his worst. Her heart hardened against him. She had been a fool to think that she would be happy with such a man. His smiles had deceived her foolish heart. She would not weep and ask for forgiveness, she would not beg for his affections.

Annelise's mind was uneasy as she drifted into a restless

sleep. Justin could rage at her all he wished, and she would remain cool and aloof; he should not have best of her.

If there had been anyone she could have turned to, she might have been reckless enough to leave her guardian's house that very night, but there was no one—nowhere she could go. It was no use; she must stay here until she found a way of escaping from her misery.

Her dreams were far from happy. Several times she cried out in her sleep, and tears slipped down her cheeks. Twice she called Justin's name, but he was not there to hear her.

Chapter Five

Justin left Ralph sleeping on the settle in his library. They had both sat drinking far into the night, something neither of them had done for a long time. It brought back memories, both bitter and sweet.

They had first met on the field of battle, just after Justin's father had been slain. Finding the youth, bloodied sword in hand and a look of stunned horror in his eyes, Ralph had given up the search for fallen friends and helped Justin to bury his father in a quiet spot by a church. After that, they had fought and lived as comrades for the remainder of the war.

In France, Ralph had found himself a niche at Court, while Justin had ventured further afield, serving as a mercenary for foreign rulers—but he had returned after each campaign, each voyage, once he had his ship—and their friendship had never wavered. Sometimes Justin thought that without his steady counsel and warmth he would have sunk into the mire of blood and war never to resurface.

'Sleep well, good fellow,' Justin murmured, a smile on his lips as he covered the bulky figure with his own cloak. 'You little know how I value you.'

His expression was grim as he went out, carrying a

chamber-stick to light his way. Ralph was right, of course; the King would be angered by news of a duel fought within the very bounds of the palace. Charles frowned on violent disputes amongst his courtiers, and who could blame him? There was enough unrest without petty disputes between men made ill-tempered by years of war and exile. Justin would no doubt be summoned to explain, and all hope of favours from His Majesty would be at an end for a time. It was as well Justin had not allowed his anger to cloud his judgement.

He had wanted to kill Rathbone when he saw him trying to force himself on Annelise. The foolish, wilful wench! What had she been thinking of to allow Rathbone to lead her into such a trap? He shuddered to think what might have happened had he not arrived in time.

'Oh, Annelise,' he murmured to himself. 'You little know what you did—or what might have been lost.'

What could have been in her mind? She could surely not have wanted Rathbone to make love to her? Only the worst of women could want a man like that!

No, no, he did not believe it! He had heard her cries, seen her struggle to fight off the foul beast who would have raped her.

Then why had she gone with him? Justin's brow furrowed as he wrestled with the problem. He wanted to drag the truth from her, his feet following a path of their own choosing until he found himself at the door to Annelise's boudoir. For a moment he stood there, wrestling with himself. Wild thoughts filled his mind, thoughts of her lying flushed in sleep, her lovely hair spread out upon the pillows.

He could go to her, make her confess her innermost secrets—but that way would lead to her destruction!

No! He would not give way to the temptation that plagued him endlessly. Despite her reckless behaviour this evening, she deserved her chance to find happiness. He must fight this selfish urge to take what *he* wanted, what *he* needed. For once in his life, he must put another person's well-being before his own. Annelise must marry a man who would worship her and treat her gently. Justin would do nothing to rob her of that right.

Ralph had named men who were free of the blood that stained his own hands, men who had not lost all their softness, all their gentleness. Annelise would turn from him in horror if she ever learned how he had spent the last few years of his life—of the ships he had sent to the bottom of the sea.

Like all those who had sailed with him, Justin hated the Spanish, enemies of England since the time of the glorious Elizabeth, despite any declarations to the contrary. He knew his own fate had he ever fallen into the hands of the Inquisition, knew the torture and bitter death that would have awaited him at their hands. They had called him Satan when he'd raided their ships, taking the silver they had plundered from the New World. Sometimes he would let the crew limp home in a disabled ship, but some had defied his orders to surrender and had paid the price by going to a watery grave.

Yet he had felt no shame in this, for the men he had condemned had blood on their own hands, innocent blood. Few who defied them had escaped the torture chambers of the Inquisition, but Justin had harboured those who had, the scars they bore hardening his heart against the enemies he waylaid and robbed of their ill-gotten treasure.

He had ventured to the New World himself, seeing the way the natives of that land were exploited and tortured by their masters. He had rescued one such creature: a man whose tongue had been torn out by the Inquisition.

Poor Carruda still served on the ship Justin had gifted to his crew when he had decided to give up his old life and return to England with the King. He was rich enough not to need more plunder, besides, he'd had no heart for it…after the mistake.

Justin blotted the memory from his mind, shutting out the screams of the damned. What had happened that dreadful night was a thorn in his conscience, a regret he would carry with him to his grave.

He would not permit himself to remember, though the horror of it would never leave him.

Turning away from Annelise's door, Justin knew that he had drunk unwisely that night—enough to bring back the memories, but not enough to dull the pain.

Annelise waited in her room until past noon the next day. She had expected Justin to come storming in, demanding an explanation, but there had been no sign of him. No message. No summons.

Perhaps he did not care. He had been angry when he discovered her with the Earl, but the duel had been fought for Madame Varennes's sake, not hers. It was the beautiful Frenchwoman he wanted, not Annelise.

She sat up straight as she heard a knock at her door, expecting the worst, but a second later Lady Emily entered and her fluttering nerves quietened.

'I thought we might go shopping,' her hostess suggested. 'I have not bought anything new for more than a week. La! I feel positively dowdy.'

Annelise smiled at this nonsense, for Lady Emily was one of the most elegant ladies at Court and had several admirers of her own.

'Should I not wait here in case Justin wishes to speak to me?' she asked in a small voice.

'You are not in a quake over what happened last night?' Lady Emily trilled with laughter. 'Justin is unhurt—a tiny scratch, no more. Did I not tell you how it would be? Rathbone was a fool to tangle with him, and has his just deserts.'

'I am glad Justin is unhurt,' Annelise said, dropping her gaze. 'But he was angry…'

'I dare say he has forgotten it,' replied Lady Emily with a reassuring look. 'I spoke to him this morning and he made no mention of wanting to discipline you. Besides, he has other things on his mind. The King has sent for him.'

'The King…' Annelise turned pale, her heart catching with fear. It was easy to tell herself she would not let herself care for Justin, but less easy to put him out of her mind. 'Will he be angry with Justin because of what happened?'

'I dare say he may be reprimanded,' Lady Emily said. 'Do not be anxious, Annelise. It will do my son no harm to have His Majesty ring a peal over him. Sometimes he is too arrogant for his own good—but you need not fear. The King is not ungrateful. He will not punish Justin too severely, though he may be cold towards him for a time.'

'He will not help him to recover his estates.'

'My son needs no royal intervention,' Lady Emily said. 'From what I hear, the case is almost won. He should recover the house and lands quite soon—though whether that will ease his black moods I cannot say.' She frowned. 'I think something else plagues him, but it would be useless to ask. He would not unburden his soul to me. Only when Justin learns to love can he hope to lift the despair that eats at him…to hope for some measure of happiness.'

'Do you not think he loves Madame Varennes?'

'Justin love her?' Lady Emily frowned. 'I pray he does not, my dear. She is a shrew—and too much like me. Justin needs a very different woman, someone who will give him what he needs…a woman with a tender heart, very like you, Annelise.'

'He does not care for me.'

'No?' Lady Emily arched her brows. 'Then he is a fool—

and whatever else he might be, I have never thought my son a fool.'

'He loves Madame Varennes. She told me so last evening.'

'Did she indeed?' Lady Emily's eyes gleamed. 'Was she very angry, Annelise?'

'Yes. She called me terrible names and blamed me for putting Justin's life at risk.'

'How interesting,' said Lady Emily. She smiled inwardly. It was most intriguing. Had Mirabelle been certain of Justin's affections, she would have ignored his ward. The very fact that she had raged at Annelise told a story in itself. 'Well, for the moment, we shall forget both my son and the lady he chooses to waste his time with, my love. We are going shopping…'

Justin was thoughtful as he left the palace. His interview with the King had been uncomfortable to say the least. For a moment he had believed Charles would have him imprisoned in the Tower.

'You knew my feelings on this matter,' the King had said in the icy cold manner that concealed his rage. 'Oddsfish, Saintjohn! You try my patience to the limit. I have a mind to let you cool your temper in the Tower. You may think yourself lucky that I remember your father's service to me—and your own.'

'You are gracious, Sire.' Justin's stubborn expression did not help his cause. 'But you would not have me allow Rathbone to insult my ward?'

'Your quarrel with the Earl is no concern of ours,' Charles replied testily. 'Had you killed him in France, we should have applauded you—but we will not have this undignified brawling at our Court.'

Justin smiled inwardly. Charles was taking refuge behind the royal We, a sign that his temper had cooled. Justin was going to be warned, but no more action would be taken—this time.

'Forgive me, Sire. Had I known you wished it, Rathbone would have died months ago.'

Charles turned aside, not wanting Justin to see that his boldness amused him. 'My wishes have nothing to do with this matter, Saintjohn. I tread a perilous path still, and cannot afford to lose my most faithful supporters.'

'I am ever that, Sire.'

'Then do not cause me more trouble.' Charles sighed. 'There are enough of those who bay for the blood of my father's enemies. For myself, I would have an end to these trials and executions. I would be merry and have my people sleep easily abed at night.'

'Amen to that,' Justin replied. 'I had no wish to fight Rathbone, Sire—he forced it upon me by doing what he did last night. It was quite deliberate, believe me. Had he wished to conceal his actions, he would have been more cautious, made more effort to sneak my ward away. He wanted me to challenge him to a duel.'

'And why should that be?' Charles looked at him curiously.

'He hoped to defeat me, to kill me…I can only guess at the reasoning behind his behaviour. It seems that my case will be settled favourably very soon. Rathbone's cousin will be forced to give up the house and lands he stole from my family.'

'Bought, Saintjohn. It was the rogues in Parliament who stole your estate,' Charles reminded him with a smile. 'It is Rathbone's cousin, Sir Roger Courtney, who stands to lose all, not you.'

'Justice will be done when my lands are restored to me.'

'Indeed?' Charles arched his brows. 'We have no love for Sir Roger, Saintjohn. He bore arms against our father…which makes it all the more surprising that Rathbone should kill for his sake. He fought at our father's side and we had thought him loyal to us.'

'Unless he plotted together with Courtney against the throne, Sire?'

'What mean you? What is this talk of treason?'

'I have been followed,' Justin replied. 'My life has been at risk on at least two occasions. Some nights ago near the theatre there was a protest concerning the latest arrests of the regicides, which Ralph and I managed to break up quite easily—perhaps too easily—and I saw Courtney in the crowd, though he hid his face and did his best to keep his identity from me.'

'You think he would have done murder to keep your estates?'

'I have no doubt of that…but unless I much mistake the matter, he is embroiled with men who would cause trouble for you, Sire. There are many who do not rejoice at your return…'

'Say you so?' A mocking smile touched Charles's mouth. 'You speak more truth than others, Saintjohn. If you have more news of a plot, bring it to us, and we shall listen.'

'If I am at liberty to do so, Sire, I shall always serve you.'

Charles smiled, a wry amusement in his eyes. He waved a scented kerchief in Justin's direction. 'Go, knave! We shall not smile on you at Court, but you hath not displeased us.'

Justin bowed deeply before him and went from the audience chamber.

He was thoughtful now, as he left the palace gardens and began to walk through the streets. At first he had believed the disturbance near the theatre had been meant as a cover for his own death, but further enquiries had led him to believe that there was more behind the noisy protest than had seemed likely at the time.

Charles had no legitimate children, and his brother James was not generally admired, was in fact a Catholic—something that would not be tolerated by those who had fought to cast out the perceived evil of Popery. Charles might incline towards the bishops and much of the old ritual of the Star Chamber, which had been the cause of so much dissent, but he was wise enough to bow to the wishes of the many and hide his own faith if it be other than he professed.

If Charles should die without issue, blood would once again run in the streets and fields of England. Once Charles was crowned, it would be harder to take the country back to what it had been before the Restoration—thus, if there was a plot against his life, the traitors would move soon and swiftly.

Justin had no way of knowing if his suspicions had any substance. He had paid agents to make enquiries, and he knew that Rathbone and Courtney had met in secret—and that some of the men who met with them were known to be opposed to the Crown—but so far he had no direct knowledge of a plot to kill the King.

It was something Rathbone had said as Justin's blade had pierced his side which had made Justin suspect it.

'I am well served for my traitor's heart,' the Earl had gasped, sinking to his knees. 'You have killed me, Saintjohn. Better the deed than you know. Greed destroyed me. I repent. Long live His Majesty.' He had pitched forward on his face, sinking into unconsciousness as the blood flowed from the deep wound in his side.

Rathbone was not dead, but any part he might have played in the plot was at an end. Why had he forced a duel on a man who was known for his skill in swordplay? Did the traitors suspect Justin knew more of their intentions than he'd actually learned?

It was possible, and would explain the attempt to stab him a few nights previously. He had wrestled with his attacker, forcing him to drop the knife and run off. Suspecting a deeper trap, Justin had not followed. The attack could just have been the work of a footpad intent on robbing him of his purse, but Justin did not think it was so simple.

Had Rathbone's attempt to rape Annelise been the calculated action of a man who wanted to destroy an enemy—someone who might somehow have stumbled on a wicked plot and was a danger to these shadowy men? Or was Justin allowing his imagination to run wild?

He could not be certain, and until he was, there was no more to be done. He frowned as his thoughts turned from treason to the appropriate punishment for a wilful girl.

What was he going to do about Annelise? The fact that Rathbone had used her as his tool made Justin even more wary of showing interest in her. If there were others involved, she might be at risk—and next time he might not be there to save her.

The thought of her in danger worked powerfully in him, giving him more pain that he would have thought possible.

It would be best for all concerned if she were to marry soon.

Annelise did not see Justin again until they dined that evening. For once, Lady Emily had chosen to spend a quiet night at home. They had no guests as the three of them sat down together at table, and for the first few minutes they ate in silence.

'Do you not think that shade of blue favours Annelise?' Lady Emily asked her son after he had been staring moodily at his plate for some time. 'You do not eat, Justin. Have you no appetite?'

Justin put a piece of chicken that had been cooked until tender in a piquant sauce into his mouth, chewed without seeming to relish the delicious taste and swallowed. He glared at his mother, as if daring her to speak to him, but Lady Emily only smiled serenely. She was reminded of the young boy who had been sent away from her and her heart twisted at the memory.

'Surely such succulent fare does not take so much chewing?' she asked, deliberately provoking him. 'Or have you the toothache, Justin? Should I have the servants fetch some oil of cloves?'

A choking sound from Annelise made him frown all the harder. 'No, Mother, I do not have the toothache. Nor does my head ache, or my stomach. I am in the best of health.'

'I am glad to hear it—but it makes me wonder if your hearing is failing.'

'Annelise looks lovely whatever she wears. She needs no compliments from me.'

Annelise stared down at her plate, willing herself not to let him see her hands were trembling.

'A woman can never have too many compliments,' Lady Emily persisted.

'The colour is most becoming,' Justin said, giving his mother best, a gleam of wry amusement in his eyes. 'But the gown she wore last night was even more so; that green is not a colour every woman can wear, but it looked well on Annelise.'

Annelise glanced at him. Why was he reminding her of her shame? She had given the gown to a maid and would never wear it again.

'I prefer blue,' she said, looking at him coldly. Why was he smiling at her? It was merely a trap, to lull her into a false sense of security, to make her believe that he had forgiven her—and then he would pounce and make her sorry she had dared to presume herself forgiven. He was heartless and she hated him!

'Then we must agree to differ on the subject,' Justin said

in a tone so mild it immediately set her teeth on edge. He *was* mocking her! How dared he? 'I have no engagements this evening, Mother. I believe I shall stay here with you and Annelise.'

'That will be very pleasant,' Lady Emily replied, her manner so exact a copy of his own that Annelise was struck. How very alike they were! Their smiles, their way of saying one thing and meaning another! Why could they not see that and find joy in each other? 'Do you not agree, Annelise? Will it not be a pleasure to have Justin at home with us?'

'Oh… Yes, of course.'

Her answer was so obviously forced that a gleam of dark amusement leapt up in Justin's eyes. His black mood lifted, the imp of mischief reared its head, and he discovered he was looking forward to the evening ahead.

'We shall dance, Annelise and I,' he announced. 'You will play for us, Mama.' It was more a command than a question.

'Most willingly,' Lady Emily answered. 'I own I am surprised, but perfectly happy to oblige.'

'I think my ward needs to practise her steps,' Justin went on smoothly, the devil at his shoulder. His eyes were full of a wicked intent as he looked at her, as though he found his revenge sweet. 'Some of your movements are not quite as elegant as they might be, Annelise. You need further instruction.'

He was mocking her! Deliberately provoking her, trying to make her answer back. So this was to be his way of punishing her. She had expected him to lose his temper, to rage at her, but this ridicule was more subtle, more hurtful.

Well, two could play this game!

'You are too good to take an interest in my dancing skills, sir,' she replied gravely, her tone and expression schooled to modest acceptance. 'I shall be glad to learn what you care to teach me, sir.'

'Ah, the dutiful ward at last.' Justin struggled to hide his amusement. This was the little Puritan she had once pretended to be—what an actress she was! 'Why do we not begin at once?' He pushed back his chair and stood up. 'We none of us seem hungry—so let the instruction commence.'

'An excellent idea,' said Lady Emily, watching the exchange between them with an expectant eagerness. 'Annelise should practise all the arts of a courtier since she may need them in the future.'

Justin's eyes narrowed dangerously as he glanced at his mother. However, he asked no questions, made no comment, merely bowing reverently before offering his arm.

Annelise followed as they led the way to the music room. It was a long, narrow chamber, with various instruments set about and a boarded floor which was very suitable for dancing.

She had thought her guardian merely jesting to discomfort her, but when Lady Emily began to play she discovered that Justin was very much in earnest. For the next hour he put her through rigorous instruction, making her curtsey to him again and again until she did it to his satisfaction; he showed her how to hold her gown, how to move more elegantly in the dance, and she discovered that she was learning things Lady Emily had not made clear. Not only was he an excellent teacher, he knew how to dance with an exquisite grace himself.

'No, no, Annelise,' he said when she moved too swiftly. 'Imagine you are a swan gliding on the water. Your gestures are too jerky. You should be graceful, a great lady—not a country wench romping on the village green.'

'Justin!' Lady Emily protested. 'That is unfair. Indeed, you go too far. Annelise dances very well.'

'"Very well" is not good enough for my ward,' he replied. 'I would have her outshine every other lady at Court,
not just in looks but in manners.'

'But why?' Lady Emily frowned as a thought occurred
to her. Had Justin seen it too? Was that the reason for his
sudden interest in her dancing skills? Was he grooming her
to take a very exalted place at Court? 'You are not thinking
of… Justin?'

The look he sent her was enigmatic, giving nothing
away. Lady Emily was conscious of both anger and disappointment. How could Justin think of using his ward to
gain favour at Court? She had hoped so much that he would
fall in love with Annelise himself, that at last he might find
the happiness which had eluded him so far.

'Point your toe more!' Justin commanded, his attention
concentrated on Annelise. 'No, no, you obstinate girl. Have
you not listened to a word I have been saying? Lightness!
You must be thistledown—light as air.'

'I am trying,' Annelise said, her eyes flashing with resentment. She knew well enough he was merely teasing her,
but loving him as she did it only made her heart ache the
more. 'May we not stop for a while? You have not let me
rest for an hour. I am tired.'

Lady Emily rose from the harpsichord at once. 'Annelise
is right. She has practised enough for one evening.'

'Very well.' Justin smiled oddly. 'No more dancing. Do
you play an instrument, Annelise?' She shook her head.
'No? That is a pity, but perhaps you sing? Yes, I know you
sing. I heard you in the woods…'

Annelise glared at him. 'I did not know you were there,
spying on me.'

'Spying on you?' His mouth twitched at the corners. 'No,
do not accuse me so, Annelise. I came upon you unawares—a wood nymph weaving her enchantments to snare
the unwary traveller.'

'You mock me, sir.' Her eyes sparked with temper. He had pressed her too far. She saw the gleam in his own eyes and knew she had betrayed herself. Of course, this was what he wanted!

'Indeed, I do not mock you, Annelise. Come, will you not sing for us? Mother will play.'

'Yes, Annelise.' Lady Emily added her pleas to his. 'I should like to hear you sing something.'

'For you, then.' She hesitated. 'Do you know the music to ''She of her Heart's Contenting''? It is popular, I believe, but I have not heard it sung at Court.'

'Yes, I believe I have heard it once or twice.' Lady Emily plucked at the strings of the harpsichord. 'Is that the air you mean, my dear?'

'Yes, thank you.'

Annelise stood very still, bringing the words of the tragic ballad to mind. It told the story of a wilful lady who refuses to marry the man of her father's choice. Forbidden the love of her young suitor, she takes to her bed, refuses to see anyone, will neither eat nor drink. When she is close to death, her father relents and begs his only child to live and forgive him, promising to allow her to marry her lover, but it is too late, and she dies as he weeps at her side.

> *For she was fair…*
> *And she was lovely as a*
> *summer's morn'*
> *But no more shall I see her*
> *face…*
> *No more will she take the*
> *sweet air.*
> *And I am left alone.*

There was silence as Annelise's clear, sweet voice ended its tale of tragic love and wilful self-destruction. A tear trickled from the corner of Lady Emily's eye, then, all at once, she jumped up and went to embrace the girl.

'That was so beautiful, my dear,' she said. 'You sing very well. Did you not think so, Justin?'

Justin was standing by the window, his back towards them. For a moment he gave no sign of having heard his mother, then at last, without turning his head, he said, 'Annelise has a good voice, but it is untrained. I shall arrange for her to have singing lessons.'

'Justin? I think that most unkind of you.'

'Do you, Mother?' He turned to look at her then, and all trace of mockery had gone from his face. His eyes were bleak, haunted. 'As it happens, I was thinking her voice deserves to be nurtured, but I would not expect you to understand. You have never known what was in my heart.' He bowed to her, then to Annelise. 'I shall send Signor Bartoli to you, Mistress Woodward—and now I ask you both to excuse me. I find I have other business this evening after all.'

Annelise would not answer him; she could not even bring herself to watch as he left the room. He had done his best to humiliate her all evening. His unkind remarks about her voice had been meant to punish her for disobeying him; they had hurt her deeply, for she had put her heart into the song, singing for him alone, so that he would understand her love could only be given to one man, that she would rather die than marry someone else.

'Annelise, my love.' Lady Emily was looking at her, pity in her eyes. 'I am so sorry. I cannot understand why Justin has been so cruel to you this evening.'

'Can you not?' Annelise blinked back her tears. She must not, would not cry! 'He is still annoyed with me for embroiling him in that duel. It was his way of punishing me.'

'Is he so unfeeling?' Lady Emily looked distressed. 'I confess I had not thought so ill of him until this evening.'

'I brought it on myself. It was my fault for disobeying him.'

'No, that I will not allow,' Lady Emily said at once. 'You were foolish, but no more. Justin knows that in his heart. I cannot understand what has happened to him. He was not like this in France. Oh, he has always had his black moods, but...' She sighed. 'I must tell you that I had hoped he might come to love you. I prayed that you might be his salvation.'

Annelise lifted her head, fighting her tears. 'I am sorry to disappoint you, ma'am. Sometimes I think he does not even like me.' She swallowed hard. 'If you will excuse me, I should like to retire. I—I have a little headache.'

'Yes, of course. Goodnight, Annelise.'

Lady Emily stood watching as the girl walked from the room with dignity. If she were not much mistaken, Annelise was breaking her heart for Justin—and her foolish son could not see it!

She was angry with him for hurting Annelise. She had grown used to his reserve towards her, to his occasional taunts, but they had always been able to laugh together. She had felt his mockery was more defensive than unkind, that beneath the crust of cynicism was a warm, loving man waiting to be released.

'Oh, Justin, my son,' she said. 'Forgive me for what I did to you—forgive yourself for whatever it is that is eating at your soul.'

Justin looked into the eyes of his mistress and felt the emptiness swamp him. Mirabelle was beautiful, witty, sensual and sophisticated—and he did not want her. He had come to her lodgings intending to make love to her, to ask her to be his wife and put an end to the torture in his mind—but he could not force himself to speak.

'What is wrong?' she asked, her voice husky with desire

as she swayed towards him invitingly, her perfume wafting upwards to fill his nostrils. He discovered he disliked it— it did not have the fresh, light piquancy of Annabel's scent. 'You look so stern, my love. Why do you not forget your worries and come to bed?'

'You think it would answer?' Justin set down his wine glass. He was standing by the fireplace in the small parlour, contemplating the open grate. 'Tell me, Mirabelle—why did you follow me to London? Was it because you hoped for marriage?'

Her green eyes narrowed, became wary. 'I have thought it might suit me to be your wife,' she said. 'But I am not a pauper, Justin. I have wealth enough. I do not need to beg for favours—even from you.'

'I am glad you feel that way.' He smiled at her, remembering that he had been fond of her in his way. 'You have always been generous, Mirabelle. We have dealt fairly with one another, I think?'

'Yes.' She curled her nails into the palms of her hands, willing herself not to lose her temper. She was afraid of losing him, had been so since she'd heard him whisper a name in his sleep. 'What are you saying, Justin? If it is that you do not wish to marry…' She turned her face aside so that he should not see what this was costing her. 'I too have had second thoughts. I believe we do well enough together as we are.'

'No,' Justin said, his voice grating against her nerves. 'No, Mirabelle, this is not fair to you. You deserve more. I have decided to end it.'

'You cannot!' she cried, whirling on him in shock and fear. 'You cannot leave me. I will not let you.'

'It is for your own good,' he said, a frown in his eyes. 'Much better to end it now while we are still friends— before I hurt you.'

'You would not hurt me,' she said, voice low, desperate.

She moved towards him, her manner pleading with him. 'You care for me, Justin. I thought you loved me.'

'Love!' he ejaculated. 'You know I never promised love, Mirabelle. It is a myth…a song, no more.'

Seeing the pain in his eyes then, she guessed the truth he would not admit even to himself and could no longer contain her temper. 'Yet you moon after *her* like a lovesick calf! Do not lie to me or yourself, Justin. You are sick for that…country wench! She has made a fool of you with her smiles and her coy looks.'

'I needed no help to make myself the fool,' Justin said, a wry twist to his lips. 'But you are wrong, Mirabelle. Annelise is not the reason I have decided to end our affair. I owe it to you because I have always liked you and I have no wish to hurt you.'

'Pouff!' She dismissed his claim with a wave of her hand. 'You deceive yourself, but you cannot blind me with your excuses. You want her.'

'That I cannot deny,' Justin said, his expression revealing more than he could know. 'But she is not for me. She would be defiled by my touch. I am unworthy of her.'

'You *are* in love with her!' His words enraged her. She struck out at him with her claws. 'Unworthy of that—that witch! You are a fool. She would bore you within a week if you wed her.'

'I shall not marry her.'

'Then why leave me?' Mirabelle flung herself at him, winding her soft arms about him. 'You know I can please you. Why not stay with me? I can make you forget her.'

'Would it were true,' Justin said, pushing her away. 'Forgive me, Mirabelle. I must go.'

'Stay. I beg you, stay.'

'I do not want you,' he said. 'Forgive me. I had not meant to hurt you—but it is over.'

'Get out!' Mirabelle screamed, her rage boiling over as

she realised it was useless. She had lost him. 'I hate you. I never want to see you again.'

'Forgive me.'

Justin bowed to her and walked from the room. She screamed and threw a vase after him. It smashed against the wall. He turned, smiled, and went out without a word. She screamed again in frustration.

How dared he prefer that country simpleton to her? She would make him pay. Somehow she would be revenged on them both!

Justin was thoughtful as he walked home. Was his former mistress right? Had he allowed himself to care too much for Annelise?

He was by turns enchanted and dismayed by his charming but wilful ward. At times she seemed an accomplished flirt, at others he knew her to be still the girl he had come upon singing in the woods. Which was the real Annelise? Or could the answer be that she was a delightful mixture of the two?

His brows furrowed in frustration, and he felt annoyed with himself for allowing himself to care.

It hardly mattered, since he was determined that he could never be more to her than a guardian.

Chapter Six

'Shall you wear your new gown this evening?' Lady Emily asked. The weather had become chillier and she had ordered new gowns for them both. 'That green velvet becomes you well, Annelise.'

'I am very pleased with it,' Annelise replied. She had lied when she'd told Justin she preferred blue: green was her favourite. 'Shall you wear your crimson brocade? It suits you well, ma'am.'

'Yes, I believe it does.' Lady Emily smiled to herself. 'Are you going for a walk this morning?'

'If you do not mind? I like to walk by the river—and I shall not be cold if I wear my cloak.'

Lady Emily nodded, kissed her cheek and went away. Annelise stared at her reflection in the mirror. Were those shadows beneath her eyes? She *had* spent a restless night—a week of restless nights!

Was it only a week since Justin had ridden off to inspect his estates? It seemed far longer.

'I shall not ask you and Mother to come this time.' He had made a point of seeing Annelise before he left, giving her a posy of late roses. Her eyes had pricked as he'd apol-

ogised for his comments about her singing and asked her
to forgive him. 'I meant no insult, believe me.'

She held the flowers to her nose, to inhale their perfume
as he went on to explain why he was leaving her in London
for the time being. 'I want to make sure the house is in a
fit state to receive you before I take you home.'

'Shall we live there in future?' she asked, surprised at
his use of the word *home*. She had thought him devoted to
the life at Court, to serving the King.

'Perhaps—at least for some part of the year. Though
Mother could not stay long away from the Court. She may
prefer to live here and you could stay with her...until you
marry.'

'Until I marry.' Annelise lifted her head proudly. 'That
may be sooner than you imagine.'

'Someone has spoken to you?' Justin frowned.

'No, not yet. I should naturally refer the request to you,
of course, but if—if I made it known that I was not averse
to a proposal...'

'I see. Then perhaps I shall have the pleasure of arranging your wedding when I return from the country.'

Justin had left her then, without waiting for her answer,
which was just as well since she could not have spoken to
save her life. Why had she sent him away thinking that she
was preparing to marry? It was only her foolish, foolish
pride!

She had missed him so! Annelise regretted so much of
what had passed between them since her arrival in London.
Perhaps if she had been more obedient...but she loved him
so very deeply, and it had hurt her to see him with Madame
Varennes.

The Frenchwoman had not been at Court this week. Annelise had thought she might have gone down to the country with Justin, but then, only last evening, she had caught

a glimpse of her at the theatre with a gentleman she had never seen before.

Walking through the gardens now, her head bent and deep in thought, Annelise considered her future. What ought she to do? Robert had already spoken to her twice of marriage. She had denied his request as kindly as she could, assuring him of her friendship and affection, but her kindness had only made him the more determined to win her as his wife. He was convinced that it was only a matter of time before she agreed.

Of all her suitors—and there were several—Annelise liked Sir Robert the most. Yet she hesitated to accept him, because he loved her too much. Would it not be cruel to wed him without returning his passion? She liked him too well to be the cause of more pain. It might be better to take one of the others, a man who was as interested in her fortune as her love.

The wind was cool by the river, but Annelise walked there for almost an hour. Her thoughts were no less confused as she returned to the house to be told by a servant that she had a visitor.

'A visitor?'

'Madame Varennes, Mistress Woodward. She has been waiting for several minutes and insists on seeing you.'

'Lady Emily is not with her?'

'The mistress went out not half an hour ago.'

'Very well. I shall see Madame Varennes.'

Annelise gave her cloak to the servant, glanced at herself in a Venetian glass in the hall and went into the parlour, where a fire had been lit and the atmosphere was both comfortable and welcoming. The Frenchwoman was warming her hands before the flames, her back to Annelise. She turned as the girl entered, eyes cold, hostile, as she looked at her.

'So you have come at last. This neglect will not go un-
noticed, I promise you.'

'Forgive me, *madame*,' Annelise said, curtseying politely. 'I was out walking and have but this minute returned.'

'So you say. Well, I suppose I must accept your word—
but Justin will not be pleased that you chose to slight the
lady he intends to make his wife.'

Annelise could not stop the gasp escaping her lips. She
had lived in dread of this, half expected it, but it hurt just
the same, sending a flame of pain through her.

'It—it was not intended, I assure you, *madame*.'

'Indeed?' Mirabelle's lips curled in scorn. 'I came to visit
you with good intentions, Mistress Woodward. When I am
mistress here, you must still feel free to remain beneath my
husband's roof—for as long as it takes you to find a husband for yourself. I came to assure you of my assistance
to that end. I have been approached by a gentleman who
wishes to make good his suit with you. The Marquis de
Montfort—a kinsman of mine. If you are at Court this evening, I will introduce you.'

'You are too kind, *madame*.' Annelise lifted her head,
eyes flashing with pride. 'But I have already received several flattering offers. I believe I may choose where I wish.'

'At your age?' Mirabelle's scornful gaze went over her
in disbelief. 'You are past the first flush of youth, but I
suppose your estates must recommend you to some who
were beggared by the war. If you will take my advice, you
will listen to de Montfort. He at least has a fortune of his
own.'

'I am grateful for your concern, *madame*, but I have already decided on my choice.' Annelise bristled with pride.
'I need neither your help nor your advice in this matter.'

'Very well.' Mirabelle's eyes narrowed. 'You will do me
the courtesy of keeping the purpose of my visit to yourself,

I trust. Justin feels it his duty to offer you a home, naturally, but he would not wish for discord between us.'

'You may be sure that I shall say nothing of this when he returns, *madame*.'

'Then I shall take my leave of you.'

Annelise watched as she swept from the room. How spiteful she was! How could Justin love her? Yet he meant to marry her.

Annelise must leave this house before that marriage took place! She would not stay beneath the same roof as Mirabelle Varennes.

'You are very quiet, Annelise,' remarked Lady Emily as they were about to leave that evening. 'I hope you did not take a chill this morning?'

'Oh, no,' Annelise said. She brought her head up, fixing a bright, brittle smile in place. 'I am very well, ma'am, and I mean to enjoy myself this evening.'

'Good.' Lady Emily patted her hand affectionately. 'I think perhaps Justin will return soon. Ralph tells me he has received a letter to say he has some business to discuss with him.'

'Indeed?' Annelise nodded coolly, but her heart jerked with pain. If Justin was coming home to be married, she must find herself a husband and quickly. 'I had hardly noticed he was gone,' she lied.

Lady Emily glanced at her anxiously. Annelise seemed to have an irritation of the nerves. What could have upset her? She had not been like this earlier in the day.

'Is something wrong, my love?'

'No, nothing at all,' Annelise denied.

But there was something. Lady Emily was certain of it. She was worried by Annelise's manner, and as the evening progressed her fears grew stronger. It was she who had taught the girl to flirt prettily, but as a game…as an amusement. There was something reckless about Annelise that evening as she laughed and threw wicked, enticing looks at the men who crowded around her.

She was a living, vibrant flame, and they were moths, fluttering their wings, singeing them against her brightness. Outwardly, Annelise was the same as always, but her anxious friend sensed her fragility and feared for her.

'Annelise, my love.' She murmured a gentle protest as the girl returned to her side for a few minutes. 'Have a care. You are attracting attention from men I would not have you encourage. Remember Rathbone! You are too heedless of your reputation.'

Annelise moved away, hiding her hurt. So even Lady Emily was turning against her. She was too miserable to heed her warning, yet she found no happiness in what she did. None of the men who fluttered about her, smothering her in pretty compliments, meant anything to her, but she seemed unable to stop herself flirting with them.

It was not until much later that she became aware of someone watching her from across the room. Her heart stopped beating for one terrible moment as she saw the look in those blue eyes and trembled inwardly; then she lifted her head, smiling up at her companion, defying her guardian even while her heart was breaking. Before she had time to make the jest that was in her mind, Justin was at her side, his hand on her arm.

'Montgomery. I beg your indulgence, sir. I must take Mistress Woodward away from you. I need to speak urgently with her.' He met Annelise's sparkling gaze with an odd, intense look that sent shivers down her spine. 'You will oblige me, I think?'

She felt the iron grip of his hand on her arm and the false gaiety drained away, leaving her subdued and fearful. She thought he was angry, but his manner was controlled, distant—as if he were labouring under some emotional conflict all his own.

'We are leaving,' he said, and led her to his mother. 'Madam, I am taking Annelise home. I would like to speak to you later. Perhaps you would follow us?'

Lady Emily saw Annelise's white face and was moved to sympathy. 'I shall come immediately,' she said. 'There was no need for this, Justin. We were about to leave anyway.'

'Then nothing has changed.'

His grip on Annelise's arm did not slacken as he led her outside. She was helped into her chair in silence, and one glance at his face made her drop her gaze. This cool restraint was worse than if he had raged at her.

Was he angry with her because she had been rude to Madame Varennes?

Justin was silent as he ushered her into the house some time later. Not until they were alone in his library, the door shut against inquisitive ears and eyes, did he look at her—and then the condemnation in his face tore her apart.

'So this is what happens when my back is turned!' His tone was measured, calm but unnerving. 'Is one man lying close to death not enough for you, Annelise? Must I kill half the Court to satisfy your vanity?'

'No!' She was stung by his accusation. 'I meant no harm. I was but playing a game—a game other ladies play.'

'But they have nothing to lose. Does your reputation mean nothing to you? Would you have them all think you a whore?'

'That is unfair!' Lady Emily spoke from the doorway. 'You judge her too harshly, Justin. Annelise was within my sight the whole evening. She did not leave even for a moment.'

'Then you have much to answer for, ma'am!' Justin glanced at his mother, his manner grave. 'If you do not care for her reputation, I must. I have business in town for the moment, but in three days from now I return to the country—and Annelise goes with me. In the meantime, she will not leave this house. Her pleasures will be confined to whatever she finds to do within these walls. Mayhap a stay in the country will teach her to obey my wishes as a dutiful ward should.'

'You are unfair, sir!' Annelise cried, driven beyond bearing. 'All you want to do is marry me off so that I am no more trouble to you. Well, I shall marry—and to the first man who asks me. Lord Montgomery was about to propose. Had you waited only a moment longer you would have been rid of me.'

Justin went white. 'You would have taken him? Do you know he has buried three wives already?'

'Better dead than live here when *she* is your wife!' Annelise gave a sob of despair, turned and ran from the room before he could do or say anything to prevent her.

'Annelise!' he called after her. 'What do you mean? Come back! Come back here, you foolish girl.'

'She will not come back,' Lady Emily said angrily. 'What do you expect after the way you have treated her? You fool, Justin. You have thrown away a treasure greater than you know—and for the sake of that French trollop!'

'What has Mirabelle to do with this?' He stared at her in astonishment. 'Do you suppose that's what Annelise meant just now? She cannot imagine I would marry… Why? Why would she think that?'

His surprise made Lady Emily laugh. 'Are you blind? Annelise is jealous, Justin. Mirabelle Varennes called when I was out today. I suppose she told Annelise of your intentions to wed her.'

'She cannot have,' Justin said, still looking at his mother in bewilderment. 'It is impossible.'

'Why so?'

'Because…' Justin shook his head, refusing to elaborate. 'She had no right to come here. No right to say such things to Annelise. None at all.'

Lady Emily did not allow her inward delight to show. 'Indeed? Annelise was not alone in believing you meant to marry Madame Varennes. Was that not your intention at one time?'

'If it was, it is no longer.' Justin saw the gleam in her eyes and laughed. 'I know your game, madam. Have known it for an age. Do not imagine you have won.'

'The game is over. I weary of it—and of you,' Lady Emily said. 'I know not what eats at you, Justin. Destroy your own life if you will—I cannot stop you—but never hurt that child again. She is more a daughter to me than you have been a son. I am warning you—destroy her and you will answer to me.'

She walked from the room, leaving Justin to stare after her in frustration. He was well aware he had allowed his feelings to cloud his judgement. Annelise had indeed been reckless, but if she had been hurt…then her behaviour was understandable. He knew Mirabelle's spiteful tongue only too well.

He would pay her a little visit in the morning and discover just what she had been up to—but for the moment he needed his bed. He had ridden hard to reach London, and the picture of a young woman's lovely face had driven him on. During the time they had been apart, he had almost persuaded himself that there might be a chance for him after all, that if he told Annelise the truth she might be prepared to give him the opportunity to redeem himself so that they could at least be friends—but watching her flirting with Montgomery had driven him near mad and he had reacted hastily.

Sighing, Justin acknowledged in his heart that this could not go on. After he had visited Mirabelle, he would talk to

Annelise—try to find some way of restoring the trust she had once had in him.

Annelise tossed restlessly in her bed for most of the night. She suffered bouts of shame, followed by rushes of anger as her tormented thoughts gave her no rest. When she rose the next morning, her eyes felt gritty and tired. What was she going to do? Had her behaviour really been so bad the previous evening—or was Justin being unfair?

Perhaps she had been reckless, but it had not seemed to matter. Her unhappiness had overshadowed everything, and now she was close to despair. How could she go on as she was, loving Justin and knowing he despised her—that he loved Mirabelle Varennes?

She would have to leave this house—but where would she go? Justin had forbidden her to go out at all. He was so unkind! Surely she had done nothing to deserve this?

She dressed simply in a grey cloth gown, face pale, eyes pricking with tears as she waited to hear her fate.

Would she be allowed to go for a walk in the gardens if she asked Lady Emily, or was she to remain a prisoner in the house? She hesitated about leaving her own apartments, not sure of her reception if she ventured downstairs. Just as she was making up her mind to risk it, there was a tap at her door and her hostess entered.

'Ah, there you are, Annelise. I am about to go shopping—would you like to come with me?'

'I—I cannot,' Annelise said, her bottom lip unsteady. But she would not give way to tears! She lifted her head proudly. 'Have you forgotten, ma'am? My guardian has forbidden me to leave the house.'

'I have not forgotten. It was unkind of him and we shall ignore it. Besides, he is out on business of his own and need know nothing about it,' said Lady Emily. 'I was very angry with my son last night, and we have had words.'

'But—but you yourself warned me to have a care last night,' Annelise reminded her. 'I know I was reckless, heedless of your advice, but it was because…' She choked back a sob, determined not to break down.

'Because you were unhappy?' suggested Lady Emily. 'I understand more than you might suppose, my love. Justin is a fool. He is not worthy of your tears. Dry them and…'

She was interrupted by the arrival of a servant. The girl knocked, entered and bobbed a curtsey; she looked flustered as she addressed her mistress.

'Excuse me, milady, but there is a…person downstairs. He insists on seeing Mistress Woodward.'

'A person?' Lady Emily's brows rose. 'Whatever do you mean, Rose. Is this person a gentleman?'

'I suppose some would say so, milady…of a common order. By his dress I would judge him a Puritan.' The girl wrinkled her nose in distaste. 'He says his name is Master Broughton, and that he has travelled a long way on purpose to see Mistress Woodward.'

'Mr Broughton?' Annelise said in surprise. She looked at Lady Emily. 'Why, he is my aunt's kinsman. He was at the house when you came to fetch me, ma'am. His errand must be important if he has come all this way to visit me.'

'Yes, indeed it must,' agreed Lady Emily. 'Do you wish to see him, Annelise? Or shall I speak to him on your behalf?'

'I think in all common decency I should see him, ma'am. My aunt must have asked him to come. I fear my uncle may be worse—or dead.'

'Yes, it would seem so. Will you see him alone—or shall I come with you, to lend you support?'

'I would much prefer you to be present, ma'am.' Annelise was a little hesitant. 'If it is no trouble?'

'You could never be a trouble to me,' her hostess replied. 'Surely you know that?'

'Thank you.' Annelise smiled. 'You have always been so kind.'

'Come, let us go down.'

They went together to the small parlour, where a man of medium height dressed in the severest black was standing with his back towards them. He was sturdy in build, but when he turned Annelise discovered that his features were pleasant enough and his hair a soft brown, slightly receding from his forehead. His eyes were serious and dwelt on Annelise for a moment before he spoke.

'Ma'am.' He bowed to Lady Emily. 'Forgive this intrusion, but I was requested to come here by my kinswoman Lady Prudence Featherstone. She asked me to beg Mistress Woodward to return home at once.'

'Return? Why?' Lady Emily's gaze narrowed. 'I was under the impression that Lady Prudence did not wish to hear from her niece again.'

Mr Broughton's steady gaze did not waver. 'I have a letter from my kinswoman. She begs Mistress Woodward's pardon for anything she may have said to offend her and asks if she will return.'

'For what reason?' Lady Emily repeated her question.

'Sir Hugh is close to death, but recently he recovered his senses and made a last request—which is to see his niece before he dies.'

'My uncle wishes to see me?' Annelise stared at him. 'Do you know why, sir?'

'No, Mistress Woodward, I do not.' Mr Broughton frowned. 'I know only that he has said he cannot die in peace unless he first speaks with you—that he must beg your forgiveness or his soul will know no rest.'

'For what? There is nothing to forgive.'

'I do not know how that may be,' replied Broughton, 'but Lady Prudence was in tears when she entreated me to come to you. She cannot bear to see her husband suffering so. Will you not at least read her apology?'

Annelise took the letter, broke the seal and read the words her uncle's steward had penned on her aunt's behalf. She turned to Lady Emily, offering the paper.

'Will you read this, ma'am? Pray tell me what I ought to do.'

Lady Emily scanned the letter, then frowned. 'It is a pretty enough apology. What do you want to do, Annelise? It seems your aunt needs to be forgiven—as does your uncle.'

Annelise hesitated. She was willing to forgive any transgression of her uncle's, though she knew of nothing he had done to cause this terrible guilt he appeared to be suffering. Despite his strictness, he had done nothing to harm her during the years he had been her guardian. It was surely her duty to grant Lady Prudence's request. Besides, it was a way of escape for Annelise, at least for a while.

'I feel I ought to go home,' she said. 'But how can it be arranged?'

'I am here to offer my escort,' Mr Broughton said. 'I rode to London on my horse, but I could arrange a hired carriage for Mistress Woodward.'

'Annelise will travel in my carriage,' Lady Emily said decisively. 'I shall send a maid with her, and you may ride beside the carriage, sir.' She looked at Annelise with regret. 'I would come with you, my love, but it is difficult, as you know—however, you will be safe enough in this gentleman's care.'

'On that I give my word, ma'am.'

'And I shall send one of our most trustworthy grooms to ride with the coachman,' went on Lady Emily. She kissed Annelise on the cheek. 'It is right that you should go, but you must promise to return to us. I cannot part with you for longer than three weeks at most.'

'Do you truly want me back, ma'am?'

'Want you? La! What nonsense is this?' trilled her la-
dyship. 'I love you as my own and would not part with
you at all—except that I believe it may serve a purpose.'

Annelise wondered at the odd, secretive look in Lady
Emily's eyes, but made no comment. She went upstairs to
order the packing of a small cloak bag; she would not
bother with much, because her old clothes had been left
behind when she came to London, and they would be more
suitable in her uncle's household.

She was a little apprehensive as she wondered what
would happen if Justin were to return before she left.
Would he try to prevent her? He had forbidden her to leave
the house and might be angry with her for disobeying
him—but Lady Emily would explain.

She kissed her kind hostess goodbye, tears hovering on
her lashes. 'Forgive me if I have been a trial to you,' she
said. 'I love you and I shall miss you.'

'La! Such foolish talk,' cried Lady Emily, and smiled
lovingly. 'You will come back to us soon, Annelise.'

Annelise nodded but did not meet her eyes. She was very
subdued as she went out to the carriage. Mr Broughton
handed her in, giving her a look of approval.

'Lady Prudence was afeared you would not come, but I
was of the mind to try. It is after all no more than Christian
duty to put a man's soul at ease if it is in your power. Do
you not agree, Mistress Woodward?'

'You are very right, sir. I thank you for the trouble you
have had in coming to fetch me.'

'It was no more than my duty.'

His pompous manner was a little irritating, thought Annelise. She had forgotten how very righteous her aunt's
people could be.

She sighed as the carriage door was shut, leaning her
head back against the squabs and closing her eyes as the

carriage lurched and the horses began to move forward. Her frantic prayers had been answered; she had found a way of escape…so why did she feel so empty? Why no elation at having defied her guardian one last time?

Justin was furious as he left Mirabelle Varennes's lodgings. She had made no secret of her triumph at what she had done, laughing in his face, her green eyes flashing with spite.

'So the little milksop told you of my visit? She swore she would not—but I might have known she would weep on your shoulder.'

'My mother told me your visit had upset her, *madame*.' His eyes narrowed dangerously. 'Just what did you say to her?'

'I made it clear she would not be welcome in my house once we were wed—I advised her to find herself a husband before she found herself passed over for a younger woman.'

'You sour-tongued witch!' Justin stared at her with something akin to hatred. 'You have done your worst, *madame*, but your spite has worked against you. You hoped to rush her into an unwise marriage for reasons of your own—but it has not happened, nor will it.'

'I suppose you mean to have her for yourself?'

'Perhaps. What I choose to do from now on is none of your affair, *madame*—and I would advise you not to cross me again.'

'I care nothing for your affairs!' Mirabelle snapped her fingers. 'I am returning to Paris at once.'

Justin nodded. 'A wise decision. I bid you farewell, *madame*. I think it best you do not visit England again for a long time.'

A vase smashed against the wall as he left, but he did not turn, nor did he smile. He was angry, as much with himself as with her. She had deliberately tried to drive a

wedge between him and Annelise, and had succeeded only
too well. Yet his innate sense of justice told him that the
fault was mostly his own.

Justin cursed himself now. He must learn to curb his
temper for his own sake, and for Annelise's. In future he
would think before he leapt—and try to treat Annelise more
kindly.

'What?' Justin's good intentions dissolved, banished by
the fear that gripped his heart. 'You let her go with that
man? Have you taken leave of your senses? You sent her
off with a stranger—alone and unprotected?'

'Her aunt's kinsman?' Lady Emily smiled inwardly. Her
little ruse seemed to be working better than she had
thought. 'Mr Broughton seems quite harmless, Justin.
Slightly pompous and self-righteous, to be sure, but not
dangerous. He may not have blue blood in his veins, Justin,
but he has unexceptionable manners—for a country gentleman. I am sure she will be safe with him. I sent servants
with her. Besides, she was determined to go. Had I not
provided my carriage, she would have gone in a hired ve-
hicle. You would not have wished her to travel so?'

'I did not wish her to go at all,' he said in a stunned
tone. Annelise gone? A sense of loss swept over him. 'I
forbade her to leave this house—had you forgot?'

'My memory is very clear, thank you,' his mother replied. 'You were abominably rude to her last night, Justin.
She was upset, as she had every right to be. It would not
surprise me in the least if she were to decide to stay at her
own estate.'

'Stay…' Justin glared at her. 'No, that I will not allow.
Have you any idea of what her life was like in that household, Mother? She was made to wear those drab gowns, to
feel ashamed of her looks, never given any freedom…'
Seeing the look in Lady Emily's face, he gave a cry of

exasperation. 'No! No, that is unjust, ma'am. I have not treated her so unfairly.'

'Have you not?' Lady Emily arched her fine brows. 'You have played the stern guardian often enough, my son. Your unkindness has reduced her to tears more than once.'

'If I was strict it was for her sake.'

'Indeed? Are you so sure of that?'

'My intention was to see her happily settled. Her behaviour last night could have been detrimental to her marriage prospects.'

'If your intention was to see her happy, I fear you have failed—for she has been miserable of late.'

'And you blame me?'

'Who else is there, Justin?'

For a moment he seemed as though he would deny it, then a wry smile lifted the corners of his mouth. 'Have I been so very difficult, Mama?'

Lady Emily caught the softer note in his voice and allowed herself to hope. Perhaps the son she loved so much was not quite gone, just hidden behind the layers of distrust and bitterness he had erected to protect himself.

'You have been impossible,' she said truthfully. 'I have found your moods hard to bear. Poor Annelise has not known how to please you. No matter what she did, you frowned on her, and found fault in everything—even her singing.'

'Has she tried to please me?' Justin frowned. 'I have found her wilful and obstinate—she tries my patience beyond bearing.'

'Then let her stay in the country.'

'Never!' His eyes gleamed. 'She belongs here. And you know well that I thought her singing delightful—that's why I thought singing lessons would please her. They were meant as a gift, not an insult.'

He turned to leave but his mother caught his arm. 'Where are you going?'

'To follow her, of course.'

'To fetch her back?'

Justin looked and saw the eagerness in Lady Emily's look. He guessed why she had been so ready to let Annelise go. 'Fetch her back?' he echoed, the devil on his shoulder. 'No, my very dear, scheming Mama! If my ward wishes to visit her estate, I shall escort her there.'

Lady Emily watched as he left the room. What a provoking creature he was! Why could he not admit he cared for Annelise?

What was it that caused him so much pain? Why did that black, haunted look he wore sometimes make her fear for him?

She had no answers to her questions, only the conviction that his salvation rested in the hands of a certain very lovely young woman.

'Please God let him realise it,' she whispered after he had gone. 'Let Justin understand before it is too late.'

They had been travelling for some hours, and with each mile that passed Annelise's heart grew heavier. She had longed to escape, but now all she could recall were the moments when Justin had smiled at her...the times when she had felt a closeness between them, when she had even dared to hope that he might care for her.

Oh, how foolish she was! She must remember his anger, his rages, the look in his eyes when he had forbidden her to leave the house—but, despite all their quarrels, she could not help loving him and her heart ached at the thought that she might never see him again.

She was beginning to feel weary and to wish they could stop for a while. Surely there must be an inn where they could rest for an hour or so? She was about to pull back the curtain and put her head through the window aperture, to enquire whether they might not stop at the next inn, when she heard shouting and the coach lurched to a sudden halt. The next moment the carriage door was wrenched open and she found herself staring into a pair of triumphant blue eyes.

'So, I have caught you!'

'Justin!' she gasped, startled. 'W-what is wrong?'

'You can ask me that?' he said. 'You run off with a stranger, alone and unprotected, and ask me what is wrong? You might have been kidnapped, killed…anything.'

Annelise felt her former weariness slough off as a discarded skin; she was suddenly alive again, her pulses racing. He had come after her!

'I am not unprotected, sir,' she said, a little smile tweaking the corners of her mouth as her spirits lifted. 'Nor did I run away. Lady Emily gave me her permission.'

'It is rather *my* permission you should have obtained.'

'You were not there, sir—and the matter was urgent.'

'So urgent it could not have waited another hour?'

'It was I who requested haste.' Mr Broughton had dismounted, coming to her aid. 'And Mistress Woodward is right. Lady Emily gave consent. I would not otherwise have…'

'Hold your tongue, sirrah!' Justin's eyes flashed with scorn. 'I could have you arrested for kidnapping my ward—another word and I vow I will have you clapped in irons.'

'My lord, I protest…' Mr Broughton's look of indignation brought a smile to Annelise's lips.

'La, Justin,' she said, her sense of the ridiculous making her find the situation comic. 'There is no need for such threats. As you see, I am quite safe—and, if you wish it, prepared to return with you.'

'Indeed, mistress?' Justin caught the note of mischief in her voice and all at once his pent-up emotion drained away.

How enchanting she was! It was his own fault if she had taken the chance to escape his harsh strictures. He knew a deep longing to make his peace with her. 'As it happens, I have come to escort you to your home.'

Annelise's heart quickened. 'That was kind of you, sir.' A little dimple appeared in her cheek, a gleam of wickedness in her eyes. 'I think my carriage must be the best-protected on the road. And I fear for any highwayman who has the presumption to accost us.'

Justin tried, but could not prevent the laugh escaping. No wonder she had half the Court at her feet! If she looked at all the men in that teasing half-woman, half-childlike way, the only wonder was that he had not been forced to fight a dozen duels over her.

'Annelise,' he murmured softly. 'What am I to do with you?'

'Do you wish to ride inside, sir?' she enquired innocently. 'Only I fear you must sit with Mary, for my gown takes up the whole of this side.'

'Never fear, I shall not squash your gown,' Justin replied. 'I shall ride beside the carriage—but we must stop at the next inn. My horse is nigh exhausted. I have pushed the poor beast hard to catch up with you and must rest it or hire another somewhere.'

'I was hoping we might rest for a while—and perhaps take some refreshment. If there is a respectable inn nearby?'

'I believe I know of such a place. We may as well take rooms there for the night. It will be dusk soon, and we cannot hope to complete our journey today.'

'As you wish, sir,' Annelise said at her most demure. 'I am sure Mr Broughton will be only too happy to be guided by your direction—as shall I, naturally.'

'Jade,' he muttered, choking back his laughter. 'You do not deceive me for an instant, mistress. We shall speak later—in private.'

With this threat, he closed the door, and she leaned back against the squabs, smiling in relief. He was not truly angry with her, and he had cared enough to come after her... For the moment that was sufficient to ease the unhappiness that had dwelt too long inside her.

Chapter Seven

'So, Annelise, what have you to say for yourself?' Justin had secured a private parlour for them, and, Mr Broughton having excused himself, they were for the moment alone. 'Why did you run off the moment my back was turned?'

'I did not run off.' Annelise met his searching gaze and blushed. It was as if he could see into her mind, her secret thoughts 'I did not run away without Lady Emily's knowledge. I would never do anything to cause *her* distress. You cannot think so ill of me?'

'Your scruples do you credit, mistress.' Justin arched his brows mockingly. 'May I perhaps enquire whether you gave any thought to *my* distress?'

Annelise studied him for a few moments before answering. He certainly wasn't angry, instead he seemed watchful—even a little offended that she had not considered his feelings.

'I did not imagine my leaving would disturb your peace of mind, sir. You had forbidden me to go out, that I admit, and it was wrong of me to disobey you—but a mercy visit to my uncle's deathbed was not, I think, what you had in mind?'

'No, that is true,' Justin agreed. 'I could not in all conscience forbid you that. If it was your only reason for leaving, we shall say no more on the subject.'

Annelise hesitated. She was tempted to tell him the truth, but knew in doing so she would betray her innermost feelings—and to confess her love for him when he did not love her would shame her.

'It was my reason for leaving, but…' She faltered, unable to continue.

'You have been unhappy, is that not so?' Justin's questing gaze made her drop her own hastily. Her heart was racing in confusion. How difficult it was to read this man with all his conflicting moods. She could almost think he really cared for her. 'And that is my fault, I think?'

She took refuge in defence. 'I—I have made you angry, sir. I should not have gone to that courtyard with Earl Rathbone. Nor should I have flirted so heedlessly with those gentlemen at Court. It was wilful and foolish of me.'

'No, you should not have done those things,' agreed Justin, but in a gentle tone that made the tears rush to her eyes. 'No, no, do not weep, Annelise.' He smiled wryly, offering his own kerchief. 'I would not have you shed your tears for such matters. I fear I have a wicked temper—and I beg you to forgive me.'

'You ask forgiveness of me?' Her head came up, tears forgotten.

'Is that so very shocking?' A puzzled look came to his eyes. 'Have I seemed such an ogre to you, Annelise? Did you think me incapable of any decent feeling? A monster who wanted only to crush all the joy from your life?'

'No! Of course not,' she said, a blush creeping into her cheeks. 'I—we have sometimes seemed to tolerate each other's company quite well. It is only when you are…'

'In one of my black moods?' He reached out to wipe the last tear from her cheek with his fingertips. 'My mother has taken me to task over them, I assure you. I am sorry if I have been unkind. Sometimes there is a devil in me and I lash out, hurting those I care for most. You once told me I was not caring enough towards my mother. You thought I hated her, but if ever I felt something near to hatred for her that time is long past. I do care for her. If I seem not to…' He shrugged. 'I have reasons enough for my moods, but not to hurt others. In future I shall try not to inflict them on her—or you.'

Annelise swallowed hard. This new gentleness in him was so surprising that it made her ache to take him in her arms, but of course she could not be so forward. If he did care for her at all, it was as his ward, as a friend of his mother's.

'You…I do not know what to say.'

'Say only that you will try to forgive me. And that we may begin again. I would be your friend, Annelise. I would have you smile at me—as you do at Ralph and Robert.'

'Oh, yes!' Her eyes glowed. 'I would like so much to be your friend, Justin.'

Impulsively, she darted forward and kissed his cheek, then blushed a fiery red and stood back, her heart thumping. Justin seemed stunned. Why did he look at her so strangely? Had she been too forward? Pray God he was not angry again!

'Thank you,' he said in a rueful tone. 'I do not…'

Whatever he was about to say was lost as the parlour door opened and the landlord came in bearing a tray; he was followed by a sheepish-looking Mr Broughton.

'I have taken the liberty of ordering supper, my lord,' he announced in his rather pompous manner. 'Have I your permission to dine with you and Mistress Woodward?'

'Yes, yes,' said Justin. 'I could hardly deny you after your trouble. If I was sharp with you earlier, sir, I apologise.'

'No need, my lord. Your concern was for Mistress

Woodward's safety and does you credit. Indeed, I am heartily glad to discover that my kinswoman's niece has been
in such good hands. Lady Prudence feared it was not the
case; I told her I was sure you were a man of good reputation and honour, and now we have met I shall be able to
confirm that and set her mind at rest.'

Mr Broughton's words were meant in good faith, but had
the effect of rousing Justin's hackles. His expression was
one of deep affront, and it was all Annelise could do to
hold back her laughter.

'You are very good, sir.' Justin's reply was forced, but
then, meeting his ward's wicked gaze, he saw how ridiculous it would be for him to lose his temper over such foolishness and relaxed, a gleam of mischief in his eyes. 'I shall
rely on your kind recommendation to Lady Prudence.'

Annelise blew her nose hard, muffling the laugh she
could not quite prevent escaping. 'Shall we eat?' she asked,
looking innocently from one man to the other. 'I am starving.'

'Forgive me,' said Justin, an answering gleam in his
eyes. 'I have neglected your well-being, Annelise. I would
not have your friends think you had been deprived of any
comfort.'

'No one could think that,' she replied. 'I am sure you
have paid me every attention, sir. Indeed, my uncle could
not have guarded me with more vigilance—and so I shall
tell my aunt.'

'You are too kind, Annelise.' His deceptively mild tone
made her want to box his ears. 'I find myself indebted to
you.'

She threw him a speaking look, but declined to continue
their sparring. It was unfair to Mr Broughton, who seemed
to her a worthy man, but whose intellect was not capable
of seeing beyond the obvious. He did not realise Justin was
making game, and she would not join in this mockery.

During their meal, Mr Broughton made several derogatory remarks about the Court, and told them seriously of Lady Prudence's very great fears about the effect mixing in such licentious company might be having on her niece. He appeared not to realise that his aspersions on the courtiers might be offensive to Justin, and indeed to Annelise herself.

She held her breath on at least two occasions, fearing an outburst, but Justin's manner remained outwardly calm. In truth he seemed to take a malicious pleasure in drawing the other man out, exposing him as rather too pompous and a bore who imagined himself to be vastly clever.

At last, seeing Annelise vainly trying to hide her yawns, Justin decided to show mercy.

'You have entertained us well, sir,' he said. 'But I believe my ward grows weary. If you will excuse us, I shall escort her to her bedchamber and then seek my own.'

'Indeed, the hour is late—it must be past nine,' Mr Broughton said, getting immediately to his feet. He looked at Annelise in concern. 'Forgive me for keeping you up, Mistress Woodward. You must rest if we are to make an early start the morrow.'

'I thank you for your consideration, sir.'

Annelise wished him goodnight. She led the way upstairs, keeping silent all the while until they reached the door of her room, then glanced frowningly at Justin.

'That was not well done of you, sir,' she reproved. 'You were not kind to make game of poor Mr Broughton.'

'Better to make game than test his wits against the scorn I feel for such as he. Had I not laughed, I might have been tempted to take a horse whip to him—it was such men brought England to bloody war.'

'Are you still bitter?' Annelise glimpsed pain in his eyes. 'Can you not forgive…after all these years?'

'Forgive those who killed my father? For murdering my King—and being the ruin of men I loved as brothers?'

Now she was seeing behind the mask to the real man, beginning to understand what might have made him sometimes harsh. And her heart ached for love and the pity of his suffering.

'It was over long ago.'

'For some perhaps. Not for others.'

'But unless you forgive, you will find no peace.'

'I expect none,' Justin replied. He smiled wearily, then leaned towards her. His kiss was soft, the merest touch of his lips on hers, and set her heart fluttering like a caged bird. 'Do not frown so, Annelise. I am not worthy of your concern. And I would not have your life blighted because of my past.'

'Justin…'

'Sleep and rest,' he said. 'One day perhaps I shall tell you why I have this devil inside me, but not tonight. I would not give you nightmares.'

His smile twisted the heart in her. It held bitterness, regret and something more. Was it only her imagination, or had his eyes begged for understanding…for forgiveness?

Annelise felt the carriage slowing to a halt. They were almost there. She had mixed feelings about her homecoming. The parting from her aunt had been acrimonious, and she was apprehensive as the carriage door opened and Justin helped her down. He smiled at her, as if sensing her nervousness.

'You need fear nothing,' he said softly, giving her a look that sent her heart racing. 'No one will force you to do anything you do not wish; I give you my word.'

He had mistaken her mood. She was not afraid of her aunt's power, only of the reception she might receive.

'Annelise, my dear niece. How good it is to see you.'

Seeing the sheen of tears in her aunt's eyes, Annelise realised she need not have worried.

'Aunt Prudence,' she said, kissing her cheek. 'I am happy to see you again. How is my uncle?'

'Very close to death,' her aunt said, smothering a sob. 'He asked for you an hour ago. I pray he will know you have come. It has lain heavy on him…this need to beg your forgiveness.'

'But he has done nothing to harm me.'

'Yet something haunts him, giving him no peace,' said Lady Prudence. 'Please go to him, Annelise—grant him absolution so that he may die in peace.'

'Yes, of course.' She glanced over her shoulder at Justin. He nodded encouragement and she went without another word, walking up the stairway and along the gallery to her uncle's apartments.

Master Blackwell, her uncle's steward, was standing by the bed as she entered. He looked at her with a strange, frowning look, then turned away as if disapproving. Annelise hardly noticed. She was aware of Parson Hale reading from the Bible, and of one the maids sniffling as she made up the fire with sea coals.

A silence fell as Annelise moved closer to the bed, and she looked at the parson uncertainly. 'Is he…?'

'Sir Hugh is alive,' he said. 'He sleeps…'

'I can wake him,' said Master Blackwell.

'No, please,' Annelise protested. 'Do not disturb him if he is resting.'

'It was his wish…should you return in time.' There was a cold disapproval in the steward's eyes. He shook his master's shoulder. 'Sir! She is here. Mistress Woodward has come.'

Seeing her uncle's eyelids flutter, Annelise moved to stand by his side. She bent over him, her hand touching his cheek for a moment.

'I am here, Uncle. What is it you wish to tell me?'

The dying man opened his eyes. His hand reached towards her and she took it in her own. 'Annelise? Is it you, child? Are you truly here?'

'Yes, Uncle. I am here.'

'Forgive me, child. I have wronged you. It was not my intention…but I have failed you.'

'No, Uncle,' she said softly. 'You were always just and fair. You have not failed me.'

'You do not know…' His eyes closed. It was clear the effort was too much for him. 'Blackwell has…' A sigh escaped him. 'The letter…it will explain.'

'Rest, Uncle,' Annelise said. She bent to kiss his withered cheek. 'If there is anything to forgive, I do so freely. Be at peace, sir. You have done nothing to harm me.'

His eyelids flickered open once more and for a moment he seemed to smile. 'May God bless and…' The rattle of death was in his throat. His eyes closed and Annelise knew it was for the last time.

'God bless and keep you, Uncle,' she said, then turned her head as she heard a cry from the doorway. Her aunt stood there, fear and distress in her eyes. 'He is at rest, ma'am.'

'You forgave him? He knew you?'

'He knew me,' Annelise said. She moved aside so that her aunt could take her place. 'I believe his mind was eased.'

'Thank you.' Lady Prudence blinked away her tears. 'You were generous to come…after what I said to you when we parted. My words were harsh and spoken in haste, Annelise. I have regretted the manner of our parting and do sincerely repent my unkindness to you.'

'Please do not reproach yourself, Aunt.' She touched Lady Prudence's hand. 'We shall talk later.'

Leaving her uncle's chamber, Annelise went to her own.

It was unchanged, her things just as she had left them, as if awaiting her return. She was saddened by her uncle's death, and by the marks of grief in her aunt's face. They had both done their duty by her as they saw it, and she might have fared far worse had Sir Hugh not protected the estate at the end of the war. She had often resented her uncle's strictness in the past, but now saw that in his way he had cared for her.

She glanced at herself in the tiny hand mirror. Even her simple travelling costume seemed too elegant, too ostentatious for this house of mourning. She decided to change into one of her old gowns. Looking through her linen chest, she pulled out a suitable grey dress and a plain white collar.

Once changed, Annelise looked at herself again. She was not the girl who had formerly lived in this house, even her drab gown could not disguise the vitality…the zest for life that her time in London had awakened in her. No, she would never become that meek Puritan again, but for the moment, out of respect, she would wear the apparel her aunt approved.

Leaving her room, Annelise went downstairs, her intention to find Justin and discover whereabouts her aunt had lodged him in the house. She was told he had stayed only long enough to greet Lady Prudence then gone on to Longton Hall.

'The Marquis said he would stay at Sir Robert's house,' the maid informed her. 'He bade us tell you he will call on you tomorrow morning, Mistress Woodward.'

'Thank you,' Annelise said. 'If Lady Prudence should ask for me, I shall be outside in the gardens.'

'Yes, Mistress Woodward.'

Was she imagining it, or was there a new respect in the servants' manner towards her? In the past she had often felt herself treated as little more than a lodger in the house, tolerated but not valued, not really wanted here.

She left the house and went out into the gardens, which were beginning to wear the colours of autumn. Could she live here again? Annelise wondered. It was her home, and as its rightful mistress she could order the running to suit herself—employ servants of her own choosing. Yet she would need a husband at her side. Even though the estate was hers, it would be impossible for her to manage it alone. This was a small village peopled by gossips, many of whom still clung to the Puritan ways; they would not be slow to point the finger if she tried to defy the laws by which they lived.

So she must marry. Nothing had changed. She had made her peace with Justin for the moment, but nothing would persuade her to live beneath his roof once he married Madame Varennes. Yet she had only the Frenchwoman's word that such a marriage would ever take place.

Perhaps Justin would change his mind. Annelise could only wait and hope.

She stopped walking and glanced over her shoulder, shivering as a cool breeze seemed to pass over her. She had the oddest feeling…as if she were being watched. And in a secretive way.

Who would want to spy on her? No, no, she was letting her imagination run away with her. No one was watching. It was merely the wind rustling the leaves of a tree.

Sighing, she turned and went into the house.

'Of course you are welcome to stay here for a few days,' Robert said, staring moodily out of the window. 'Without your help I would not even have been able to repair the roof.'

'You need not feel obliged because of that,' replied Justin. 'Let us be plain, Rob. I am aware of your feelings for my ward—but I cannot force her to accept you. She must make her own choice.'

'Ralph says you're in love with her yourself.'

'Ralph says a good deal too much!'

'She would be a fool to take me if she could have you.' Rob turned, a rueful smile in his eyes. 'Damn it, Justin! I'll admit I came rushing down as soon as Lady Emily told me where she had gone, but I doubt it will do me much good. She has already refused my offer twice, but I shall not give up. I cannot!'

'Refused you?' Justin frowned. 'You had no right to ask without my consent.'

'I know it,' Rob confessed. 'She told me so herself. She is far above me, Justin, but, fool that I am, I love her.'

'Then you must be patient. She will marry—must marry soon. If you wait, she may turn to you.'

'I think there is someone else...' Robert's expression hardened. 'But I shall win her if I can. Neither friendship nor gratitude will prevent me from having her if she will consent.'

'I would expect nothing less,' Justin said. 'Now to other matters. I think I was followed here. For the moment I believe I am in no danger—but we should both do well to be on our guard.'

'Sir Roger Courtney?'

'Or one of his henchmen.'

'But why? What could he hope to gain by your death now? The judgement went against him.'

'I have no male heir.' Justin shrugged. 'My mother would sell. She has no love for the country.'

'You are keeping something back,' Robert said, his gaze narrowing. 'I pray you, tell me all. I would be of service to you in this if I am able.'

'You can watch and listen,' Justin said, and grinned. He offered his hand to Robert. 'We are friends still? The matter of Annelise set aside, nothing has changed between us. I may count on your sword, Rob?'

'As always.' Robert smiled. 'I shall win her from you if I can, Justin—but you once saved my life and in all else I am yours to command.'

'Then listen well, my friend. For more may depend on this than you yet guess…'

Annelise moved amongst the small gathering of mourners come to pay their respects to Sir Hugh. She offered cider, ale and wine to the gentlemen, and her aunt's own raspberry cordial to the ladies.

'A sorrowful day,' said Mistress Hale. 'Sir Hugh will be greatly missed. He was a good man.'

'Yes, he was,' Annelise replied. 'I am saddened by his passing.'

The parson's wife crossed herself piously. 'And you, Mistress Woodward—what are your plans for the future?'

'I am not yet certain. I shall stay with my aunt for at least another week, then I may return to London. It depends on my guardian.' She glanced across the room at Justin, who had been speaking to Sir Robert, but was now standing alone by the window.

Mistress Hale nodded. She glanced in the direction Annelise's gaze had taken a moment earlier and frowned. The Marquis was dressed soberly, as befitted the occasion, but his hair and bearing proclaimed him what he was—a Royalist and a disciple of the devil!

'Why do you not wed a godly man and stay here?' she asked, looking pointedly at Lady Prudence's kinsman. 'Master Broughton seems a worthy choice.'

'He has been kind,' Annelise said. 'But my marriage is a matter for my guardian, ma'am. Excuse me, if you please; I think the Marquis wishes to speak with me.'

It was with a sense of relief that she went to Justin.

'I saw you beckon,' she said. 'Did you want something? May I serve you wine or food?'

'I want for nothing,' he replied, a wry smile about his mouth. 'I thought you looked as if you longed to escape.'

'Did my looks so betray me?' Annelise smiled. 'I have forgotten how to hide my thoughts.'

'You were never able to hide them from me.' He studied her face, seeing the faint shadows beneath her eyes. She was as lovely as ever, but looked strained and tired. 'What troubles you, Annelise? Have you had enough of this place? Of these sour faces? Do you want me to take you home?'

How she longed to say yes! She wanted to be with him, living in his house, seeing him every day, but knew she must not give way to her desires. He was promised to Madame Varennes and she must never forget that.

'I must stay a few more days,' she said. 'It would be unkind and discourteous to leave too soon.'

'Another week, then.' He laid his hand on her arm. 'I think we might leave them to it, Annelise. Come, walk with me. I should like to see more of the estate—and I must leave tomorrow.'

'Leave?' She stared at him, her dismay writ plain upon her face. 'Must you go?'

'I have an errand,' Justin replied, a look of mischief in his eyes. 'Fear not, Annelise. I shall not forget you. A day or two at most, and I shall return to rescue you.'

She averted her face, knowing she had betrayed herself once more. He must be aware of her feelings for him. How could he not be? Which meant that he did not return her love.

Her heart was heavy as she allowed him to lead her from the parlour out into the gardens.

'What would you like to see, my lord? There is a fine orchard, the soft fruit beds—or perhaps the carp pond?'

'We shall stroll down to the stables.' He glanced at her. 'Do you ride, Annelise?'

'My uncle taught me when I was a child, but he did not

think it seemly for me to ride alone once I had become a woman. I have not ridden for years.'

'Then you should take it up again. When we go to Hampshire I shall provide you with a mare of your own. We shall ride together, Annelise. We might even go hawking—if the idea does not displease you?'

'I should like to share your pleasures, my lord.'

'Would you, my ward?' Justin smiled, amusement lurking in his eyes. 'There are many things we might enjoy together, Annelise—since we have decided to be friends.'

Annelise caught his mood. The shadows left her face; she tucked her arm through his, smiling up at him as hope renewed itself once more. Perhaps he did care for her just a little.

'You were the one who decided, sir. I have always wished to be on terms with you.'

'Indeed? Then I must have imagined all your little tricks, mistress. Did you not set out to tease and torment me? To sharpen your kitten's claws on my wits?'

His eyes teased and challenged, lifting her heart. Oh, if only it could always be this way between them!

Annelise's laughter rang out. 'La, sir! I do not know what you mean. At least, I meant only to play a little game with you. It was never my intention to make you angry—except once.' She dimpled charmingly, her manner deceivingly demure. 'That was wrong of me. For that, I do most humbly beg your pardon.'

'And promise never to plague me so again?'

'Most humbly, my lord.'

'Minx! Why do I suspect you, Annelise?'

'It is your nature, sir. A severe fault, but one we must hope can be cured with time.'

'Impertinent wench!' He laughed, entranced. 'You bewitch me, Annelise. What am I to do with you?'

'Perhaps you should beat me?'

'Do not dare me, wench!' He threw a speaking look at her. 'I may yet decide to teach you obedience.'

Annelise laughed again. She glanced up at him, a hint of wickedness in her eyes. 'In what way would you have me serve you, my lord?'

Justin caught his breath. She looked so lovely, despite the drab gown she wore, her eyes bright with mirth, yet somehow untouched…the innocent wood nymph he had seen singing in the woods. Here in the gardens of her home she seemed to have shed the veneer of sophistication she had acquired at Court, to be the girl who had first stirred something he had thought long dead inside him…the girl he had loved from the very beginning.

Loved? Justin felt the shock run through his veins as he looked down into her face. Love! *He* contemplated love? What foolishness was this? How could he offer love to this girl? It was impossible. Unthinkable! Yet he could no longer deny this feeling inside him. It was stronger, more powerful…more tender than anything he had ever experienced in his life.

The desire to kiss her was overwhelming. Without realising what he did, Justin reached for her, drawing her to him, close to his breast. His heart was pounding like a war drum; he seemed to be drowning in her eyes, losing all control as he bent his head, his mouth drawn to hers irresistibly. Then he was kissing her, hungrily, with a passion that threatened to sweep away all restraint, a desire more desperate, more compelling than any he had known before.

He loved, adored, wanted this woman more than life itself.

'Mistress Woodward! Mistress Woodward…'

Justin released her as they heard the servant calling. For a moment he hardly knew what he did, so great was his need to hold her again, so fierce his longing to make her his own. He fought the raging desire inside him, regaining his senses, his will taking control, banking down the fires until they merely smouldered deep inside him.

'Forgive me,' he croaked. 'I should not have done that. It was both unwise and wrong of me.'

'Justin...' She could not breathe, could not speak. 'I...'

'Mistress Woodward! Everyone is leaving. Lady Prudence begs you will come to her at once.'

Annelise saw the disapproving expression in the steward's face. Had he seen her in Justin's arms? She could not be sure. She had sensed Master Blackwell's hostility towards her many times, now she felt it like a physical thing. He did not just dislike her, he hated her.

She looked at Justin, silently begging him to understand what was in her heart. 'Shall I see you again before you leave, sir?'

'No, I think not.' Justin was fighting his baser instincts. He wanted her, desired her—loved her. God have mercy! If this was love, it was a fearful thing. No wonder men killed for it...died of it. 'I shall return soon—in two days at most. For now, I bid you farewell.'

Annelise ignored the steward's impatient looks as she watched Justin walk away. She longed to call him back, to tell him she wanted nothing more than to be in his arms— but what had brought that shuttered look to his face? Why had he kissed her like that and then withdrawn from her? Surely it could not be only that he was her guardian? He must know that such formalities could be overcome.

'You would not be wise to walk alone with that man.'

'What did you say?' Annelise blinked as the steward's words got through to her. 'Do you speak of the Marquis, Master Blackwell?'

'I speak of the devil who killed my master...that spawn of Satan!' He spat on the grass, his eyes glowing strangely.

'Hold your tongue, sirrah!' Annelise gave him an angry

look. 'How dare you speak to me so? The Marquis Saintjohn is my guardian and a man I hold in respect.'

'Then you are a fool,' Blackwell said. He took a sealed
document from inside his leather jerkin. 'My master bade
me give you this after he was dead. If you will not heed
my warnings, read this and learn the truth. Discover where
your wilfulness may lead you, Mistress Woodward, and
save your soul.'

'What is this?' Annelise made no attempt to take the
packet from him so he thrust it into her hands. 'You are
impertinent, Master Blackwell. I have a mind to dismiss
you from my service.'

His eyes were contemptuous as he looked at her. 'I
stayed here only for my master's sake. Now that he is buried, I shall seek employment elsewhere. I would not want
to serve a man who carries the mark of Satan—nor his
whore.'

'Leave at once! I shall not tolerate such foul talk. You
are dismissed and shall have no reference of me.'

He took a step towards her, seeming as if he would strike
her. 'Be warned, Mistress Woodward. My master cared for
you, and so I would have you take heed. The shadow of
evil hath fallen upon you. Your only salvation is prayer.
Down...down on your knees, Jezebel! Beg for God's help
and you may yet be saved.'

'You are mad,' Annelise said. 'Go! Leave me! I will hear
no more of this wickedness.'

'The fires of hell await those who do not repent. Fire
shall take thee and all those who live in sin...the torment
of the damned be on thy head.'

Annelise stood watching as he walked away. She was
trembling as she turned towards the house. How dared he?
How dared he say such terrible things to her?

She was so upset that she did not notice Robert leave
the house and come towards her.

'Is something wrong?' He stared at her. 'Annelise—can I be of service to you?'

'Just leave me alone,' she cried, and ran past him into the house. 'Why will no one leave me alone?'

Robert watched her disappear, then turned and walked off in the direction of the stables.

Annelise wept for several minutes. It was not until the storm of grief had passed that she remembered being sharp with Robert. Oh, how careless of her! She would not have hurt him so for the world. Her nerves had been in such a state! First that wonderful, heart-stopping kiss which had seemed to draw her very soul from her body, then Justin's abrupt withdrawal—and that unpleasant, frightening confrontation with Master Blackwell.

Annelise glanced at the crumpled packet he had so dramatically thrust at her. She realised that this must be the letter her uncle had tried to tell her about just before he died.

What could possibly be in it that was of such significance? Master Blackwell obviously knew its contents. Sir Hugh must have dictated it after he became too ill to write himself.

She had always known that the steward disliked her, but had not been aware of his hatred until now. His furious tirade must have been brought on by something. He *must* have seen her in Justin's arms!

Why should that make him angry? It was none of his business what passed between her and her guardian. Perhaps her behaviour was not entirely correct, but neither was it sinful. Only an accident of fate had made him her guardian. There was no true reason why they should not love each other.

Annelise had not yet experienced enough of the world to understand that there were many kinds of evil, many degrees of lust and envy. She saw Master Blackwell as a devout Puritan, a godly man who adhered strictly to the creed of his chosen doctrine, but could not guess at the canker of his tortured mind or know that he wore a hair shirt beneath his clothes because he could not control his thoughts of her—that he writhed beneath a desire he believed sinful yet was unable to banish: a desire he would never seek to ease as other men, but which made him hate her for what she unknowingly inflicted on him.

Unaware that for a few minutes that afternoon he had been driven near to breaking point, and that she had been in danger of losing not only her innocence but her very life, Annelise stared at the letter Master Blackwell had thrust upon her. She was unwilling to open it, knowing somehow that its contents would cause her pain.

Should she tear it to pieces? She did not have to read it. No one could compel her.

She took it between her hands as if to rip it in two, but, folded as it was, the parchment was too thick for her to tear.

She would throw it into the fire! Yet that would leave a nagging doubt at the back of her mind. Her uncle's warnings combined with Master Blackwell's threats were forcing her to face the inevitable. She had to read the letter, because she would never be at peace unless she did—but she did not want to know!

Several times she almost broke the seal, then threw the crumpled parchment down again. How could she be sure that whatever was written there was the truth? No, she would not read it. She would not let her mind be poisoned by lies!

'Annelise…are you there?'

'Yes. Come in, Aunt.'

She wiped her cheek as the door opened and Lady Prudence entered.

'Is something wrong, Annelise? Why are you sitting up here alone?'

'I—I wanted to be quiet for a while. I am sorry for leaving you to cope, Aunt. Has everyone gone?'

'Yes, at last.' Lady Prudence sighed. 'They meant well, but…I confess I am glad it is over.' She hesitated, then looked at Annelise with a slight frown. 'Tell me, is it true that you have dismissed Master Blackwell?'

'Yes. I am sorry if you are displeased, Aunt. Another steward will be found to take his place.'

'Was he impertinent?' Lady Prudence pursed her mouth when Annelise nodded. 'I suspected as much. I have not liked the way he looked at you of late. With your uncle's illness he was given too much authority; he has got above himself. We shall do better with a new man. I shall speak to your guardian when he returns, Annelise. The Marquis Saintjohn seems a very reasonable man to me.'

'I am glad you approve of him, Aunt.'

'Most understanding.' Lady Prudence went on. 'I told him your jewels had been sold—without my knowledge at the time, Annelise. Your uncle invested the proceeds in some venture.' She pulled a wry face. 'He would never discuss business with me, as you know—but I had my own ways of finding out. Sometimes I listened when he was closeted with Master Blackwell. That is how I knew about the will making you the Marquis's ward—and the venture that unfortunately failed. I imagine it was the loss of that ship which caused your uncle so much anxiety. He was afraid of what the Marquis would have to say about the misuse of your property.'

'A ship was lost?' Annelise stared at her. 'Are you saying that was why my uncle was so upset—why he became ill?'

Lady Prudence nodded. 'I heard them talking. Your uncle had some kind of partnership—with a Portuguese gentleman, I believe. They had invested in a rather risky venture which was supposed to bring in huge profits. It involved trading in the New World, for a cargo of silver. Unfortunately, the ship was sunk. It went to the bottom of the ocean with all its crew and cargo still on board.'

'How did that happen? Was there a storm?'

'No, I do not think that was the case. I am not certain, but I believe the ship was attacked by pirates.'

'They sunk it with all its crew?' Annelise was shocked. 'That is terrible—wicked! How could anyone do such a thing?'

'I believe it happens often. These pirates call themselves privateers, and usually attack Spanish treasure ships. What went wrong I do not know. For some reason the ship was given no chance to surrender. It was sent to the bottom with all its crew. And that is still not the worst of it, Annelise—there were women and children on board. The captain's wife, her sister and two young boys.'

'They were killed?' Annelise felt a chill of horror run down her spine. 'That is horrible! To kill women and children...without mercy. How could anyone be so cruel?'

'It gave me nightmares to think of it,' Lady Prudence said. 'What kind of a monster could do such a thing? I am sure I do not know how the captain who gave the order can live with himself.'

'No, nor I.' Annelise shuddered. 'He can have no conscience.'

'Well, we shall never meet him. Your uncle told Blackwell that the Spanish call the pirates' captain the devil. As well they may!' She smiled at Annelise. 'I shall leave you to rest. Pray come down when you feel able.'

'Yes, Aunt. I shall come soon.'

After Lady Prudence had gone, Annelise picked up her uncle's letter again. It must contain an account of the sale of her mother's jewels—and the fateful venture which had ended in disaster.

She understood now why her uncle felt he had failed her. It was unfortunate that such a venture had ever begun. Had she been consulted, she would have preferred to keep the jewels. Indeed, they had been her personal property, and Sir Hugh had been wrong to sell them without her consent.

At least she had nothing to fear from opening the letter. Breaking the seal, Annelise began to read what was written there.

As she had expected, her uncle started with an apology for selling her jewels. He had regretted the impulse and had hoped to buy them back with the proceeds of the venture.

'I was persuaded to it,' he confessed. 'I am no man of business, Annelise, and should have been a more careful steward of your fortune. I can only beg you to forgive me and believe that I meant well.'

He went on to tell her how the ship had been lost, omitting nothing.

Guilt pertaining to the deaths of Captain Mendoza and his wife and children has lain heavy on my soul. God may forgive me, but I cannot forgive myself. Had I not been motivated by greed this dreadful thing might not have happened; it is a terrible sin and one I shall carry to my grave. But there is something that weighs even more heavily on me, my child, something that makes me fear for you. I have recently learned that the ship which wreaked such evil on ours was owned and captained by a man the Spanish call Satan…

Annelise stopped reading. Her heart had begun to pound and her mouth had gone dry with sudden fear. Where had she heard that before? It had been quite recent….

From Lady Emily! No! Oh, no, please let it not be true. Annelise wanted to stop reading, to destroy the letter before it destroyed her, but her eyes moved inexorably to the final paragraph.

I can scarcely believe this, Annelise, but I fear it is the truth. The man who sank our ship—who sent women and children to a cruel death—was none other than the Marquis Saintjohn. You know nothing of him as yet, but your father's will made you...

The letter had been dictated before her uncle's last illness. He had not known that Lady Emily had been sent to fetch her—that she had indeed become the ward of the man he'd feared.

Annelise screwed the paper into a ball and flung it from her. It could not be true. This story was wicked, wicked lies! It must be. She would not believe that Justin could do such a terrible thing. She would not believe it!

Surely it was a lie? Justin was not capable of such a cruel act.

She knew that he had killed in anger and in war. He had almost killed a man for assaulting her!

Yet that had been to save her—and she was as much to blame as he for the duel that had left Rathbone seriously injured. While her woman's soul shrank from all acts of violence, she understood that there were times when a man must kill—in defence of his home and loved ones it was an honourable thing.

But to send a ship with women and children on board to the bottom of the sea—to offer no mercy, no chance to surrender—that was a cruel, vengeful act. Why had he done it? There was nothing to be gained by such wickedness, no profit to be had in such senseless waste.

Why? Why? Why?

Annelise paced the floor of her bedchamber as she wrestled with her shock and disgust. Could there be some mistake? Was Justin really guilty?

She would not believe it! Justin must tell her the truth. She would ask him when he returned.

Not until she heard it from his own lips would she believe that the man she loved had done this terrible thing.

Chapter Eight

'Mistress Woodward!' Annelise had stopped by the carp pond that afternoon, to feed the fish with bread she had begged from the kitchens, and was watching them rise to the surface when Mr Broughton came up to her. He was breathing hard, as if he had hurried to catch up to her, and looked rather red in the face. 'Forgive me if I intrude—but I would speak with you a moment, if I may?'

'Of course, sir.' She turned to him politely. 'May I be of some service to you?'

He hesitated, clearly ill at ease. 'I would not have you think me forward, Mistress Woodward, nor careless of your grief for your uncle—but I must leave here in the morning, and if I do not speak now the chance will be lost.'

Annelise guessed what he meant to say next. It was embarrassing but must be endured. Her uncle had invited him to make her an offer of marriage, and she must listen to him out of courtesy. She was silent, waiting for him to continue.

'I am not a rich man, Mistress Woodward, nor yet handsome or clever, but I deal fairly with the world and can offer a steadfast character. As you will know, it was Sir Hugh's wish that we should marry—and from the first moment of seeing you it has been my own earnest wish to make you my wife. I have come to regard you highly for your modest manners and your good nature, Mistress Woodward, and would consider myself honoured if you would permit me to approach your guardian for his permission to ask for your hand in marriage.'

Seeing that he had at last finished his unwieldy and laborious proposal, Annelise steeled herself. 'You are kind, sir,' she said. 'I must thank you for your flattering attention, but…' She halted abruptly, her throat tightening as she saw Justin coming towards them. Her heart jerked and she was suddenly in a fret of nerves. She could not speak to him! She was not ready. 'Excuse me, sir. I must leave you.'

'But, Mistress Woodward, you have not answered me.'

'I cannot. Pray forgive me.' She began to walk away, her heart racing.

'But may I speak to him?'

'Do as you please, sir.'

Annelise was in a hurry to escape. She could not meet Justin yet. She must have time to prepare, time to think what to say to him.

She did not glance back, so was not privy to the meeting between her guardian and Mr Broughton.

'Good afternoon, my lord.'

'Good afternoon, sir. Where has my ward gone in such a hurry?' This with a frown from Justin. 'I wished to speak with her.'

'I fear it may be my fault, my lord.'

'Why so?'

'I was asking her for permission to speak with you.'

'You wished to speak to me on a matter concerning Mistress Woodward?' Justin's brow furrowed. 'May I ask what business you could possibly have with my ward?' He was very much the aristocrat as he stood there that autumn afternoon, eyes cold, a sneer of barely held contempt on his lips.

'I wanted to ask for…' Mr Broughton quailed at the look in the Marquis's eyes, then bolstered up his courage. 'It was Sir Hugh's wish that we marry. And I would wish to…to make you aware of my own feelings in this matter.'

'Your feelings and Sir Hugh's wishes are as one to me,' replied Justin. 'I am Mistress Woodward's guardian, sir. I alone and none other—and I must make it plain at once that your suit is not acceptable to me. I have other plans for my ward.'

'But—but Sir Hugh asked…' Mr Broughton blustered, a fiery colour creeping up his neck into his face. The Marquis's bluntness had shocked him. 'You have not consulted Mistress Woodward. You do not know what she may feel on this matter.'

'Her wishes are my concern alone,' Justin said. 'I suggest you waste no more of my time or your own, sir. My answer is no. Let that be an end to it.'

'You are very plain, sir!' said the outraged Mr Broughton. 'I dare say you think me unworthy of her?'

'Exactly so,' replied Justin, his lip curling. 'You are far beneath her. I would not even consider the match. You have my leave to go.'

Justin left him gaping, striding off in the direction Annelise had fled a few moments earlier.

He was frowning as he set out in search of her. His business had taken him three days, three long days in which he had thought of little else but the way she had responded to his kiss. He was anxious to see her again, to speak with her. The sweet taste of her lips had stayed with him these past days, haunting him, making him think very hard about the future.

He had believed himself incapable of love, had held back from her because he'd thought his desire to make love to

her could only cause her harm. In the past no woman had
ever had the power to hold him, but now he had begun to
understand the strength of love—and to realise that there
might be another way to live. Perhaps he might be able to
make Annelise happy. She might be his own salvation; in
devoting his life to caring for another person, he might
make amends, atone for his sins.

If she could come to care for him... Sometimes he had
thought she might. Her response to his kiss had convinced
him that she felt something for him—passion, perhaps.
Many women had responded to his lovemaking, but he
wanted more from Annelise. Much more. He would have
her heart, her body—her very soul.

Justin laughed outloud at his own thoughts. How demanding he was, how greedy! Why should he expect Annelise to love him with a passion to match his own? That
was ever his way. He must have all. He must hold what
was his, like a jealous dog with its bone.

If he were not careful, he would frighten her away. She
had run from him once, driven from his protection by his
rages and his demands. He must tread carefully. First of
all, he must win back her trust; he must court her gently,
as befitted a lover, and then perhaps he could begin to speak
of the secrets in his heart.

Ahead of him, he could see a pretty summerhouse. It
was fashioned like a small temple, with a circular domed
roof and smooth columns of white marble. Annelise was
sitting on a bench just inside, her head bent. She seemed
to be lost in thought, but then, becoming aware of his approach, jumped to her feet, as if she were a startled deer
about to flee from the hunter.

'Annelise,' he called to her. 'Where are you going? I
pray you, stay a moment. I would speak with you.' She
halted, standing where she was, face averted, pale of cheek,
plainly agitated. What could be wrong? What had upset

her? Could it have been that kiss—or the way he had left her afterwards? 'Does something trouble you? Have I offended you, Annelise?'

She turned slowly to face him. When she did, there was such accusation in her eyes, such condemnation! What had he done to make her look at him that way? Justin felt that look strike him deeper than a sword-cut, thrusting at his heart.

'I *have* offended you,' he said as she was silent. Her gaze fell and he was aware that she was trembling, close to tears. 'Was it because I kissed you? Are you angry because of that—or because I left you?'

'Neither.' Her throat was so tight she could hardly speak. She kept her eyes downward, unable to raise them...unable to look at him after that first glance. 'I wish you would let me go, sir.'

'Why? Why do you not look at me?'

She shook her head. 'I cannot. Please, I beg you. Let me go now and we shall talk another time.'

'Tell me why you are so distressed.' He caught her arm as she would have passed him. 'Is it because of Broughton? He told me he had asked permission of you to speak to me. The impertinent fool! He will not bother you again with his unwelcome attentions, I'll swear.'

'Are you so sure that his offer was unwelcome to me?' Her head went up, her expression proud, challenging.

'What?' Justin was incredulous. 'You would consider wedding that—that pompous idiot? When you have twice refused poor Rob! Have your wits gone begging? You would die of boredom married to that sanctimonious fool!'

'He is a good, godly man who has done harm to no one.'

'And for that you would waste your life on him? No, that I vow you shall not!' Justin stared at her, frustration mingling with disappointment. 'What is this, Annelise?

What has changed you? I do not understand this coldness in you. You were not thus three days ago.'

'I…' Her mouth trembled; her eyes filled with tears. 'Please, I beg you, do not make me speak of it. I cannot bear…'

'What is it that you find so unspeakable, Annelise? Come, tell me. Say whatever is in your mind.'

She lifted her head then, and her eyes reproached him. 'I… My uncle left me a letter. I wish I had not read it. God help me! I would give anything not to have read it…not to know. I have tried not to believe it, Justin. I vowed I would have the truth from your lips, that I would believe only what you told me—but it haunts me. I have not slept in three nights for thinking of…' A shudder ran through her and she turned away to hide her revulsion.

Justin had noted the shadows beneath her eyes and won-dered at them, then, seeing the way she stood, her body sagging as though beneath a great burden, his heart stopped for one wrenching moment. The ice was spreading through his veins, driving all warmth and feeling before it.

She knew… How could she? He had told no one of the nightmare that had haunted him for months. And yet *she* knew. Somehow her uncle must have learned his shameful secret and had written it down in a letter.

Justin shuddered inwardly as he imagined what that letter contained—the plain, damning version of the truth that was all others would know—imagined the horror she must have felt as she read it. No wonder she had looked at him so accusingly.

'What have you been told—that a ship was sent to the bottom of the ocean with all its crew on board?'

'Women…' she whispered through bloodless lips. 'There were women and children on board, Justin.'

'Do you think I do not know?' His eyes mirrored a ter-rible, haunting grief. God damn it! Had he not seen their faces, heard their screams a thousand times in his dreams? 'Do you think I do not know…?'

'Justin?' She stared at him, catching something in his voice, sensing the pain he had kept hidden so long, the inner torment—the guilt. 'Tell me…tell me it was all a lie.'

'Is that what you want, Annelise?' he asked, voice hoarse, face gaunt and weary. 'Do you want me to make it all go away—to pretend it never happened? I cannot do that, not if you hate me for it. Despise me if you will. The truth is ugly, but I will not deny it even for your sake. The ship caught fire; flame spread through its holds and there was an explosion. Nothing could be done. My crew had to fight to save our own ship.'

'Please do not…' she begged, feeling faint as she smelt the stench of burning wood and tar, witnessed the scene as she had in her dreams. 'Those poor women…and the children, the little children.'

'We looked for survivors but there were none.'

His voice was harsh, his face hard as granite. Yet she sensed the emotion he kept in check, felt his pain.

'It was my uncle's ship,' she said. 'His and a Portuguese merchant he had taken as a partner.'

'We thought it Spanish,' Justin said, his voice husky, eyes staring through her, beyond her, to that terrible night. 'We had followed Don Sanchez's ship for half a day. In the mist we lost his ship and at first light…we did not realise our mistake until it was too late. No one saw the women and children until after the ship was fired…'

'It was a mistake?' Annelise stared at him, a mixture of doubt and hope in her eyes.

'We meant to sink the ship of Don Sanchez,' Justin said grimly. His face was white, his eyes icier than the North Sea in dead of winter. 'Make no mistake, Annelise. My men and I preyed on ships loaded with silver from the New World. We sank those we could not force to surrender,

though most were glad to give up their treasure and escape
with their lives. There is no escaping the truth—we were
desperate men who had been robbed of our homes, our
fortunes and our pride. We took what we could by force.
And sometimes we took lives.'

'Yes, I understand that.' She clung to hope desperately.
'But the Portuguese ship was a mistake. You did not mean
to—to kill innocent women and children.'

'No, we did not intend that,' he said gravely. 'But what
does that signify? Does it change what we were—what we
did? Can it wash away the blood, Annelise?'

She gazed into his eyes, saw the hell there and gasped.
How he had suffered for his mistake! She wanted to run to
him, to hold him in her arms and ease his pain, to tell him
that she loved him, would always love him, but the words
would not come. And then it was too late.

'No, of course it cannot,' he said bitterly. 'You are right
to despise me, Annelise. I despise myself. Will do so until
my dying breath. Believe me, if I could undo...if I could
prevent that ship from sinking, bring back to life those I
killed... But to wish for the moon is senseless. I have done
what I have done and must live with my conscience. I ask
for no one's sympathy, for no one's forgiveness.'

And with that he turned and walked away from her.

Annelise stood watching as he strode away. She longed
with all her heart to go after him, to comfort him, but it
was as if she were turned into a pillar of stone. Her heart,
her mind, her thoughts went out to him, but her feet stub-
bornly refused to move; her mouth stayed closed, the words
she wanted to cry out unspoken.

She knew it would be useless. He was unreachable.
There was a barrier of thorns between them, too painful,
too bitter to be torn down by futile words.

Oh, Justin, she whispered in her heart. I did not know,

my love. Forgive me…forgive me for causing you such
pain.

When they met again later that afternoon it was at the
house, in Lady Prudence's parlour. Justin was a polite
stranger. Annelise was chilled by his manner, so formal, so
distant. He had withdrawn from her so completely it was
as if they were meeting for the first time. This was not the
man she had teased, not the laughing Cavalier she had met
in the woods—nor yet the stern guardian who had fought
a duel to save her honour. She did not know him. She could
not penetrate the barrier he had erected between them; she
was afraid to try.

'Tomorrow we return to London, Mistress Woodward,'
he said. 'I trust this meets with your approval?'

'Yes. Yes, of course.'

'Lord Saintjohn has arranged for someone to look after
the estate,' Lady Prudence told her. 'He has begged me to
continue to make my home here…and invited me to visit
you in London, Annelise. I shall not, of course—but was
that not kind of him?'

'Yes, Aunt. Most kind.' She spoke stiffly, finding it hard
to form the words.

Lady Prudence looked at her oddly. 'You will visit me
sometimes—and write to me?'

'Yes, of course.' She forced a smile. 'I give you my
word, Aunt.'

Annelise felt so cold. It was all she could do to keep her
teeth from chattering. Her body ached as if she had been
ill. What was wrong with her? Why could she not be natural? Why could she not look at Justin? She longed to tell
him she did not hate or despise him, that she had been
shocked—was still!—but did not blame him, had not meant
to turn from him in horror. The words would not come.

How could she speak to this stranger who looked through her?

She had offended him by showing her horror too plainly. It was her own fault. She had vowed not to accuse him, not to believe him guilty, to ask for his own story—to listen and understand. But three days had been too long to dwell on the terrible discovery she had made; too many hours spent in thought had brought her to a state of acute distress and made it all come out wrong.

Justin had withdrawn his friendship from her. She could not reach out to him because he did not want her to—he was too proud to ask for understanding or forgiveness.

'Oh, my dearest girl!' Lady Emily cried, rushing to embrace her, to sweep her up in a hug as she entered the house. 'How are you, my love? It has seemed an age. Was it very terrible?' She looked beyond Annelise, frowning as she saw she was alone. 'Where is Justin? Is he not with you? Surely he did not let you travel on your own?'

'No. He escorted me to your door, ma'am.' To her dismay, Annelise dissolved into tears. Justin had remained polite but coldly aloof during their journey, speaking to her only when necessary, and then with that distant manner she found so wounding. 'He asked me to send you his compliments and say he would see you later.'

'Did he indeed?' Lady Emily frowned. 'Now what has that wretched son of mine been up to, pray? Why are you so upset, Annelise? Has he been unkind to you?'

'He—he has done nothing.' Annelise accepted the kerchief she was offered and wiped the tears from her cheeks. 'I am very much afraid I have offended him, ma'am.'

'Why? Please, Annelise—you must tell me. Something has been playing on Justin's mind for a long time now. Do you know what it is? If you do, you must speak. He needs help, my love—and we are the only ones who can give that help.'

Annelise was silent as Lady Emily drew her into the small parlour, where a welcoming fire of scented logs was burning merrily in the open grate. It was only when they were seated, sipping a glass of warming cordial, that she began haltingly to tell her story.

Lady Emily heard her out in silence, then stood up to take a turn about the room, the rustle of her silk gown the only sound apart from an occasional crackle from a log. She was clearly distressed, and did not speak for several minutes, then at last she turned to look at Annelise.

'I have known there was something,' she said. 'He has not been himself for almost a year now. He always had a temper, even as a child...' She smiled to herself as she remembered the child she had adored; the young man who had come back to her so changed and yet so charming. 'He could always wound with his tongue—but these sudden rages, these black moods, are not like Justin. He was used to laugh at everything. Indeed, I was wont to scold him for not taking life seriously enough.'

'I think he blames himself, ma'am. He has taken the deaths of those women and children on his shoulders.'

'Yes, of course. He could not do otherwise. It was his ship. The responsibility is his. Justin never shirks responsibility.'

'But it was a mistake. He could not have known when he gave the order to fire.'

'You make excuses for him, Annelise. Do you not condemn him for what he has done? It is a fearful thing—a terrible sin.'

'I do not forget that, ma'am. It was a terrible tragedy,' Annelise said. 'But I love him. I cannot stop loving him. I think that I should love him even if he had meant to...yet

I know that could never be. The man I love is too fine, too honourable to do such a thing.'

'Then you truly know him at last,' said Lady Emily. 'It is because of his nature that he suffers as he does, that he feels things so deeply. Another man in his position might count this accident as the misfortunes of war—but not my son. No, Justin must be right. He must do what is right—and his conscience is a hard taskmaster, believe me. He has been punished for his sins, Annelise, whatever they might be.'

'Yes, I know.' Annelise raised her lovely eyes to meet the other woman's. 'What can I do to help him? He has withdrawn from me. I cannot reach him—I do not know how.'

'You must wait. He is bleeding from his wounds. The time will come when he may reach out to you. And you must be ready to give your love—for it is only love will save him.'

Annelise was silent. In her heart, she did not believe that Justin would ever turn to her. He was too proud. She had shown her feelings too plainly. He would not forgive her for doubting his integrity.

Even though Justin had caused that ship to sink, he was not guilty of murder. He must have had good reason for what he did. Another man might have sought to escape the responsibility, to throw off the burden of blame and make excuses. Not the Marquis Saintjohn.

Yet Annelise was suddenly certain that something had not been revealed to her. The man she loved would not have ordered his crew to fire on a Portuguese merchant ship!

There was some mystery here. Something that Justin would not tell her.

*   *   *

'Will you not speak to me?' Annelise asked. 'Will you not forgive me for doubting you, Justin?'

It was three days after their return from the country. She had hardly seen him. He came home late at night and was out early in the morning. This was the first time she had managed to find him in the house.

'Forgive me, Mistress Woodward,' Justin said, his eyes looking at something beyond her, deliberately avoiding hers. 'Is there something I may do for you?'

'Please do not call me that,' she begged, her voice little more than a whisper. 'Do not look at me as if I were a stranger, Justin. We were friends. I am sorry for doubting you. Please forgive me.'

'For what? You have no need to beg my pardon. You asked for the truth and I gave it—there is no more to say.'

'I should not have asked. I should have known that you…you could not have given the order without good reason.'

Something flickered in his eyes, emotion, memory— what? She could not be sure but it was there.

'Could I not? How little you know of me, Annelise. I am capable of many things.'

'But not of murder,' she cried. 'Yes, you would kill in war or in the heat of battle—but you would not order the sinking of an unarmed merchant ship.'

'We believed her to be a Spaniard. I told you.' There was a guarded look in his eyes as if he was fighting her— or himself. 'You would do well to forget this. Put it from your mind. I would not have your dreams haunted.'

'As yours have been.' She dared to press for she did not fear his anger now. She understood what drove him and her love was all the stronger. No longer the timid fluttering of a foolish girl's heart, but the deep, warm love of the woman she had become.

'You have not told me all, Justin. Why were you pursuing that ship—the ship of Don Sanchez?'

'To take her cargo, of course.' He turned away, the shuttered expression on his face. 'Excuse me, I have an appointment.'

She let him go, but there had for a moment been something in his eyes. Something he had not been able to hide. A glimmer of hope, a plea for forgiveness? She could not be sure but she was certain of one thing. There was more to this—and she would not let it rest until she had the truth of him. No matter how he fought her, no matter how he tried to avoid her, she would not let him go.

'Justin!' Annelise caught him as he left his apartments. 'Do you not think my gown is pretty? They call this colour emerald-green. Do you not think it suits me?'

Justin's eyes swept over her. For a brief second she thought she caught a glimmer of amusement.

'It suits you very well, Annelise. I think I told you before—green favours you above all other colours.'

'That is why I chose it,' she said, her eyes lifting suddenly to meet his. 'Because you admired me in green.'

'I am not the only one,' he said, the shutters coming down once more. 'Enjoy yourself at Court this evening.'

She placed herself in his way as he would have passed her, waving her fan a little so that her perfume wafted towards him, enveloping him in a warm, sensual mist.

'Shall you be there, Justin? We hardly see you these days.'

'I have business,' he said. 'Forgive me. I must go.'

'You had a good reason for sinking Don Sanchez's ship,' she said as he went down the stairs. 'Was he your enemy, Justin? Had he done terrible things? Is that why you were determined to give no quarter?'

She saw him stop, saw his shoulders stiffen, but he did not look back nor did he answer her.

She stood watching as he continued down the stairs and disappeared from her view.

'You stubborn, foolish man,' she said softly, a smile about her lips. 'You will not answer me—but I shall not give up. I shall have the better of you yet, my love. In the end, I shall make you tell me the truth…even if you hate me for it.'

'Justin—will you look at the clasp of my pearls please? I think something is wrong with it. Perhaps you could take them to the goldsmith for me? I am very fond of them and should not want to lose them.'

'Let me see.' He frowned as he took the pearls from her hand, examining the gold fastener. 'It was merely bent a little out of shape. I have straightened it. It will hold now.'

'Will you fasten them for me?'

'Of course. If you wish.'

She smiled at him over her shoulder, but it was the smile of a friend, not a courtesan—a smile that spoke of love and hope and understanding. His hands brushed against her neck, seeming to linger for the merest instant.

'Thank you,' she said, turning to look at him. 'Shall you come to Court this evening? Ralph asked me where you had disappeared to—everyone asks about you.'

'Tell them I have business elsewhere.'

He turned to leave. She laid her hand on his arm, the pressure making him look round at her, into her eyes. What he saw there made him look away for fear of her. She was too strong for him—and yet he must not weaken for her sake.

'Why was Don Sanchez your enemy?'

Justin's eyes narrowed. 'Have you heard of the Inquisition?'

She shook her head. 'Are they not members of the church?'

'They are cruel fanatics who do the most unspeakable things in the name of their god—not God as you know him, but a vengeful, cruel being. Sanchez was one of them—a man of God, but also a monster. He was returning from a voyage to the silver mines, his ship laden with treasure to enrich his cause. One of my crew was a native of the New World. They tore his tongue out because he spoke of his own gods and would not bow to theirs. Another saw his wife raped before his eyes by one of Sanchez's men; his brother had his eyes…'

'Enough!' Annelise put her hands to her ears. 'So you had cause for what you planned. Why torture yourself for what you did? Such men deserved to be punished. Had I been with you, I would have cheered as they died.'

'But it was the merchant ship we sank,' he reminded her.

'Come to Court,' she called as he walked down the hall. 'We all miss you, Justin.'

'Justin!' Lady Emily waylaid her son as he came from his apartments two days later. 'You are to attend the Court this evening. His Majesty commands it.'

Justin stared at her, a spark of annoyance in his eyes. 'Your doing, Mother? I suppose Annelise put you up to it?'

'It was the King's own idea,' Lady Emily said, lying serenely. 'Unless you wish to find yourself in the Tower, my son—you *will* come to Court this evening.'

'You win,' Justin said, a harsh laugh escaping him. 'You and Annelise. Since I have no choice, I shall attend the Court this evening.'

Justin had promised to come, but half the evening had already gone and there was still no sign of him. Annelise sighed, her lovely face clouding with disappointment. She did not know what she hoped to achieve from dragging Justin back to Court, but at least it would be a beginning.

It had started as a battle of wills, a faint crack in the armour of his resistance showing her the way. If only she could break down the barrier he had built between them, make him come back from wherever he had gone inside himself!

Her own return to Court had been greeted by a rapturous welcome from several gentlemen. However, Annelise had learned her lesson, and her new manner had left the boldest of them disappointed; she still smiled and teased those she trusted most, but some of the flirtatious looks had gone, and not even the most hopeful of them could think she favoured one above another. They were all her friends, all given the same smiles, the same welcome, but nothing more.

It was generally thought she had given her heart to some fortunate gentleman outside the Court, and though some took wagers as to his identity, none were willing to give up the chase. She was sought after as much as ever, and had not lacked for partners all evening, but now she had taken a moment to cool herself and was standing alone by a window, gazing out at the moonlight.

'Why so sad, Mistress Woodward?' Annelise turned in surprise as she heard the King's voice. 'Are you not pleased with the company?'

'Why, yes, Sire,' she replied, and laughed up at him. The King was one of her favourite companions, for his dry wit and sly looks amused her, and though she knew his reputation with the ladies, she had never felt other than at ease with him. 'Especially now. Do you not think Mistress Langdon looks very fine in that crimson gown?'

The lady she had mentioned had been throwing languishing looks at Charles all evening, and the latest whisper amongst the courtiers was that she had taken a wager she would snatch him from beneath Madam Barbara's nose within the year.

'Mistress Langdon looks well enough,' Charles murmured, 'but I do not care for that shade particularly.' His eyes went over Annelise, a hint of mockery in their slumbering depths. 'My preference is for green—emerald-green, mistress—a colour not all ladies can wear as well as you, Mistress Woodward.'

Annelise's heart fluttered. There was no mistaking the invitation in his eyes. Yet still she had no fear, for she knew it was not in his nature to take what was not freely offered. She smiled demurely and thanked him for his compliment.

'It is also a favourite of my guardian,' she said, and then, as she saw Justin walk into the room and stand looking in her direction, made a little curtsey. 'I see he has this moment arrived, Sire. Perhaps I should go and greet him?'

'And Barbara comes this way,' the King replied, a faint sigh escaping him. 'Methinks the Langdon hath put salt on Madam's tongue.' His eyes met Annelise's briefly. 'We shall talk another time, Mistress Woodward.'

'As you wish, Sire.' She smiled at him, then left him to make her way across the room towards Justin. But before she could reach his side, she was detained by a gentleman who took hold of her arm with such determination that she was startled. She glanced up at him. 'Yes, sir? Did you wish to speak with me?'

'You have not danced with me in an age, Mistress Woodward,' complained Lord Montgomery. 'I swear you have fallen out with me—though I cannot think why.'

'No, indeed, sir,' Annelise said, and smiled as he sighed heavily. She knew his reputation as a rake, and since Justin had shown his disapproval so plainly had not sought his company, but she could not avoid him completely without being discourteous, and he had never done more than flirt with her. Instinctively, she knew that he would never seek

to use her as had Earl Rathbone. 'Why should I be so unkind?'

'I vow I have racked my brains for cause and can find
none,' he said, giving her a challenging look. 'Can it be
that you have heard ill of me from another—someone who
would keep us apart?'

'Should I have been warned, sir?' Annelise asked, her
mouth quivering. 'Would I do better to heed that warning?'

'If you were any other woman the answer would be yes,'
Montgomery said, startling her with his honesty. 'But I vow
I would reform my ways for you, mistress. I might even
be persuaded to marriage, should that be your desire.'

'Not for the first time,' she reminded him.

'But this time I should take better care,' he said. 'If you
were my wife, I should not want to lose you.'

Annelise began to grow uncomfortable. It seemed he was
in earnest this time, and she had no wish to be his next
wife. She glanced towards Justin and saw that he was glaring at her.

'You must excuse me, sir,' she said. 'My guardian
wishes to speak to me.' Her heart began to race as she saw
Justin was coming towards them. 'See—he comes this
way.'

Lord Montgomery looked at Justin's scowling counte-
nance and bowed to Annelise. In this case, absence might
be the better part of valour. The Marquis Saintjohn was too
dangerous an enemy. 'Methinks I would be better employed
elsewhere,' he murmured. 'But consider my offer, Mistress
Woodward—it was sincerely meant.'

Annelise made no reply. As he walked away, she turned
to meet Justin with a smile of welcome on her lips. 'Were
you coming to ask me to dance, sir?'

'No, I was not,' Justin said, his eyes smouldering with
banked-down fires. 'But if it is your wish, I shall of course
oblige you.'

He was jealous! Surely he was jealous? Once she would have taken his stern look for anger, but now she thought that anger was Justin's way of hiding his feelings. Her conversation with Lord Montgomery had displeased him. Her heart began to beat very fast. It was the first sign of emotion she had seen in him for an age.

'I thank you for your kind offer, sir,' she said, giving him a teasing look. 'But I have danced sufficiently this evening, thank you. I am a little tired and would take my ease.'

'Then perhaps we should go home?' Justin said. 'If you are ready, I shall escort you.'

'But you have only just arrived,' she said, wanting to provoke him a little. 'I must not make you rush away too soon or His Majesty will be displeased.'

'What was he saying to you when I arrived?' Justin asked, his brow furrowing. His manner was controlled, as if he were trying very hard not to quarrel with her. 'I thought you had learned your lesson, Annelise. But now I find you at your old tricks. The King is as dangerous as Montgomery or any others of their disposition.'

'How can you cast such aspersions on His Majesty's intentions?' Annelise said, suddenly annoyed by his assumption that she had flirted with either gentleman. She had behaved with perfect propriety all evening. 'He was merely making polite conversation. And Lord Montgomery has just proposed marriage to me.'

'Oh?' Justin looked at her intently, his eyes narrowed. 'The matter of your marriage. I have been giving much thought to that of late—and I have decided you should be wed before Christmas. It is only right that you should have a husband to take you in hand. I have neither the time nor the inclination.'

A cold arrow pierced her heart. How could he say such a terrible thing to her?

'Christmas?' Her voice shook a little even though she did her best to control it. 'But that is only two months away. I cannot marry so soon…I cannot. You must not ask such a thing of me.'

Justin had a grip on her arm. He was forcing her to leave the ballroom. She glanced at him, feeling chilled as she saw the hard set of his mouth, the determination in his eyes.

'Nevertheless you *will* marry,' he said. 'And to a man of my choosing.'

'Your choosing?'

They were in a passageway, alone apart from a footman standing wearily by the door that led to one of the private apartments. It was late and Annelise shivered, feeling suddenly cold.

'My choosing, Annelise,' Justin replied harshly. 'I have decided there are three gentlemen who might tame your wilful heart—and you shall have the final say. In that I think you will at least find me just, if not complaisant.'

She looked up at him, eyes bright, head held proudly, defiantly. 'And who are these men?'

'My first choice is Robert…'

'He is too young and too much in love with me,' she said, eyes flashing. 'I should break his heart. You cannot wish me to do that, Justin?'

'Then take Ralph,' Justin said, his mouth hardening. 'He knows you for what you are and loves you anyway. He would take good care of you, Annelise.'

'Ralph is my friend. I would rather he stayed my friend.'

'Then you will marry Sir Edwin Rushton. He has approached me in the proper manner and I have promised him an answer soon.'

'He is at least sixty if he is a day,' Annelise said in disgust. 'And this is all you can offer? What of my other suitors? Why may I not choose for myself?'

'If your previous behaviour is anything to the point, you

have no notion of what kind of man would suit you,' Justin
said. 'Sir Edwin has an heir. Once you are wed he will turn
a blind eye to your affairs, and is a gentle man, a considerate man. He will neither beat you nor create a scandal
every time he finds you with a lover.'

'How dare you!' Annelise cried. She was furious at his
high-handed manner—his assumption that she would cheat
her husband. 'I should not take lovers if I loved my husband…'

'Is there someone you love?'

Annelise felt something snap inside her. He was impossible! She would not humble herself by confessing her love.
If he did not know her heart now, he never would.

'No, there is not,' she said angrily. 'Why should I care
for one man more than another when you are all such selfish creatures? I do not care what you say, Justin. I shall
not marry any of the men you have suggested. Nor shall I
marry anyone until I am ready.'

'I think you misjudge the matter,' Justin said, taking hold
of her arm. 'You are my ward, Annelise—and you will do
exactly as I tell you. I am tired of your tantrums and your
wilful disobedience. I have made up my mind to see you
wed—and that is exactly what you will do.'

'You cannot force me,' she cried, losing all caution. 'Or
will you drag me to the altar?'

'No, I shall not do that,' Justin said, looking grim. 'But
neither shall I allow this wilfulness to continue. You will
stay in your room until you come to your senses. I threatened once before to teach you better manners, Annelise—
and this time I shall carry out my threat.'

'Then you had best be prepared to let me die there,'
Annelise said, meeting his eyes with stubborn defiance. 'I
told you once in my song that I would never marry unless
I loved—and I shall not. Neither you nor any power this
side of heaven will force me to it…'

Chapter Nine

'Don't make me do this,' Justin said. Annelise recognised the pleading note in his voice, but she was too angry to respond, too stubborn to give in. 'Come, say you will be sensible. Otherwise you leave me no choice. My duty as your guardian will not permit me to stand by and see you ruin your life.'

'I shall not marry unless I choose.' Her eyes met his defiantly. 'You cannot make me. Beat me, starve me, as you will—I shall never marry against my wishes.'

'Then I have no choice.'

Justin flung open the door of her apartments. She resisted him, clinging to the doorpost, pulling back as he took her arm, fighting his attempts to make her enter. Looking at her wilful, obstinate face, he gave a sigh of exasperation, then swooped on her, lifting her in his arms and carrying her despite her struggles and furious yells into her bedchamber.

'Now, my sweet vixen,' he said, depositing her none too gently on her bed, where she lay looking up at him, her eyes flashing her defiance at him. 'You see that it is useless to defy me. You are here, and here you will stay until you have calmed down sufficiently to behave with the proper decorum.'

'You are a cruel tyrant and I hate you!' Annelise cried. 'I shall never, never obey you in this! Do what you will with me, sir, I shall not give in to your demands.'

'Do what I will with you?' An odd, rueful smile touched his mouth. 'Ah, my ward, you know not what you say. Do not tempt me, for you would end by hating me.'

'I hate you now!'

'Would you rather I let you go your own way? Do you wish to become the King's whore, Annelise? Or shall I let you marry a pox-ridden roué? A man who would use you for as long as you pleased him and then take his pleasure in breaking your spirit until you whimpered at his feet like a whipped cur?'

'I have no intention of becoming any man's whore—or wife,' Annelise muttered, her eyes flashing with temper. 'You are all selfish brutes, and I want none of you. I would rather die than marry. I promise you, for as long as you keep me a prisoner in this house, I shall neither eat nor drink.'

'Like the foolish girl in your song?' Justin's eyebrows arched in mockery. He was suddenly amused. She was the most stubborn, wilful wench he had ever known! 'Romantic nonsense, Annelise. You will discover it is most unpleasant to go hungry—and thirst is a fearful thing. No, my sweet, I think you will soon change your mind, and then, when you are ready to apologise, we shall discuss this matter again.'

'Go away!' Annelise said. 'You are a monster. I hate and despise you. Leave me alone to die, as you left…'

The smile faded from his lips and she realised she had gone too far. She had not meant to say those cruel words; her temper had led her on and at once she wished them unspoken.

'No, Justin! I did not mean that. You know I did not.'

'Do I?' His face was white, his eyes bleak as he looked at her. 'But it was in your mind, Annelise. You believe that I would condemn women and children to a watery grave, don't you? That I would stand by and do nothing as they died…'

'Forgive me. I was angry.'

'You spoke what was in your heart.' Justin walked to the door, then looked back. 'I know you hate me, Annelise. I could in all honesty expect nothing else. But believe at least this…I would never stand by and watch you die. I would rather suffer the fires of hell than do that.'

Annelise stared at him in silence, her throat caught with emotion, too shocked by what she had said to speak. And then he was gone, the door closed and locked behind him.

What had she done? She had driven him away! He would never love her now, never smile at her in the way that made her heart leap for joy.

But he did not want her anyway. She had tried so hard to win him, but it was useless…hopeless. He loved Mira-belle Varennes. Annelise was nothing to him, nothing but an unwanted duty—a troublesome burden placed on him by her father.

She lay down on the bed but did not weep. She was no longer a naive girl. He was an impossible, foolish man but she loved him, and would find a way to reach him. With this thought in her mind, she slept at last. In her dreams she was drowning. She could not breathe and her chest felt as if it would split apart with the pain as the water closed over her head. She was dying…and then she heard some-one calling to her, calling her back to life.

'Believe at least this…I would never stand by and watch you die.'

She woke with tears on her cheeks. Justin had said he

would not let her die, but her heart was breaking. She did not want to live without him.

'Justin!' Lady Emily confronted her son as he was about to leave the house the next evening. 'Where are you going? I wish to speak with you, sir.'

'I have an appointment, Mother. May we not talk later?'

'No we may not!' The look she gave him was laced with equal quantities of anger and contempt. 'You *will* listen to me now, Justin. I am furious with you. How dare you lock Annelise in her room? How dare you threaten her so cruelly? Your behaviour is unspeakable. I can hardly believe you would stoop to this!'

'I am merely giving her time to reflect,' Justin said mildly. 'She has not been harmed, nor will she be. The servants have taken her food and drink.'

'Which she has not touched!' Lady Emily said. 'She is distraught with grief and vows she would rather die than marry this man you would force on her. How could you, Justin? How could you?'

'I have said she must marry, which is not unreasonable. She refused both Robert and Ralph—Sir Edwin is a good man who will look after her.'

'He is an old fool,' snapped Lady Emily. 'Annelise deserves better. I shall not permit this.'

'Indeed?' Justin raised his brows, a faint smile in his eyes. 'Do you imagine you can prevent me if I am determined on the match?'

'If need be I shall put my case before the King,' Lady Emily said. 'Even you may not defy him. You are my son, Justin. I have loved you dearly, little though you believe it. It was not my wish to have you sent away. I lost as much as you—perhaps more.'

'Say you so, madam? Then it must be true.'

'I lost a child I loved,' she went on, ignoring his sarcasm.

'Annelise has given me so much joy…so much love. I have
found myself again in her, Justin. I would not turn against
you lightly—but unless you relent I shall do what I must.'

'Do you really imagine I would let her die?' Justin stared
at his mother, anger hiding the hurt. 'You think me such a
monster?' His mouth twisted in a rueful smile. 'Perhaps I
deserve it. Do as you wish, dearest Mama. Let her out. Take
her to Court—make a present of her virtue to the first man
who asks. It matters not to me. I have finished with her—
she is in your tender hands.'

'Justin! You cannot mean that?'

'Can I not?' He bowed his head. 'Since you know me
so well, discover my meaning for yourself. And now I must
go. I have important business elsewhere.'

Lady Emily stared after him as he walked past her. How
fiercely he protected his inner self. It was impossible to
know for sure what was in his mind or what he truly felt.
Yet she sensed the struggle going on inside him and it gave
her hope. Perhaps there was still time to save him from
himself.

Justin's mind wrestled with his confused thoughts as he
walked towards the inn where he had pledged to meet
Ralph that evening. Of late he had made several discoveries
concerning the plot against the King, and he had sensed
that his own life might soon be forfeit. It was time to pass
on what he knew, to reveal names and places to the friend
he trusted most—in case he were to be assassinated before
he had had time to present his evidence to His Majesty.

It was important that he keep a clear head. He needed to
be alert, to watch for enemies—but his thoughts would not
give him rest. No matter how hard he tried, he could not
blot the picture of Annelise's pale, defiant face from his
mind.

She had sworn she would die rather than marry against

her will. He had thought her words merely wilful temper, but now he had begun to wonder. Even before his mother told him he had known of Annelise's refusal to eat or drink.

The foolish, wilful wench! Her stubbornness frustrated him, yet at the same time he admired her courage, and the thought of her suffering made him wretched. To think that he had caused her pain! Curse his evil temper! Better he had never been born than that it should come to this.

He had gone unwillingly to Court the previous night, forced to attend and smarting at the machinations of his mother, yet drawn also by his longing to make his peace with Annelise. He had been aware of her attempts to break down the barrier of his pride, admitting reluctantly to himself that it *was* mostly pride that was holding him back. If he told Annelise the truth… But only a weakling begged for forgiveness.

It was pride that had kept him from speaking the words which would have cleared him of the stain of murder. Justin had never asked for quarter, never permitted himself to make excuses. It had been his ship, his guns that had sent the Portuguese merchantman to the bottom, therefore he was responsible. The fact that he had not ordered the attack was irrelevant.

His pride demanded that she love him as he was, with all his faults, which were many. Fool! His true self rose up to mock him. Love him? She hated him—and who could blame her?

A wry smile twisted Justin's lips. Why had he behaved so abominably the previous evening? He had never meant to force her into marriage with anyone—but the sight of her smiling at the King and then Montgomery had near driven him mad with jealousy.

The truth was, he was not sure he could stand to see her married to any man other than himself, selfish and unworthy as that was.

He had reacted instinctively. And her defiance had aroused his worst instincts. What a blind, stupid fool he had been.

Justin laughed harshly. He had made a mess of this business from start to finish. Well, he would put an end to it. Since he could not trust himself near Annelise, he would leave her in London and go down to the country. Perhaps then he could drive her out of his mind and find some sort of peace at last.

Just as soon as this other business was finished. He glanced over his shoulder as he paused outside the inn. For some minutes now he had felt that he was being followed. His hand rested on his sword hilt as he peered into the shadows. He would rather they came at him, gave him a chance to fight them, but as yet it seemed they were content to watch and wait.

Annelise was so hungry! Her stomach would keep rumbling and she felt awful. She had not been able to resist drinking a little water, but she was determined to eat nothing. Surely Justin would relent soon? He would not let her starve herself. She did not really believe he could be so cruel—and yet he was determined to make her marry against her will.

She had vacillated between misery and anger, but now pride had reasserted itself. Somehow she would force Justin to change his mind. Even if it meant going back to the country to live with her aunt.

Her head lifted as she heard the sound of a key in the lock. Was that Justin? Had he come to persuade her to accept his wishes? She would not! She would not give in even though she was so terribly hungry!

'Annelise, my love—how are you?' Lady Emily entered, carrying a tray containing some soft rolls and a pot of honey. 'I want you to eat this for me. I know you are angry with Justin, and indeed I do not deny that he deserves some punishment—but think of me. It would break my heart if anything were to happen to you; I do not think I could recover from it. You could not want to hurt me so?'

'No, ma'am, I do not,' Annelise said, a lump in her throat as she saw the anxiety in her friend's face. 'I love you truly, you know I do—but I will not marry this man Justin has chosen for me.'

'Nor shall you, my love.' Lady Emily set the tray down on a table and came to sit beside Annelise on the bed. 'Did you think I would let him force you into such a match? I have remonstrated with him over it and he has washed his hands of you. I am to have the care of you in future.'

'Justin said that…he has washed his hands of me?'

'That was a figure of speech,' Lady Emily corrected herself. 'He meant only that he would not interfere in your life again. I am to be your guardian in future—and I shall never force you to marry anyone. Indeed, I should be loath to part with you, and would do so only if it were for your happiness.'

Annelise blinked hard, holding back the rush of tears. So it had come to this. Justin had given her up to his mother. He wanted to be free of his burden. Well, she could not blame him. She had caused him nothing but trouble from the beginning with her wilfulness.

'Will you keep me with you here, ma'am?' she asked in a small voice. 'I do not want to go back to my aunt.'

'Nor shall you,' said Lady Emily. 'You are as dear to me as the daughter I never had, Annelise—and that is just what you shall be.' She smiled and wiped the salt from Annelise's cheeks with her own kerchief. 'Now, will you not eat a little of this bread and honey for me? Just a very little, to please me?'

'Perhaps…in a moment,' Annelise said. 'You are very

kind to bother about me when I have been so much trouble to you.'

'You have been no trouble—it is my foolish son who causes me pain,' Lady Emily said, and sighed. 'But it was ever thus. He is too proud, too stubborn for his own good.'

Annelise was silent. She watched as Lady Emily spread soft butter and honey on the rolls and handed one to her. Her stomach rumbled, reminding her she had not eaten all day, and she took the offering, biting into it with relish and eating every crumb. Oh, it was so good, tasted so sweet, and she had been starving.

Lady Emily watched with satisfaction. 'Will you try another, my love?'

Annelise laughed and reached for the rolls. 'I confess I am very hungry, ma'am—but I was determined not to give way. Justin made me so angry. I did not mean to quarrel with him, truly I did not—but I cannot marry…anyone.' She smothered a sob and put down her roll. 'Why can he not see it is impossible?'

'My son is a law unto himself,' Lady Emily said with a faint smile. 'And blind when it comes to you, it seems. He cannot see what I have seen for months—that you are in love with him. Of course you cannot marry anyone else.'

'Is it so plain, ma'am?' Annelise blushed. 'I have tried to hide it from him, because I know…I know he intends to marry Madame Varennes.'

'Did she tell you that herself the day she came here?'

'Yes. She made it plain I would not be welcome here when she is mistress. I could not stay here if Justin brought her home as his bride…I could not live in the same house as her.'

'Nor I,' said Lady Emily, smiling inwardly. 'But we need not trouble ourselves. Justin has no intention of marrying her. I believe she has already returned to France.'

'Returned to France?' Annelise stared at her. 'Why would she do that?'

'I have no idea. Perhaps Justin knows. Why don't you ask him, Annelise?'

'I—I am not sure he will speak to me at all.'

'Oh, I think perhaps he might,' Lady Emily said, and leaned forward to kiss her cheek. 'You know, I sometimes think some men are like small boys—they do not know what is good for them and need to be shown what they cannot see for themselves.'

'I do not see Justin as a small boy, ma'am,' Annelise said, an impish smile tugging at the corners of his mouth.

'No? Do you not? Perhaps it is easier for me because I am his mother—but one day I think you will see that deep inside him there is a child who cries out for love. I failed to give him the love he needed, but perhaps you will make amends for me.' She smiled and stood up. 'Finish your rolls, Annelise. I shall not ask you to come to the theatre with me this evening, because you need to rest—but tomorrow we shall go shopping. I think it is time we both had a new gown...'

Annelise made no reply as her friend went out. She drew the rolls towards her, munching thoughtfully. Lady Emily's words had given her a spark of hope. Was it possible that Justin's moods had been brought on by her behaviour?

Surely not? He had tried to persuade her to marry Robert or Ralph, his two best friends. Why would he do that if he cared for her himself?

Could it be that he wanted her to be safe—married to someone he knew to be trustworthy?

She had been so cross with him that she had not considered such an idea for a moment, but now she wondered.

If there was a chance...she would do anything, take any risk to make him speak. She knew he was out, but she would wait for him; she would sit by her window and watch for him to return, and when he did…she would confront him in his own apartments.

'I'll walk with you,' Ralph insisted as they left the lights of the inn behind. 'No protests, Justin. After what you've told me this night, I could do no other. Besides, my friend, you have drunk more than usual this evening.' He looked curiously at him. 'Is something troubling you—other than this business of the traitors?'

Justin smiled wryly. 'I have been a severe trial to you of late, I think? Why have you not complained of it, Ralph? My mother is not so reticent, I assure you.'

'Lady Emily is very fond of Annelise,' Ralph replied. 'Why do you blind yourself to the truth, Justin? Why not admit you love her—want her for your own?'

'I should have known you would find me out.' Justin laid his hand on Ralph's shoulder. 'How can I ask her to marry me? After all I have been—all I have done?'

'What have you done? No more than any other soldier, I'll warrant,' Ralph said, then, seeing the haunted look in Justin's eyes, 'Why torture yourself over that merchant ship? From what I've been told it was not your doing.'

'I have told you nothing.' Justin's eyes narrowed. 'How do you know of this?'

'Have I no ears, no eyes? I've witnessed the change in you—and I've wits enough to listen when men talk. I know that you were asleep in your cabin when the first shots were fired, and I know that they had to knock you unconscious to keep you from trying to board that ship once you saw the women and children. You would have saved them if you could, Justin. You should not torment yourself. It was a mistake. In the poor light your crew saw what they wanted to see. And the Portuguese was showing a Spanish flag. No one wanted to kill those women…'

'They had been using a Spanish flag to cover their illicit

trading for silver,' Justin said, his voice tight with suppressed emotion. 'Had they been caught by the Spanish
they would have died by the sword…instead they were
caught by us. Carruda's village had been put to the torch.
The men were thirsty for revenge. Normally they would
not have attacked without my order, but they were so sure
it was Sanchez's ship…'

'And you blame yourself for that?'

'I should have been there—I should have controlled
them. It was my ship, my responsibility.'

Ralph nodded, understanding him. 'And that's why you
gave them your ship—because you could not bring yourself
to sail with them again?'

'They had reason for their hatred. I blame no one but
myself.'

'Of course not. It is your way—but I do not believe
Annelise would blame you if she knew.'

Justin turned on him fiercely. 'I shall not tell her. And
nor must you! Give me your word on it, Ralph.'

'If she is to be told you must be the one,' Ralph said.
'For goodness' sake, Justin! Don't you know the poor girl
loves you? She is breaking her heart over you. You must
be blind or mad if you cannot see that.'

'She hates me. She told me so. I have made her hate me,
Ralph.'

'You have driven her to say it out of self-defence,' Ralph
said with a wry twist of his lips. 'Your moods would drive
a saint to madness—and Annelise is not a saint. She is a
beautiful, wilful woman and you would be a fool to let her
go. Get down on your knees if you have to, my friend, but
make your peace with her. Fail in that and you will never
cease to regret it.'

'I know it,' Justin admitted ruefully. 'But, fool that I am,
I cannot do it. I think perhaps…I am afraid that she will
turn from me…that I will see disgust or hatred in her eyes.'

* * *

Justin was thoughtful as he parted from Ralph and made his way slowly to his own apartments. The walk and the night air had cleared some of the confusion in his mind, but he had drunk more than he ought. It made him feel reckless. He wanted Annelise. Why should he not have her for his own? Ralph was right. He would be a fool to let her go. Why should he give her to another man? She had said she cared for no one—that she would be wife to no man. But she was made for love. He had seen the passion in her, felt the pull of her sensuality. If she married an older man, she would soon grow tired of him—and then she would return to Court.

She would take lovers. Already she had attracted the attention of the King. Charles was a fickle lover. He would not long be content with any one woman—even with a woman as beautiful as Annelise. And then what? Montgomery…and others after him.

Justin felt the worm of despair turn and twist inside him. How could he stand by and watch that happen? Why should he not have her for himself?

His tortured thoughts had brought him to her door. He paused before it, his hand reaching towards the latch as he pictured her lying in her bed, eyes closed, flushed in sleep. He wanted her, burned for her! Yet his hand fell to his side and he turned away, mocking himself as he did so. He softly quoted a line of the poem he knew she loved.

> *I could not love thee (Dear) so much*
> *Lov'd I not honour more…*

Reaching his own apartments, Justin inwardly admitted he loved Annelise. It still surprised him, this tenderness she aroused, this need to protect her, to nurture her. She haunted his every breath, his every thought, his every sense.

He could smell her perfume always, lingering in the air...
He could smell her perfume!

Justin looked about his chamber. The air was full of her.
Was he going mad? She had never been in this room, which
was filled with his books, maps spread over a desk, and
various paraphernalia. It was his private sanctum where he
sometimes sat of an evening, reading or studying, and Annelise had never entered here. Yet the scent of her filled
his nostrils, was all around him, inflaming his senses.

'Annelise...' He was like a man thirsting in the desert,
his imagination run wild. Surely his desire for her had
robbed him of his wits? 'Annelise? Are you here? Speak
to me for I feel your presence. Are you truly here—or am
I mad?'

The curtains at the windows stirred, and then she was
there, in the room with him, wearing only a flowing velvet
drape over her night-chemise. Her lovely hair was hanging
loose, spilling in shining tresses over her shoulders and
down her back, and her perfume—her perfume was all
around him, enveloping him in a sensual mist that set his
pulses racing.

'Annelise—why have you come?'

'Justin...' She moved towards him. 'Please don't be angry. I had to come. To beg you to forgive me for all the
terrible things I said to you. I did not mean them. You know
I did not. I cannot bear it when you are angry with me.
I've been so miserable. Please don't make me marry that
man...don't send me away from you.'

'Send you away?' he echoed hoarsely. 'How could I send
you away? I want you, Annelise. I want you desperately.
Why should I let anyone else have you? You are mine. I
shall never let you go.'

What was he saying? She could hardly believe her own
ears. Surely she was dreaming?

'Justin…' She whispered his name and took a hesitant step towards him. 'Justin, I…'

Then he had covered the ground between them. He reached out for her, gathering her up in his arms. She could feel the throb of his heart as she clung to him, half fainting, feeling as if she dreamed as he carried her through to his bedchamber and laid her gently down. Was this happening? Her lovely eyes widened in surprise as he bent over her, his lips seeking hers in a hungry, searching kiss that made her sigh and smile up at him in sweet content.

'Don't be frightened, my little love,' he murmured huskily. 'I shall not harm you. I want only to pleasure you, to make your body sing with delight.'

'Yes,' she murmured, her lips soft and moist, parting invitingly as she gazed up at him. 'Love me, Justin. I want you to love me—to teach me what it is to be truly a woman. I want to please you.'

'You do please me,' he whispered, mouth against her throat. 'You please me as no other woman ever could.'

Annelise was aware that what was happening was morally wrong. She ought not to have come here like this. Justin should not have brought her to his bed. Yet she could no more have refused him then than she could cease to breathe. He *was* her breath, her heart, her love. She wanted this meeting of their bodies, craved it with all her natural woman's passion.

Her body opened to him willingly, giving up all its secrets, all its warmth and welcoming moisture as he caressed and kissed her, lips moving tenderly from her breasts to her navel and then slowly, surely on downwards to the very centre of her femininity. She cried out in pleasure as his touch awoke the desire slumbering within her, and the waves of sensation began to run through her, making her flesh tingle. Then his body was lying on hers and she could feel the silken heat of his masculinity pushing at her, seeking entry to that most secret place of love.

He was inside her, gently at first, easing himself into her welcoming moistness, tantalising, teasing until she whimpered and arched beneath him, then thrusting suddenly, piercing her maidenhead. His kiss stifled her cry of surprise at the sharp pain, and then it eased. She was carried on a floodtide of passion, happiness overcoming any discomfort as she gloried in the sense of belonging to him. For she *was* truly his at last, and nothing else mattered.

He loved her, must love her. He could not feel such passion, offer such tenderness if he did not feel deeply for her. She snuggled into his body when the heat of passion had died, tasting the salt of his sweat, inhaling the musk of his body, her own flesh yielding and pliant, fitting with his as if they were but two halves of one whole.

'Justin?' she whispered. 'What…?'

'Hush, sweeting,' he murmured against her hair. 'Sleep now and tomorrow we shall talk…

When Annelise awoke again it was to find herself alone in her own bed. She yawned, stretched, and then sat up with a start as she remembered what had happened the previous night. Surely it was but a fevered dream? She could not—had she really gone to Justin's room? Allowed him to make love to her? No, no, it had not been like that. She had almost thrown herself at him, not making the slightest resistance when he took her to his bed.

What must he think of her? He could only imagine she was the whore he had thought her for going with Earl Rathbone to that courtyard.

Hot shame washed over her, making her cheeks flame and her body wriggle with unease. What had she done? What had she done?

Someone knocked at her bedroom door. She shrank back

beneath the covers, half expecting it to be Justin and overcome with embarrassment.

'Yes, come in,' she said, feeling relieved as a maidser-
vant entered.

'Your bath is prepared, Mistress Woodward. Lady Emily
said she thought you would like to bathe this morning?'

'Oh…that was kind of her.'

Annelise felt her cheeks heat once more. A bath was just
what she needed—but why had Lady Emily ordered it for
her? Did she know what had happened? Was she aware
that the girl she had welcomed to her house had spent the
night in her son's arms?

How could she? Justin had carried her back here as she
slept to prevent gossip—and yet it was impossible to keep
secrets in a house this size. One of the servants could have
seen Justin carrying her back to this room…and that meant
they must all know!

She waved the maid away and sighed with relief as she
entered the tub of hot water alone. What was she to do?
She had thrown herself at Justin shamelessly and now she
was ruined, a fallen woman in the eyes of the world. A
part of her was fearful, aware that she had behaved badly,
and yet she could still taste Justin's kisses and feel the
imprint of his flesh on hers, the moment when they had
seemed to be completely one. Surely there could be no
shame in sharing such glorious sensations as both she had
Justin had experienced together?

Had she been certain how he felt about what had taken
place between them, she thought this might have been the
happiest day in her life—but was Justin regretting what had
happened in his bed?

She had been very sleepy when he'd carried her back to
her own room, hardly registering what was happening at
all. She seemed to recall twining her arms about his neck,
her head against his breast, but he had been so silent. Why?

Was he angry because she had made him forget his duty as her guardian?

Annelise's thoughts were uneasy as she summoned the maid to help her dress after her bath. What would Justin do now? Honour demanded that he marry her—but it could not make him love her.

Chapter Ten

'Ah, there you are, my love.' Lady Emily entered Annelise's boudoir just as she was about to leave it. 'All ready for our shopping trip?'

'Yes, ma'am.' Annelise's heart fluttered and she felt suddenly shy, hardly daring to look at the older woman.

'Good.' There was an expression of satisfaction on Lady Emily's face. 'Before we leave…my son has informed me that he wishes to speak with you. In his library, if you please. He says we shall not be long detained from our pleasures. I wonder what he can have to say. Perhaps he means to apologise to you, Annelise.'

'Perhaps.' Annelise's cheeks flamed. 'If you will excuse me, ma'am?'

'Of course. Run along, my love.'

There was a knowing look about Lady Emily that made Annelise tingle with shock. She knew! Somehow she knew what had happened. Had Justin told her?

Annelise's heart was beating wildly as she made her way down the stairs and through the long gallery to the library. How could she face Justin? She thought she could hardly bear to look at him. What was he thinking? Was he disgusted with her? Please do not be angry! she prayed inwardly.

She knocked timidly at the door and was invited to enter. He was standing by the fireplace, one booted foot resting on the iron fender, his arm against the mantle, head bent and deep in thought. He turned as she entered, his expression grave but not angry.

'Ah, Annelise,' he said, his manner studiously polite and somehow chilling after the passion they had shared the previous night. 'Thank you for coming.'

'Lady Emily said you wanted to speak with me?' Her voice was scared, little more than a whisper. 'Justin, I…'

'Forgive me.' He smiled at her. Not with the mocking grin of old, but the uncertain smile of a gentleman who knows himself at fault. 'Please allow me to speak first. It is my pleasure, my honour and my duty to ask you to be my wife, Annelise. I have already informed Mama of my desire to marry you, and she has accepted the office of guardian so there is no longer a conflict of interest.'

'A—a conflict of interest?' she faltered, half afraid to look at him. 'I do not understand you.'

'Mama will oversee the marriage contracts—your settlement. I would not want it to appear that I had married you for financial gain. Your estate will be held in trust for your children.'

'Oh…' Annelise blushed and dropped her gaze. 'I see…'

'Do you?' he murmured half to himself. 'I wonder.'

'You feel bound by honour to marry me after…what happened last night.' She turned to the window, her shoulders stiff as she hid her face from him. 'But it was my fault. I was wrong to come to your room as I did. I behaved foolishly.'

'What is done is done,' Justin said. He was frowning as she swung round to look at him, her eyes wide. 'We neither of us planned what happened last night, Annelise. It might have been better had it not occurred, but there is no use in crying over spilt milk. I have taken the rights of a husband and therefore I shall marry you. There is no more to be said.'

He was so calm, so controlled—as if they were discussing the weather!

'No more to be said?' His offhand manner chilled her, making her uneasy and angry. 'I do not believe you have asked my opinion. It might be that I do not wish to marry you.'

'You have no choice,' he interrupted harshly. His face was set, determined. 'Let us not argue over this, Annelise. I acted unwisely last night. I had taken wine too freely and was not in full control of my judgement. However, I am quite sober this morning and I know my duty. Besides, I need an heir and must therefore marry. As well you as any other woman. We shall marry as soon as it can be arranged.'

As well her as any other woman! How dared he? How could he say such things to her?

'And what then?' she demanded. He had hurt her, and now she was becoming angry. 'Am I to be sent to the country until you have your heir? You have accused me of flirting with almost every gentleman at Court—will you be as zealous a husband as you have been a guardian? Explain, if you please. What is to be our relationship, sir?'

'As I have said, I want an heir.' Justin's expression was tight and revealed nothing. 'This marriage will be... convenient. I hope we shall at least be friends, and perhaps more. May we not try to live comfortably with one another, Annelise?'

She caught the pleading note in his voice and her anger melted.

The new gentleness in his voice almost tore the heart

from her breast. She longed to rush to his arms, to confess her love for him, but pride forbade it.

'We can try,' she acknowledged stiffly, struggling to hide her feelings lest she betray too much. 'Though if you are going to lose your temper every time I so much as speak to a man you dislike…'

'No, no,' he said, a rueful smile on his lips. 'I have been at fault in this, Annelise. I freely admit I have abused you and shall not do so again. I mean to make your life as pleasant as possible.'

'Very well,' she said, gazing at him from beneath her long, silky lashes, unsure of what to make of this new Justin. 'If that is truly your intention…then I accept your offer. I shall be honoured to be your wife, my lord.'

'I hope to make you happy.' He came to her and took her left hand, raising it to his lips to bestow a brief, passionless kiss, before slipping a beautiful gold and ruby ring on her finger. 'Now, I must keep you no longer. Mama is anxious to take you shopping. I imagine you will find she is excited about choosing gowns for your wedding.'

Annelise made no reply. She gave him a reserved, cool smile and left the room, her emotions an odd mixture of happiness and despair. She longed with all her heart to be Justin's wife, and yet her heart ached because of the reason for their marriage. Justin was merely doing his duty from a sense of honour, a need to make reparation for his former unkindness.

He did not love her. He had made love to her so sweetly, so tenderly the previous night, but physical pleasure between a man and a woman was not love—not the kind of all-consuming love she felt for Justin.

Annelise held the tears inside her, putting on a brave face as she went to meet Lady Emily. Pride would see her through this. She must behave in a manner befitting her new station. No more tantrums, no outbursts of emotion.

Justin had shown her the way. His manner had been that of a gentleman towards a lady of quality—polite, considerate, but without passion.

Well, if that was how he wanted their marriage to be, she would follow his example. She would be calm, controlled, responding to his lead, but there would be no teasing smiles, no wicked looks.

At least that way she might be able to salvage some of her self-respect. Justin did not want a loving, clinging wife, so she would be the reserved, dignified lady he seemed to prefer.

Was Annelise truly a wanton at heart? Justin pondered the idea as he walked through the gathering dusk to his appointment with Ralph. It must surely be so or she would not have come to his room like that, have given herself so freely to him. He hated himself for harbouring such a suspicion, yet could not quite put it from his mind.

She had sworn she loved no one…had maintained her unwillingness to marry even after spending a night of passion in his arms.

Why? Why come to him if she did not wish to be married?

Then the memory of her loveliness as she surrendered to him so sweetly swept over him. She had come to him so willingly, offering her body—her whole self—with an eager innocence which had delighted him. If it was not love she had given him that night—what was it?

He had made it clear he would not tolerate her taking a lover as an unmarried woman—did she imagine he would condone such behaviour once they were wed?

A fierce anger rushed through him. He would never stand by and see her in another man's arms. Better they were both dead!

All women were faithless. Justin's lip curled. He had

learned that lesson long ago. But something—a little voice in his heart—told him that Annelise was different. Justin knew he must learn to believe in her, to trust her, or they were doomed to grief. His nature was too demanding, too possessive to ever accept less than perfection.

Suddenly, he laughed at himself out loud. Greedy fool! His needs, his desires! What of her—of her happiness? It surprised him to discover he cared very much for her happiness. He prayed he might serve her, might spend his life in giving her pleasure.

His laughter changed to a frown once more as he thought about her behaviour this past week. She had been unlike her usual self. She had responded to all his suggestions for the wedding most affably, her manner polite, agreeable—but distant. There had been an odd reserve in her that disturbed him and made him wonder if she was angry with him. Did she hate him in her heart for having seduced her, forcing her into a marriage she did not want?

His thoughts had been distracted, but, hearing a sudden noise behind him, Justin swung round just as the two men rushed down on him. He needed no one to tell him their purpose and instantly drew his sword. It was two to one, but he was ready for them, alert, his mind concentrated now on the task ahead.

'Come, gentlemen,' he said, though they were plainly rogues, roughly garbed and harsh-featured. His blade sang out in a wide arc, keeping the distance between them. 'Why do you tarry? I await your pleasure.'

'Kill him!' One of the assassins urged the other on. 'Remember what we were promised for his death—there's a hundred silver pieces in it!'

'What—would you sell your lives so cheaply?' laughed Justin, his mood lifting at the promise of a fight. It was just what he needed to banish his unwelcome thoughts.

The braver of the two ran at him. Their blades met and

clashed furiously in a swift, fierce flurry. The assassin was lacking in skill but attacked boldly, thrusting and cursing as he realised he was up against a master swordsman. He pressed hard for a few moments, but was soon outclassed as Justin's sword arm came up suddenly in a twirling movement that plucked the other man's weapon from his hand and sent it flying into the air. It landed a few feet away and went skittering across the road to lie in the gutter amongst the rotting filth. For a brief second its owner stared fixedly at Justin, rather like a rabbit might at a stoat, then he gave a cry of fear as he felt the cold tip of Justin's sword at his throat.

'Help me!' he cried despairingly, but his companion was already backing away into the darkness, running like the coward he was, afraid for his own life. His face held a plea as he continued to look at Justin. 'Spare me. I beg you.'

'Who sent you?' Justin demanded. 'Who was it—Courtney? Speak up before I kill you!'

'Mercy, sir. Have mercy,' the man begged, his face a ghastly white in the moonlight. 'I was forced to do it. I swear!'

'He offered you money. You were not forced to take it.' Justin's sword pricked his throat, making the blood spurt. 'Yet I am not a vengeful man. Go back to your master, knave. Tell him to face me like a man—not send fools and cowards to do his foul work.'

'Thank you for my life. God bless you, sir.' The man retreated to a safe distance. 'Courtney will have his revenge one way or the other. Watch over those you love…'

'What do you mean?'

Justin cursed himself as the would-be assassin melted into the darkness. He ought to have questioned him more forcibly, but he had no taste for torture and the ease with which he had disarmed the rogue had given him a false security. His skills as a soldier made him confident of protecting himself from such attacks—but what of his mother and Annelise?

A chilling fear gripped his heart. It would be his wife they might try to kill, he realised. It was well known that he was not close to his mother. No, it was Annelise who would be in danger if they tried to get to him through those he cared for.

His first thought was that he must cancel their wedding. But, no, that was not possible. It could not be done without causing a scandal. Besides, such a course of action would cause offence to both Annelise and his mother.

The wedding must go ahead. He would need to find some other way of protecting Annelise from his enemies.

'You look beautiful, my love.' Lady Emily smiled and kissed Annelise's cheek. She looked at her in surprise as she discovered she was trembling. 'You are not ill? What troubles you—you are not afraid of being Justin's wife?'

'No…of course not,' Annelise denied, her cheeks a becoming rose. She was dressed in a gown of pale cream brocade, its full skirts embroidered heavily with pearls and small brilliants. Around her neck, and falling almost to her waist, was a long string of huge, flawless pearls, which were Justin's wedding present to her. 'Just of… disappointing him.'

'La! What a foolish child,' said Lady Emily, and patted her cheek lovingly. 'How can you imagine such a thing? My son is very fortunate to be gaining such a lovely bride. It is he who should be afraid of disappointing you.'

Annelise shook her head but said nothing further, which made Lady Emily frown.

'You have seemed a little quiet of late, my love,' she said. 'You are not regretting having accepted Justin's offer? It is not too late to change your mind. I could always take you away to avoid scandal.'

'Oh, no, no, ma'am,' Annelise cried. 'Believe me, I want to be Justin's wife with all my heart. It is only…I wish so much that he loved me.'

'Why else would he marry you? It is not for your fortune, Annelise. Believe me, my son already has far more money than he truly needs. Besides, I know him better than he guesses. He loves you—he simply does not know how to express his feelings. Once you are his wife that will change. It may take him some time to come to terms with what is in his heart, but in the end you will know—even if he never says it in so many words, you will feel it in your heart.'

'You are so kind to me.' Annelise kissed her, her lovely eyes sheened with tears. 'Thank you, ma'am.'

'I pray you will call me Mama from now on.' Lady Emily looked at her with warm affection. 'And now we must go down, Annelise. Ralph is waiting to escort us to the church.'

Annelise nodded. Her throat was tight, her heart too full to speak. In another hour or so she would be Justin's wife for good or ill. She could only pray that Lady Emily was right—that one day she would be certain of his love.

Annelise looked pale but lovely as she stood at Justin's side to take her vows. A wintry sun shone through stained-glass windows, throwing a rainbow of colours on to the altar, and for a moment the silver cross seemed to turn blood-red.

She was reminded of her uncle's warnings. Was this an omen—a sign of impending disaster? She was trembling as the moment came for Justin to slip his wedding ring on her finger. It was heavy gold and set like her betrothal ring with a dark red ruby.

Again she was aware of a feeling of apprehension, and she wanted to cry out that this could not be. This was

wrong! She could not marry a man who did not love her—
yet to refuse would break her heart.

She made her own vows in a soft, whispery voice that
could barely be heard, but Justin's voice rang out in the
church strongly. Somehow that steadied her nerves, and she
was able to smile at him as they knelt together for the
blessing. Then the bells were pealing joyfully as she was
walking out into the frosty air, her hand on her new husband's arm.

'Do not despair, Annelise,' he murmured close to her
ear. 'Marriage may not be as terrible as you fear.'

Her eyes flew to his face. Was he smiling, teasing her in
his old way? She could not be sure, though some of the
tension inside her began to melt away, taking with it the
ice that had been formed about her heart these past days.
She smiled again, more confidently this time.

Throughout the wedding breakfast, Annelise was aware
of her husband watching her, his eyes darkly blue and intense. She found herself laughing, responding to the good
wishes of their friends, and all the while the excitement
was beginning to build inside her. She was his wife! Nothing could change that now. Soon they would be alone together. Justin would take her in his arms as he had the night
she had gone to his room…and perhaps he would speak of
love.

Surely he must care for her a little? She knew he wanted
her—their night of passion had shown her that. Was it possible that he also loved her?

Annelise knew she was to be spared the customary ceremony of the bedding before her guests. Lady Emily had
declared it outmoded and embarrassing.

'I shall accompany you to your bridal bed and no other,'
she had told Annelise. 'I stand in place of a mother to you,
my love, and if there is anything worrying you about your

wedding night—anything you wish to ask me—please do not be afraid.'

Annelise had blushed and shaken her head. Lady Emily believed her still innocent. It seemed she did not after all know that Annelise had anticipated her wedding vows in Justin's arms.

As the celebrations wore on, Annelise began to think more and more of the moment when she would be alone with her husband. Would he make love to her as sweetly as he had the first time? The ice had all gone now, melted by the warmth of her anticipation and her love.

Perhaps it did not matter if Justin did not love her as she loved him. She thought she might find contentment in sharing her life with him—and bearing his children. A hot, fierce heat spread through her as she imagined herself in Justin's arms…saw herself holding his son in her arms.

'What are you thinking, wife?' Justin's breath was warm against her ear, making her jump because she had been far away and not noticed him come up behind her. 'Why do you smile like that, Annelise? What mischief goes on in that head of yours?'

She blushed and could not answer him truthfully. 'La, sir!' she cried, after taking a moment to control her frantic heart. 'I did not notice your approach. You startled me.'

'You have secrets in your eyes,' he said, a teasing note in his voice. 'But I shall not press you for answers just yet. Mama is looking this way. I believe she thinks it is time for you to slip away. The hour grows late and our guests will not leave before you.'

'Oh…yes, of course.' Annelise fluttered her fan of painted chicken skin. 'Excuse me, my lord. I was dreaming.'

She moved towards Lady Emily, smiling shyly at guests who pressed their good wishes on her, showering her with dried rose petals. For a moment she paused as Robert laid a hand on her arm. He pressed a small silk-wrapped parcel into her hands, and when she hesitated smiled ruefully.

'Only a string of garnets. A small gift from one friend to another,' he said. 'Justin won you fairly, Annelise. I have regrets, but no recriminations, though I would have had you for my own if I could have made you love me.'

'I love you truly as a friend, Robert. Forgive me if I have hurt you. It was not intended.'

'I know that,' he replied, and smiled. 'You will always hold a special place in my heart. If ever you are in need of help, you have only to ask.'

'Thank you,' she said, then leaned forward impulsively to kiss his cheek. 'I am glad we can still be friends.'

She was still smiling as she reached Lady Emily's side. They left the salon together, walking in silence to the suite of rooms she would in future share with Justin.

'So here we are,' Lady Emily said. 'Let me unfasten your pearls, Annelise. Then Bertha shall unlace you. She will attend you in future. As Justin's wife you will have your own dresser, as well as ladies to wait on you should you wish it. You are the mistress here now, my love.'

'But you will not desert us?' Annelise knew a moment of alarm. 'Please, Mama! Do not think of leaving us.'

'Not immediately,' Lady Emily promised with a smile. 'I do have plans of my own, but I shall see you properly settled before I think of myself.'

Annelise made no further protest. Much as she loved her mother-in-law, she must not be selfish in her demands.

'You know I would always welcome you here.'

'I shall visit you and Justin sometimes,' promised Lady Emily. 'Now, my love, sit down and I shall brush your hair. You may go, Bertha. Your mistress will ring if she needs you again.'

Annelise sat on a padded stool as Lady Emily began to brush her hair. The action was soothing, comforting. She

closed her eyes. The feel of soft hands touching her hair
was so pleasant. She was sorry when it ceased. Opening
her eyes, she was startled to discover that Lady Emily had
gone. In her place stood Justin. He was wearing a long
black velvet robe over his nightrail and he held her hair-
brush in his hand.

'Would you like me to continue?' he asked, brows
slightly raised, a faint smile on his mouth.

'Yes…please,' she whispered. 'I like having my hair
brushed. It is soothing.'

He began to smooth the brush over her hair, which
gleamed like pale silk in the candle-glow. Annelise was
immediately aware of the difference. Lady Emily's touch
had been comforting; Justin's was firm, sensual, making her
heart race with excitement and her body tingle with a slow
trickle of desire that reached down to her very toes.

She closed her eyes again, letting the sensations of pleasure wash over her, filling her. It felt so good having Justin
perform such an intimate task for her. Her lips parted in a
sigh, and when she felt the touch of his lips against the
sensitive nape of her neck she trembled, aching with the
need he had aroused in her.

'Annelise,' Justin said hoarsely. 'Are you prepared to be
a wife to me—and all that entails?'

'Yes, Justin,' she whispered. She stood up, turned and
looked up at him invitingly. 'Yes, I want to be your wife—
to bear your children.'

'So be it.' His eyes seemed to burn into her, lighting a
fire deep down within her, a fire that threatened to flare out
of control. 'It might have been better for you had this marriage never been necessary—but we are bound to one another, Annelise. You are my wife. And I am content that it
should be so.'

There was a dull ache of disappointment somewhere inside her. He was saying that he did not love her but would

make the best of things now that they were wed. For a moment the pain was almost unbearable, but then he was lifting her in his arms, carrying her towards the bed—and as she melted against him Annelise forgot everything in the bittersweet joy of his loving.

Her body responded instantly to his touch. His kisses drove all emotion other than desire from her mind as she trembled beneath him, no longer a separate being but part of him, flesh of his flesh. He lavished her breasts with his tongue, teasing, caressing, arousing such sensation, taking the nipples into his warm mouth. Oh, oh, it was so good! She arched her back, welcoming the thrust of his throbbing manhood against her, drawing him inside to the heat of her moist femininity. He was moving in her, deep, deep within her, slowly, deliberately, in a way that made her gasp and cry out in her pleasure.

This time there was no pain, no hesitation. Her body arched into his, her hips meeting him, begging him to drive deeper, ever deeper into her inviting warmth. Such glorious sensation! Such pleasure! It made her writhe beneath him, her head moving restlessly from side to side on the pillow. She was calling his name aloud, her nails scoring his shoulder as their passion mounted.

She had never imagined anything could feel so exquisite! Even their first night of loving had not approached this. She was dying…falling…falling into this wonderful feeling, melting into Justin, becoming lost in him.

When at last it was over and he lay still, breathing hoarsely against her neck, Annelise tangled her fingers in his hair. She had tears on her cheeks, her lashes spiky and dark. He raised his head, looking down at her, a wry smile twisting his mouth.

'So, my love,' he murmured, a note of mockery in his voice. 'It seems marriage may not be as terrible as you feared.' And then he rolled away from her, leaving her bereft of his warmth.

It was a moment or so before she realised he was leaving their bed. She raised herself on one elbow, gazing up at him, her lovely hair falling forward like a curtain to hide her face. 'You are leaving?'

'I have something I need to do,' Justin said. 'Go to sleep now, Annelise. I am taking you to the country early in the morning.'

'To the country...we are going to visit your estate?'

'I have business here, and must return almost immediately,' he said. 'I shall leave you there for a time, Annelise. You will want to become accustomed to your new home.' He frowned as he saw the stricken look she could not hide. 'It is not a punishment, Annelise. I shall introduce you to your neighbours before I return. You will not be lonely, I promise. You will make new friends. Besides, I intend to live mainly at my estate in future. Once my business here is safely done, I shall join you.'

Annelise was silent. She turned her face to the pillow as he walked to the door. *He was sending her to the country!* He might claim it was not a punishment, but it was...it was! Justin had married her from a sense of duty, but he did not love her. It was his intention to leave her at his estate and return to London alone. She would be exiled from everyone she knew...alone.

She recalled being told by Lady Emily that Madame Varennes had returned to Paris, but that did not necessarily mean Justin would be faithful to his new wife—the wife he had never wanted. Perhaps he had a new mistress and wanted to be with her.

How that thought hurt! The iron entered Annelise's soul as she realised that this was the most likely explanation. Justin needed a wife for the purpose of gaining his heir, but that would not stop him from taking lovers as he pleased. What other business could be so important as to keep him from his bride?

At the door, Justin turned to look at her. Because she had turned inwards in her grief, she did not see the doubt and anguish in his eyes.

'So you are to go down to Ravenscourt,' Lady Emily said as she kissed Annelise goodbye the next day. 'Well, my love, I hope you will not be so enchanted by your new home that you will want to stay there for ever.'

'Never fear, Mama,' Justin said, an odd note in his voice. 'I am certain nothing will prevent my wife from returning to Court before too long has passed.'

'Of course she will visit us sometimes,' Lady Emily said, a challenging lilt to her voice. 'La, Justin! You do not intend to keep her hidden away in the country, I hope? She is far too lovely to stay there all the time.'

'No, Mama, I do not.' His eyes gleamed with a wry amusement. 'I am certain you would not permit it even if I had some such notion.'

Annelise saw the glint of mockery and wondered at it. He seemed almost regretful, disappointed.

Disappointed in her? Had the previous night, which had seemed so wonderful to her, meant nothing to him? Was she too inexperienced, too innocent to please him? She loved him so much, had given all she had to give. If it was not enough, she could not hope to make him love her— and yet was it possible for a man to be so tender, so passionate and not love? She could not tell. Justin hid his feelings too well.

Annelise's head went up. Her nature was too resilient, her spirit too strong to be downcast for long. For her pride's sake she would not play the part of the injured wife. Nor would she be humble! When Justin came to her bed, he would find a warm welcome, but she would not beg him to love her. Other than at times of passion, she would hold a tiny part of herself back from him.

'Do not worry, Mama,' she cried, laughing carelessly. 'I have been promised a mare of my own when we are in the country. I shall ride often—and if my husband does not bring me back, then I shall ride to London myself and visit you.'

'I almost believe you would.' A rueful smile tugged at the corners of Justin's mouth. For a while he had thought his clumsy efforts to protect her had hurt her, but now he saw that he was mistaken. She was a willing partner in lovemaking, but so were others. She did not love him. She had told him as much when they had quarrelled and he must never forget it. 'Come, Annelise. The carriage awaits. We must not keep the horses standing.'

'Oh, Justin!' Annelise cried as she saw the house for the first time. 'How beautiful it is. I did not imagine anything like this.' She turned to him in understanding. 'Now I know why you fought so hard to win back your estate.'

'Do you, my love?' A gleam of amusement appeared in his eyes as he sensed her pleasure. 'I am glad you approve of our house.'

'Who could not?' she said, giving her approval warmly. 'It has such charm—such grace.'

She could be happy here always, if only he was with her!

They had travelled for some twenty minutes through the grounds, which were extensive and included a large lake with a waterfall at one end and was banked by trees. There was also a pretty park, where it would be pleasant to ride or walk on fine days, and then a formal knot garden before the house itself was reached, but now at last they were here and Annelise was enchanted.

The house was built of a honey-coloured stone that

looked warm and cheerful even on the dullest day, and the windows reflected the rays of a dying sun, the thick grey glass turned to rose. It was shaped as an E, and Annelise knew there would be sheltered courtyards at the back, rose arbours and fountains, the gardens in which she would grow herbs to make the simples and common cures known and trusted by country housewives.

Justin helped her down from the carriage himself. He had sent servants on ahead to warn of their arrival, and the household had gathered in the main hall to greet their master and his bride.

'This is Holmes,' Justin said, introducing her to his steward. 'Holmes served my father before the war. He left when the estate was sold to run a tavern of his own—but has been persuaded to return to take care of us.'

'You are very welcome, my lord—and we are all happy to welcome your lady wife.' Holmes bowed to Annelise. He was a man of advanced years, wiry but strong, with white hair and merry eyes. 'With your permission, milady, I would like to introduce Mrs Holmes—your housekeeper.'

Annelise was passed on to the comfortable person of a rather plump lady whose smile was so warm that she immediately felt herself truly welcome.

'My lady.' Mrs Holmes curtsied. She was several years younger than her husband and had been trained as a lady's dresser in her youth. 'May I have the honour of presenting your household?'

Annelise was taken down the line of menservants, maids and finally the kitchen wenches and gardeners; she smiled and greeted each in turn with a friendly word. After the little ceremony was completed, the housekeeper led the way upstairs to a large and very luxurious suite of rooms.

'These have recently been refurbished according to his lordship's instructions,' Mrs Holmes said. 'You will find the bedchambers have access through his lordship's dress-

ing room, milady. And you have your own parlour where
you may be peaceful, should there come a time when you
do not wish for company.' She glanced around the rooms,
showing each in turn to Annelise. 'I do hope everything is
to your liking?'

The apartments were spacious, elegant and comfortable,
the colours shading from the palest duck egg-blue to rich
emerald-green velvet drapes about the bed in her own
chamber. Annelise felt as if they must have been chosen
just for her sake. Yet how could that be? The work must
have been commissioned when Justin had first taken possession of his estate—before she had so recklessly gone to
his bedchamber. Before her shameful behaviour had made
it necessary for him to offer her marriage.

'It is all perfect,' she said, smiling at the housekeeper,
who had obviously gone to some trouble to make the rooms
welcoming. 'Quite perfect. You've even picked roses.'

'The very last of them before the frosts,' Mrs Holmes
said. 'I am afraid the bitter weather last night spoiled all
but these few. Sometimes we have roses at Christmas, but
these are the last this year. I picked them yesterday before
the frost closed in especially for you.'

Annelise was touched by the woman's thoughtfulness. 'I
can see you mean to spoil me, Mrs Holmes.'

'Those were his lordship's instructions,' replied the
housekeeper with a smile. 'You are to have everything you
wish for, milady. We are here to serve you at any time of
day or night.'

Annelise thanked her and she departed. Once alone, Annelise spent some minutes exploring her apartments on her
own. It seemed that every possible comfort had been provided: an armoire for her clothes, a chair with soft cushions
for her back, and a table at which to write her letters, padded stools, a settle by the fire—and fine tapestries to give
warmth and added colour. Here she could sit with a book

or some fine embroidery on a cold winter's day and see out of her window across the park. She would be able to see visitors approaching long before they arrived—and also the deer who roamed at will.

She was standing at the window, watching a fine stag who had ventured as far as the edge of the formal gardens, and was not aware that Justin had entered the room until he spoke behind her, making her start.

'It is a fine view, I think. One of the best from the house. On a clear day you can just see the lake from this wing.'

Annelise swung round to look at him. 'Is that why you chose these rooms—for the view?'

'In part,' he said, a wry twist to his mouth. 'They had been guest rooms but I had them opened up and made larger. I did not care to use the suite that was once my parents'.'

'Why?'

Annelise wondered at the odd expression in his eyes. It was customary for the heir to move into the master's apartments. Why had Justin chosen instead to refurbish this wing?

'Because it pleased me.' He gave her an enigmatic look. 'More importantly—do they please you?'

'Yes, very much,' she replied. 'You have commissioned all my favourite colours. They might have been chosen just for me.'

'Perhaps they were. Perhaps I saw you here as my wife when I chose them, Annelise.'

His smile mocked and challenged her. She answered him in kind.

'But I recall now. You told me once how much you admired a certain shade of green.'

'And you told me you preferred blue. Here we have both, blended in harmony. Think you we can do as well, my love?'

He called her his love, but in a light, careless way which meant nothing. She lifted her head, eyes bright, smile cool and proud, hiding her hurt.

'If we do not it shall not be my fault, sir.'

'Indeed?' Justin's mouth quirked. 'So I am to be on my mettle, madam? Then I shall not try to quarrel with you— at least not more than once a day.'

His teasing brought a smile to her face. She sighed inwardly. When he chose he could be such a charming companion, such a pleasing personality.

'That will be a considerable improvement, my lord.' Her head tipped to one side, her manner challenging him.

'Oh, Annelise, my love,' he murmured huskily, a gleam of desire in his eyes. 'When you look at me that way I am tempted to forget duty and stay here with you.'

'Why do you not?' she asked. She little knew how her eyes invited or how sorely he was tempted. 'What business can be more important than our getting to know one another?'

'Forgive me, but there is something which makes it imperative that I leave the day after tomorrow at first light.'

'Must you go so soon?' she asked, giving him a provocative look. 'Would you not stay if I asked it of you?'

'No, not even then.' He looked at her gravely. 'Even if you hate me for denying you, I must go back.'

'And I must stay here alone?'

'You will not be alone.' His hand moved as if to reach out to her, then fell back. 'Tomorrow we shall entertain our neighbours to dinner, Annelise—and Ralph will be here. I have asked him to bear you company while I am gone.'

She was surprised. 'You have asked Ralph to stay? Will that not seem…will it not occasion talk?'

'I think not.' Justin smiled wickedly. 'Ralph will not be alone. He brings a lady with him. A respectable widow who has promised to wed him. You and Lady Beatrice will be chaperons for each other, my love.'

'Ralph is to marry?' Annelise smiled in pleasure. 'That is indeed good news, Justin. I am so pleased for him.'

'It is the best thing that could have happened to him. I have loaned him money to have his own house rebuilt, but until then…' He opened his hands. 'I believe we have enough space to accommodate them here. The wedding is to be held in two months' time, after which they will move into their own home—and you might be pleased to know that they will be settled not more than twenty miles from here.'

Annelise was too delighted at the news to question him further. It did not occur to her that it was odd he should have invited Ralph and his promised wife to stay in his absence. She was pleased that she would not after all be condemned to a lonely exile. The house was large enough to accommodate many guests. Indeed, she hoped it would often in the future be full of them. Her pleasure was dimmed only by the need for Justin to leave.

'You are very thoughtful, Annelise?' He raised his brows at her. 'What is in your mind?'

She smiled openly at him. 'It is only that I wish…I wish you had no business to take you away.'

'Do you, my love?' He moved closer to her, a certain look she had come to recognise and welcome in his eyes. 'Then I shall return as soon as I may…and for the moment we are here together.' His eyes met hers, seeking an answer. 'Has the journey tired you?'

'A little,' she admitted, 'but I believe a rest on the very large and comfortable bed in my chamber might restore me.'

'Do you wish to rest alone?'

'No, Justin,' Annelise said, and took a step towards him. 'I would much rather you...'

She had no chance to say more for his arms were about her. Then he was kissing her with such passion that all need for words was swept away.

Chapter Eleven

Justin watched with growing pride as Annelise played hostess to their guests the following evening. She welcomed them with all the natural grace and charm of a great lady. No one looking at her now could guess how passionate she was in the curtained privacy of their bedchamber—but his mother was a consummate actress and no doubt she had taught her protégé well.

He was not being fair to either of them! In his heart, Justin knew that as a young woman Lady Emily had had good reason for taking lovers; his father had not treated her well. He knew also that Annelise was not his mother. Her foolish escapades at Court had been caused by various factors, the chief of which was innocence. He had taken her from her sheltered background and thrust her unceremoniously into a sophisticated world of courtiers who were often licentious and cruel. The wonder was not that she had lapsed occasionally, more that she had held her own so well.

He must learn to trust his wife, to enquire before judging her—to wait before losing his temper. Loving her was not enough, Justin realised with a new humility. His happiness depended on hers—and she was not happy at being left behind in the country.

'Why do you not tell her?' Ralph asked when they stood alone by the windows of the great parlour, watching her from a distance. 'She must wonder at your leaving her so soon after your wedding. And to bring her here, Justin— away from all her friends. It must seem to Annelise that she is being abandoned.'

'You know why,' Justin replied, looking serious. 'Would you have her go in fear? No, it is best if she knows nothing for the present—and it should soon all be over. We have most of the names. All we need is the location and time of their next meeting, so that they can be taken in the act of their treason.'

'I still think you would do better to warn her, Justin.'

'You are here to watch over her, Ralph. She is safe enough in the country, and that is what matters. While I am in town where they can see me, it is my life they will try to take if they can.'

'And if they succeed?'

'Then you have my permission to tell her everything.'

'Very well.' Ralph gave in reluctantly. Justin was too stubborn for his own good, but it was useless to argue once his mind was set. 'It shall be as you wish, my friend.'

'Take good care of her; that's all I ask. Protect her from those who would harm her—and let her not be too sad.'

'I know how much she means to you.'

But did Annelise? Seeing the hurt in those lovely eyes when she looked at her husband without his noticing, Ralph wondered. It seemed so strange to him that neither of them should understand the other's heart—but they were both so proud. More alike than either of them realised.

Theirs would no doubt be a stormy marriage, Ralph thought, his eyes coming to rest on Lady Beatrice with a smile of content. No beauty, perhaps, but a good-natured woman who had offered generously of herself and her small but welcome estate. He had been lucky to find her, and since he had never expected to win Annelise he had no feelings of regret or disappointment.

'What were you whispering about with Justin? I hope you do not mean to keep secrets from me?'

Ralph turned as he caught the teasing note in Annelise's voice. He smiled at her. 'Could I hope to keep secrets from you? If I had some, you would soon have them out of me, madam. My poor wits are no match for yours.'

'Oh, Ralph!' Annelise shook her head at him. 'You do not fox me with your uncalled-for humility. I know you too well. You are not the fool you would have us believe— but I shall not tease you. If your word is given to Justin, you must not break it for my sake.'

'He will tell you himself when he can,' Ralph said. 'Believe me, Annelise, he does only what he thinks is right. It was ever thus with him—he is a man of commitment.'

'Yes.' Her eyes were bright with the tears she held inside her. 'I know my husband thinks much of honour.'

She turned away, hiding her hurt. Justin had married her from a sense of honour. Since their wedding he had behaved towards her with kindness and a genuine concern for her welfare. Sometimes, when they made love, he said things which made her think he must care for her—and yet he was leaving her here in the country while he returned to town. How could he do that if he really cared for her?

Annelise washed her face clean of the tears she had shed after Justin's departure. She had hoped he might say something to comfort her before he left…speak of his love or his regret…but he had merely told her to enjoy her new home.

'I shall return as soon as possible. Until then you have complete freedom to do as you wish with the house, Annelise. I thought it best to have our own apartments refurbished before you came, but I dare say the rest of the house needs some attention. I shall leave everything in your capable hands.'

It seemed clear to Annelise that she was being given all the privileges of a favoured wife. Justin was determined to make her life as easy and pleasant as possible. She would have everything she could possibly desire—except his love.

It was more than many women received from their marriage. She was fortunate in having such a generous husband. He had already given her several presents of jewellery, plate and silks, and had promised more on his return from town.

'What would you have me bring you, Annelise?' he had asked her with a look of indulgence. 'A ring—or perhaps bracelets?' He'd placed a kiss on the sensitive inner side of her wrist.

'I need nothing but your speedy and safe return, sir.'

'I promise to do my best to obey your commands, madam.' He had smiled, and kissed her mouth this time. 'How could I not when I have such a modest and obedient wife awaiting me?'

He had left her with a look that had challenged her, arousing her pride—but after he had gone pride had given way to regrets.

Now, as she allowed her maid to dress her, Annelise recalled the odd expression in his eyes. She had thought it mockery at first, but now she wondered. Why had he looked at her so strangely? And why had his last kiss held a kind of hunger…almost desperation? It was almost as though he could hardly bear to tear himself from her side.

'Will you wear a lace cap, milady—or the linen?'

Annelise mustered her wandering thoughts. 'The linen this morning, Bertha. I have asked Mrs Holmes to show me the west wing, which I understand had not been used for some time and may be dusty. I mean to examine the drapes for signs of the moth, so I shall be better served by a plain cap.'

Leaving her apartments for her appointment with the housekeeper, Annelise made a determined effort to forget her disappointment at being deserted by her new husband. She had longed with all her heart to be Justin's wife, and her wish had been granted. Now she must do her best to turn this huge house she knew he loved into a home of which they could both be proud.

'I am going to feed the swans,' Annelise said to Lady Beatrice some six days later. 'Would you care to walk with me, ma'am?'

'Would you forgive me this afternoon? For some unaccountable reason I have been suffering with a headache all day.'

'You must go and lie down.' Annelise sympathised at once. 'You do look a little pale. Ask Mrs Holmes to prepare you one of her soothing cordials.'

'You are always so thoughtful.' Lady Beatrice kissed her cheek. 'Why do you not ask Ralph to bear you company?'

'I believe he rode out to speak with one of Justin's tenants. Some problem over a leaking roof, I think.'

Lady Beatrice smiled and nodded. 'Then do not stay out too long, Annelise. The wind is quite cold today and you do not want to catch a chill.'

Annelise acknowledged her kindness, and they parted. Over the past few days she had come to like the lady Ralph was soon to marry, and was glad of their company. Having them at Ravenscourt had helped to make her life less lonely than it might otherwise have been in Justin's absence, though she was finding more than enough to keep her busy.

A household such as this needed a great deal of supervision, and though Mrs Holmes and her husband were re-

liable stewards of the house, there were many things that
needed the attention of the mistress. Annelise had been
shown trunks full of beautiful and costly tapestries which
had been packed away in disused storerooms when the estate had been sequestered at the end of the war.

'We did not see why everything should be handed over,'
Holmes had informed her with a smile. 'Nor was there any
need to mention the trunks during the years of his lordship's absence.'

'Then we shall have the tapestries brought down and
hung,' Annelise had told him with a twinkle in her eye. 'It
will be a pleasant surprise for the Marquis when he returns.'

'And when do you expect him, milady?'

'I am not perfectly sure—as soon as his business is
done.'

The trouble was, Annelise reflected now, as she walked
slowly towards the lake that day, she had no idea what
Justin's business was or why it had taken him from her
side. Over the past days she had come to the conclusion
that it must be something serious. Her first, painful suspicions that he was leaving her to go to a mistress had faded
after she had given them proper consideration. If Justin had
married her from a sense of honour, would that same honour allow him to go straight from her bridal bed to another
woman?

The sensible answer was no. So what could be so important—and why had he had such an odd look in his eyes
when he kissed her goodbye?

Was he in some kind of danger? Had he brought her to
the country for her own protection?

She was suddenly convinced that she had stumbled on
the truth. His stubborn refusal to defend himself from ac-
cusations of murder had shown her what manner of man
her husband was, and now she saw that his bringing her
here without explanation was more of the same stubborn

pride. He had not told her what was happening because he did not want her to worry—but she was worried!

Their parting had made Annelise realise just how much she had to lose. Perhaps he did not love her in quite the way she loved him…and yet how could she think that? Reviewing his past behaviour from a distance, and with her new insight, it struck Annelise that his black moods and sudden rages might well have been brought on by jealousy and despair.

She knew he had thought himself unworthy of her because of the life he had led since the war—was it possible that loving her, believing himself unfit to wed her, he had still hated the idea of her marrying anyone else?

Such thoughts put their marriage in a very different light. If Justin loved her—and it was just possible that he did!— she was indeed the favoured and adored wife his servants seemed to think her.

How could she have been so blind? Annelise remembered the nights of love and passion she had spent in Justin's arms, each one seeming more intense, more satisfying than the former. She ought to have known that Justin's lovemaking was too tender—at times too intense!—to be merely duty or even lust.

He had been hiding his love out of pride. Just as she had!

Justin did not know she loved him.

Astounding as it was, Annelise believed it was the truth. She had convinced him when, in a temper, she had declared she loved no man—wished to marry no man. And he had believed her.

No, surely not? He could not have thought her indifferent after their first night together? Yet she knew he believed most women faithless and incapable of constancy. Had it seemed to him that she had gone to him out of wilfulness—

did he imagine she would give herself as freely to any other man?

The thought was painful to her. Annelise knew she would never love again. She could never give herself to another man…not as she had to Justin. A smile touched her mouth. If Justin truly loved her…how happy they could be when he came back to her.

She had reached the lake. The swans had been watching her approach, and they came gliding across the water as she threw her bread for them.

How graceful they were! She glanced about her, thinking that the late autumn was a glorious time here, the colours of crimson, orange and gold giving the trees a regal splendour. Justin's estate was a place of true beauty. She understood completely why he had fought so hard to win it back.

Still deep in thought, Annelise turned to retrace her steps. Beatrice was right. The wind was very cold! She began to think longingly of the welcoming fire waiting for her at home.

'Wait, madam! I would have a word with you.'

The man's voice was harsh, and startled her. She swung round and saw him standing a short distance behind her. Dressed from head to toe in black, his cloak blown by the wind, he looked thin and gaunt of face. His appearance was so menacing that a shiver of apprehension ran through Annelise.

'Who are you, sir?' she asked. 'What are you doing here? This is my husband's land.'

'I know it well, for he hath cheated me of my rights,' the man muttered, his face tight with fury. 'This estate is mine by any true law—and I will have it back one day.'

'The courts gave title to the true owner,' Annelise replied, face pale but proud. 'I am sorry for your loss, sir— but the estate was unjustly stolen from my husband…' She stepped back as he moved suddenly towards her, a trickle of fear sliding down her spine. 'Stay! No further, sir.'

'You need have no fear, madam,' Sir Roger Courtney said, scowling at her. 'My quarrel is with Saintjohn himself. I intend to have my estate back—by fair means or foul.'

'What do you mean, sir?' Annelise's hand flew to her throat. There was such evil in this man's face. He looked like a huge black crow, flapping its wings as it presided over the carcass of a dead lamb. 'You cannot hope to win back this land; the case is over, finished. You have lost the battle.'

'What I cannot win I shall take,' he said, eyes glittering with hatred. 'When your husband lies dead, Lady Saintjohn, you will beg me to let you go in peace.'

'You are evil!' Annelise cried. She shivered in fear and distress, then, hearing hoof-beats coming fast, looked round and saw Ralph racing towards her. His imminent arrival gave her the courage to stand her ground. 'Leave my land, sir. And listen well—while either my husband or I live, you will never be master here.'

'Then I shall see you both dead.'

Courtney turned and ran towards the trees, disappearing into them as Ralph galloped up to her. He reined in sharply, his horse rearing nervously as he looked down at her.

'Who was that man, Annelise?'

'Sir Roger Courtney,' she said, her pulses racing as a feeling of terror caught up with her. 'He—he threatened Justin's life. Oh, Ralph! I fear he means to kill Justin.'

Ralph dismounted and came to her. For a moment he held her in the shelter of his arms, face grim as he looked over her head, then he let her go and stood back, recognising the very real fear and distress in her eyes.

'I was afraid of this, Annelise. I warned Justin something might happen. Come, I shall see you safely back to the house, then Holmes will summon a search party to scour the grounds—though I dare say the rogue will be long gone.'

She caught his arm, looking up at him anxiously. 'Justin is in danger, isn't he? That's why he sent me here—and you to watch over me—because he was afraid for me.'

Ralph smiled ruefully. 'I told him you would see through his ruse, Annelise. I begged him to tell you the truth, but he was determined that you should not be upset. He meant to protect you. I do not believe he expected Courtney to come here. He thought they would concentrate their efforts on trying to kill him if he stayed in London.'

'*They*…you mean there is more than one?' She stared at him in anguish. 'This is more than a quarrel over the estate, isn't it? You must tell me, Ralph. I shall worry more if you keep things from me.'

'Justin has discovered a plot to kill His Majesty…'

'To kill the King?' Annelise turned pale, her hand at her mouth as she gasped in shock. 'Oh, such wickedness! I can hardly believe…' She stopped as she realised that there were many who would rejoice in such an outcome, who would dare anything to rid themselves of a man they despised—a man they had never wanted to regain his throne. 'So, until they are arrested…Justin is at risk?'

'Exactly so,' said Ralph, and frowned. 'I ought to be there to guard his back—but you were more important to him than his own life. And he has Rob.'

'I thank you for your care of me,' Annelise replied, 'but I do not believe I am in danger for the moment. It was Justin he threatened—Justin he means to murder.'

'I gave Justin my promise that I would stay here and cannot break it,' Ralph said. 'But I shall write at once, warning him that Courtney has been here.'

'You will have your courier carry my letter with yours?'

'Of course.' Ralph smiled at her as they reached the house. 'Now you must forgive me. I have work to do.'

Annelise watched as he hurried away. Like Ralph, she was sure Courtney would have left the estate before anyone could find him.

What had been his purpose in coming here? Annelise could not be certain. Had it been to watch the house—or to threaten her? She had no way of knowing. All she could do was to warn Justin—and to tell him of her love.

Justin swore as he read Annelise's letter for the fourth time. He had hoped to have the traitors arrested and imprisoned in the Tower by now, but somehow they must have been warned, for although most had been taken, three of them had disappeared. It seemed that Courtney had fled to the country.

He had threatened Annelise! Justin's blood turned cold at the thought. If Ralph had not arrived when he had...it did not bear thinking of!

'Damn his soul to hell!' Justin cursed himself a thousand times as he laid her letter down. He had been so certain Courtney would stay close to him, watching his opportunity to strike. 'If she dies...'

The thought caused him so much pain it was unbearable. He had only one course left to him—he must go to her at once.

The King was expecting him at Court that evening. He had demanded news of the traitors who had slipped the net. No matter. Justin could send word of his unavoidable trip to the country. There was no time to be lost. Nothing was of any consequence to him now but his wife's safety.

He picked up the letter again, holding it so that he could smell the faint perfume which still clung to the parchment. She had written that she missed him...loved him. He wondered what had made her write such sweet words. In his heart he had begun to believe that she might really love him, though she had never said as much until now.

Be damned to the King's business! Had he not given long years of his life for Charles? Now at last he was thinking of his own future—of the happiness that awaited him with his lovely wife.

Annelise... His blood quickened at the memory of her lying beneath him, of the passion she had shown in their bed. He had feared she might betray him one day, that her passion would not be reserved for him alone—but now he knew he must take his chance. Only by giving her the love she deserved could he hope to be loved in turn.

He had come a long, long road, and the passage had been hard, but the feeling of having arrived at his journey's end was a good one.

Annelise was his wife. He loved her for good or ill—and he must be with her. He must protect her from those who might seek to do her harm.

It was bitterly cold and beginning to spit with rain. Justin had ridden throughout the night without pausing, except to change horses at various inns along the way. He was haunted by a terrible premonition that he would never see Annelise again. His sins, imagined or real, rose up to torture his mind. If he lost her he would truly suffer the fires of hell. He must reach her before it was too late, must tell her all the things his damnable pride had forced him to keep hidden inside.

Oh, Annelise my love... he murmured to himself. Forgive me...forgive my foolish pride.

In his haste to be home, Justin forgot the caution which had served him so well for years. His instinct for danger was submerged in the tide of emotion sweeping through him, a tide that washed clean, washed deep, taking with it the bitterness of betrayal and despair.

He loved and was loved. The certainty brought such joy

as he had never felt. Yet that joy carried a new fear—the fear of loss.

He did not sense danger for himself, only for his beloved wife. Neither did he see the dark, crouching figures waiting for him, hidden in the shadow of the trees. He was amongst them, actually on his own land, when they jumped out at him, perhaps five or six of them. Creatures of the night, brutal, mindless rogues who would murder without cause for a handful of gold. They surrounded him, halting his horse, causing it to rear up in fright.

'Out of my way, scum!' Justin struggled to draw his weapon, but it was too late. They were all over him, hands pulling at him. 'Out of my way!'

They were clawing at him, at his clothes and body, too many of them, dragging at him, hanging on to his horse as it snorted and stumbled in terror—not his own trusted steed but a hired hack that would not be gentled by his voice.

Justin fought them as they dragged him down to the ground. He hit out with his hands and feet, kicking, punching, struggling to free himself. If he could just get to his sword…but there were so many of them, and they were armed with sticks and cudgels, determined on his murder. The blows reined down on him relentlessly, hitting him again and again until one knocked him senseless.

Even after he lay defenceless on the ground, they went on kicking and hitting him until at last they were satisfied he was dead. Then, at last, their leader spoke.

'Away, lads,' he cried. 'We've earned our money. Courtney will pay handsomely for this news.'

They were laughing, excited by what they had done and the prospect of the money it would bring them as they melted like shadows, away into the darkness, leaving their victim lying bloodied and broken on the ground.

Chapter Twelve

'Will you ride with me?' Ralph asked Annelise later that same morning. 'You have not been out since—since I met you by the lake. If you do not take the air you will lose that pretty colour of yours and Justin will accuse me of neglecting you.'

She had not wanted to leave the house lest Justin should arrive while she was gone, but that was foolishness. Why should Justin come in answer to her letter? She had sent it merely to warn him, not to bring him rushing back to her side—or had she? Was she not hoping for his arrival hourly?

'I have been uneasy, Ralph,' she confessed. 'I know it is foolish. You have told me of Justin's instinct for danger—and I know his skill as a swordsman—but still I fear for him. I have this sense…a feeling deep inside me that something bad has happened.'

'You will not help yourself by staying in the house,' Ralph said. 'Come, ride with me. I must go to the village, and you would enjoy the outing. All your tenants are hoping to catch a sight of you.'

'Very well, you have persuaded me.' She smiled at him. 'Only wait until I…'

What she was about to say was forgotten as they heard shouting in the hall, then the door was thrown open and Mrs Holmes came rushing in. Her face was white with shock, her manner so distracted that it was a moment before she could speak.

'Milady…' she gasped, her hand trembling. 'Oh, milady…'

'What is it?' Annelise's heart stopped for one terrible moment. She had sensed something, known instinctively on waking that something was wrong. 'What has happened? You must tell me, Mrs Holmes. Is it news of my husband?'

'He has been…' Mrs Holmes could hardly bring herself to say the words. 'The master has been wickedly attacked, beaten near to death. A woodsman found him. He and his son carried his lordship home.'

'Justin is here?' For a moment nothing else registered. 'Here in this house?'

'Yes, milady…' The housekeeper caught back a sob. 'The men have carried him up to his chamber.'

'I must go to him!' Now it was beginning to sink in. Justin had been attacked. Beaten near to death. Annelise felt the fear rise up in her throat as she ran from the room. 'Justin… Justin…'

Her heart was hammering against her ribs. She could hardly breathe for the terrible fear coursing through her. How could it have happened? Why should Justin have been attacked on his own land?

But of course! The realisation struck home with blinding force. The assassins had been waiting for him, expecting him. Now Annelise understood the significance of Sir Roger Courtney's abuse of her. She had been meant to send for Justin. They had counted on his instant response to an urgent message from his wife.

It was her fault. Annelise was racked with guilt as she paused outside the bedchamber where her husband lay.

Why had she not thought more carefully? She ought to have suspected she was being used to draw Justin here—and in such a way that he would let down his guard. In his concern for her he had raced back alone—abandoning caution. The traitors had plotted cleverly—and they had succeeded.

'We have sent for the doctor,' Holmes told her as she entered the bedchamber, her face revealing the anguish she felt. 'Perhaps you would do better to wait until we have attended to the worst of his hurts, milady.'

'He is alive?' Annelise's eyes begged for hope, but she read none in her faithful servant's face. 'Do not send me away,' she said quietly. 'I am strong enough to bear anything but that.'

Holmes inclined his head and stood to one side, allowing her to take his place. Annelise's heart almost failed her as she saw Justin's bloodstained clothing and his battered, bruised face.

'Oh, my poor love,' she whispered. 'What have they done to you?'

'Do not despair, Annelise.' Lady Beatrice spoke from behind her. 'Forgive me for coming. I do not wish to intrude, but I have some skill with healing. Will you permit me to examine him?'

'If you can help him…' Annelise could barely hold back the tears. 'I should be so grateful, ma'am.'

'First we must cut away his clothes,' said Beatrice. 'So that we can discover whether there are bones broken. Once the blood has been washed from his flesh, we shall be able to tell more surely how severe his injuries are.'

Beatrice ordered warm water and salves to be brought up, then she took a small sharp knife and cut the laces on Justin's clothing, easing it away carefully piece by piece. His cloak had already been discarded, but soon jerkin, breeches, hose and his fine linen shirt lay in shreds on the floor by the bed.

Beatrice began her examination. She was calm, her touch firm, deft and sure. Once Justin moaned as she touched him, and Annelise looked at her in alarm. Was he dying? She moved towards him anxiously. Beatrice glanced up and smiled.

'That is a good sign,' she said. 'He feels pain, so the blows to his head have not robbed him of his senses. I believe most of it is bruising and cuts—though he does have a broken rib which will cause him pain. I believe it should be tightly strapped, but we shall hear what the doctor has to say.'

'But his face—his head,' Annelise said. 'His hair is matted with blood.'

'It may be best to cut his hair short,' suggested Beatrice. 'That way we can be sure of keeping the wound clean.'

Justin had such strong, dark hair. It would be a shame to cut it off, and yet Annelise knew her friend was right.

'We must do everything necessary to save his life—if that be possible.'

'I nursed my husband after he was fearfully wounded in the war,' Beatrice said, a shadow passing over her face. 'He lived, Annelise. It was a fever many years later that took his life. Your husband is in God's hands. All we can do is care for him and pray.'

'I shall pray,' Annelise said, her face white and strained with emotion. She was already praying with every breath she took. 'And I shall help you to nurse him, ma'am.'

'Call me Beatrice. We shall be close companions now and there should be no formality between us.' She smiled at Annelise and laid a hand on hers. 'Courage, my dear.'

Annelise nodded, saying nothing. Warm water and clean linen had been brought up. Between them, Annelise and Beatrice carefully washed away the blood and dirt from Justin's face, then Holmes cut his hair close to the scalp so that they could cleanse a deep gash and apply soothing balm. Once, Justin's eyes flicked open. He threshed wildly, as if in pain, muttering something no one could catch.

Annelise bent over him, pressing her lips briefly to his. 'I am here,' she said. 'I am with you, Justin. Do not fear for me, my love. I am safe—and we shall care for your hurts. You will be well again.'

Her words seemed to calm him, though she did not think he was truly aware of her with his conscious mind.

They had finished bathing Justin when the physician arrived. He made a brief examination and confirmed all that Beatrice had said, looking at her with respect.

'You have done everything you ought,' he said. 'I believe his lordship's injuries to be serious, but not fatal. It is the fever you must watch for, ma'am. If you see signs of infection you must send for me at once. In the meantime, I will send certain physics that may help you, but I think his lordship to be in good hands, and if he recovers it will be because of his devoted nurses.'

'Well,' said Beatrice after he had gone. 'I dare say he meant well, but I am glad you were not alone here, Annelise. I do not imagine he would have been of much comfort to you. We shall see what he sends us, but I have my own remedies. I use strange things sometimes; the knowledge was handed down to me by my grandmother, who many folk thought of as having unnatural powers. Had she not been under the protection of a great lord, I dare say she would have been burned as a witch.' Beatrice laughed. 'But she died at a great age in her own bed—so she must have had some skills.'

Annelise was standing by Justin. Tears trickled down her cheeks as she saw how pale he was, his breathing so shallow now that she was afraid he was dying.

'I do not care what arts you use to save him,' she said, looking at Beatrice through her tears. 'All that matters to me is that Justin should be well and strong again.'

'The physician spoke truly concerning the fever,' Beatrice said thoughtfully. 'I shall leave you to sit with your husband for a while, Annelise. There are certain things I need, which I believe I may find in your woods. With your leave, I shall go in search of them.'

'Pray take Ralph with you,' Annelise entreated. 'If Justin could be attacked like this on our own land…' She shuddered. 'You must take care!'

'Ralph has already summoned help,' Beatrice said. 'He has sent word to London—and several men from the village will be set to patrol the gardens. Besides, I should imagine these rogues believe they have killed your husband. For the moment his enemies will lie low, in fear of retribution from the law.'

What of the future? Annelise wondered. Would they ever be truly safe until these traitors were caught and punished?

Her thoughts were uneasy as she dwelt on the matter momentarily, then Justin moaned and she forgot all else as she bent over him.

'He feels hot,' she cried, looking at Beatrice in alarm. 'What must I do?'

Beatrice laid her hand on Justin's brow. 'It is the fever,' she said. 'Keep him cool by bathing his face, Annelise. I will go to prepare the cures that may help him.'

'Thank you.'

Annelise could say no more. Her throat tightened with emotion as she watched Justin begin to toss and jerk wildly. The fever was taking hold of him and she feared for his life.

'Do not die, my love,' she whispered, laying a cloth soaked in cool water on his forehead. 'You must be strong, Justin. You must fight this—for my sake and your own.'

Of course he could not hear her. She knew that, and yet she continued to talk to him as she kept her vigil at his side, telling him all the things she had never said as she lay in his arms.

'I loved you from the first moment I saw you,' she whispered. 'You were so bold and full of life—and your eyes seemed to laugh at me. And then, when we met in the woods, I thought you would kiss me and I wanted you to love me. Even then, I knew you were the only man I would ever love.'

Justin seemed to have quietened a little. She bent over him, stroking his brow.

'You looked so handsome. My foolish heart was yours from that moment,' she said, a little sob in her throat. 'We have cut off your beautiful hair, Justin. You do not look so fine now, my love, but it will grow again—and I do not mind it. I love you still, will love you always.'

'No...' Justin's cry startled her. 'No! Annelise...must get to Annelise...'

She touched his shoulder. His skin was so hot! He was burning up with the fever.

'You are with me, dearest,' she said, wringing her cloth out in the water. She soothed it over his shoulder and his neck, wincing as she saw him flinch. He must be in such pain, and there was so little she could do for him. 'You will get well, Justin,' she told him, a look of determination in her eyes. 'You cannot leave me. You have to fight for me—for us. I want you to hold me in your arms again. I want you to love me, Justin. I want to bear your sons. You cannot leave me. I will not let you go. I will not let you go...'

Annelise did not know how long she sat by Justin's side, talking, praying for some sign of recovery. It was dark when Beatrice came into the room, carrying a basin, which was covered by a cloth, and a small vial of dark liquid.

'Leave me now,' she said in her gentle voice. 'Yes, you

must, Annelise. You must rest, my dear. Come to me again just before dawn. We shall take it in turns to nurse him.'

'He is so hot,' Annelise said, fearing to leave him even for a moment lest he should die. 'Nothing I do seems to help.'

'Let me see what I can do,' Beatrice said, giving her a little push towards the door. 'You will gain nothing by making yourself ill.'

Annelise left reluctantly. She went through the adjoining dressing room into her own bedchamber, the tiredness beginning to seep over her as her maid came to help her remove her gown.

'You should not have waited, Bertha. It is very late.'

'I would have sat all night,' the girl replied. 'I would that I could be of real help to you, milady—but I have no skill in nursing the sick.'

'Lady Beatrice knows what to do,' Annelise said. 'Leave me now. I shall lie down as I am. I do not think that I shall be able to sleep at all—but if I do not wake in two hours, I am to be woken.'

'Yes, milady.'

After the maid had gone, Annelise lay down and closed her eyes. She wept for a few minutes as the realisation of how near to death Justin really was swept over her. Fevers killed so many—and wounds could so easily become infected. No one understood why this should be, and even the most skilled physicians were unable to help if a wound went bad.

'Please, God, do not let him die,' Annelise prayed fervently. 'Please let him live. I beg you, do not let my husband die.'

She had thought she would not sleep, but she was exhausted by grief and fear and she slipped into an uneasy dream. She woke suddenly as Bertha shook her shoulder, sitting up in alarm.

'What is it? Is he worse?'

'I do not know, milady. You asked me to wake you at dawn.'

'Have you slept yourself?'

The maid shook her head. 'I feared to oversleep so sat up all night, to rouse you at the appointed time.'

'Then you must rest now.'

Annelise went swiftly through to the next room. In the candlelight, she could see Beatrice bending over Justin. She had bound his head with linen and smeared something over his face.

'Do not be alarmed by the smell,' Beatrice said as she approached the bed. 'It is not pleasant, but it will help to heal his hurts; I promise you that, my dear.'

'How is he?'

'Still in the grip of the fever,' Beatrice replied, 'but I think he is a little easier.' She showed Annelise the tiny vial. 'This is very strong. Two drops on his tongue in another hour—and then every hour until the fever breaks. Judge the time by the glass exactly. See, I am turning it now. When the sand runs out, that will be the time. Just two drops measured into the spoon, no more or you may do more harm than good.'

Annelise laid her hand on Justin's brow. She looked at Beatrice in surprise. 'He is much cooler.'

'Yes, but the heat may return,' Beatrice cautioned. 'I believe we may have caught the fever early enough to stop it gaining too tight a hold, but I cannot be certain. Watch over him, Annelise. He may turn cold all of a sudden, and that can be just as dangerous.'

'I shall watch him,' Annelise promised. 'But you look so tired, Beatrice. You must rest now.'

'Yes, I must rest,' Beatrice agreed. 'I have done all I can for the moment—and I have one of my headaches coming on.'

'Please go to bed. You have done so much. I cannot thank you enough.'

After Beatrice had gone, Annelise took Justin's hand in her own. She began to talk to him again.

'The night I went with Earl Rathbone,' she said. 'I was so jealous, Justin. You were with that woman—Madame Varennes. She looked so beautiful—so exciting! I thought you must be in love with her and I could not bear it. I wanted to hurt you—to make you angry. When you challenged the Earl to a duel I was terrified. I thought you might be killed.' She choked back a sob. 'You must not die. I could not bear it. If you died I should want to die too.'

Justin moved restlessly. His lips parted but no sound came out.

'No, no, rest. You must rest now, my love. I am here. I am with you. I love you.'

He seemed to settle again at her words. Annelise sat quietly, waiting until all the grains of sand had run through the glass before giving him the two drops of liquid as Beatrice had shown her.

It was some while later that she noticed Justin seemed to be shivering. When she touched him, it was to discover that his skin was cold and clammy. Beatrice had warned her to look out for the change. She pulled a coverlet over him, but it did not stop him shaking violently. The room was warm enough, yet he was so cold.

Annelise slipped into bed beside him, putting her arms about him and trying to instil her own warmth into him. He moaned a little, then nestled his head against her, still obviously in the grip of the sickness.

'Annelise...must get to Annelise...'

She knew it was only the fever talking, but felt tears on her cheeks. She was humbled by his grief, his concern for her. Clearly he had been desperate to come to her. She sensed the need in him, the love he had been unable to put into words, and she understood.

'Do not weep for me, Justin,' she whispered, her lips close to his ear. 'I am here. I am with you. You are ill, but you will recover, my love. We shall be happy together.'

She stroked his shorn hair, which was damp with sweat and had begun to curl close to his scalp. 'What fools we were, Justin. Both of us—allowing our pride to keep us apart. We must never, never be so foolish again.'

He murmured something she could not decipher, his breathing seeming to ease as he rested against her breast. She realised that he had stopped shivering; he was warmer now, easier.

Had the fever truly gone? Annelise prayed it had, but a little later he began to toss and turn restlessly, and she felt the heat rising in him once more.

It was time for more of Beatrice's cure. Annelise measured two drops into a spoon and dripped them on to his tongue. He made a sound of protest, as if the taste disturbed him, but soon afterwards she saw that he was peaceful. His skin was cooler, but not cold this time.

Annelise sat in the chair by the bed. It had a high, carved back and was not in the least comfortable. Her back had begun to ache. She sighed and stood up, walking over to the window to look out. It was raining hard, lashing down into the earth so hard that huge puddles had begun to form.

'Annelise…'

She heard the whispered cry, turning back to the bed and thinking the fever must have returned. Then she saw that his eyes were open and he was looking at her…seeing her.

'Justin,' she said, her voice catching with emotion. 'You are awake, my love. How do you feel?'

'As if a carriage and six horses had ridden over me,' he said. 'My head has a thousand war drums beating inside it—and my mouth tastes foul.'

'I think that may be the drops Beatrice made for you,' Annelise said, smiling. 'You looked as if they tasted nasty the last time I gave them to you—but I think they have served you well, Justin. You have had a nasty fever. I was afraid you might…'

'Die?' He smiled oddly. 'I am too stubborn for that, Annelise. May I have some water?'

She fetched the water in a pewter cup. He tried to sit up but gave a groan of pain and fell back against the pillows, clearly exhausted. Annelise slipped her arm about his shoulders, supporting him while he sipped the cool water.

'Did the cat die?' Justin wrinkled his nose. 'What is this disgusting stuff all over me? It smells putrid.'

'It is a mixture of my own preparing.' Beatrice had come in unobserved and was watching with a look of amusement in her eyes. 'I see you are much recovered, my lord.'

'I'm as weak as a kitten,' he muttered. 'What in hell happened to me?'

'You do not remember?' Annelise stared at him. 'You were set upon and beaten by some ruffians—here on our own land.'

'Courtney's men, I suppose.' Justin closed his eyes. 'I cannot recall what occurred. I know only that I was in a hurry to reach you. I must have been careless.'

'Do not distress yourself,' Annelise said. 'It does not matter now.'

'But it does,' objected Justin. 'I dare say Courtney's rogues have been paid for their work and are gone by now. He probably imagines me dead. But when he realises his mistake…' Justin reached for her hand. 'I cannot protect you like this. You must promise me not to stray too far from the house.'

'Your wife will have no time for long walks,' Beatrice put in with a smile. 'You are unlikely to leave your bed for some weeks to come and she will naturally be here at your side.'

'Some weeks!' The look of revulsion in Justin's eyes made both women laugh. 'Good grief, woman. I cannot lie here for weeks. I should die of the tedium!'

'I see we shall have some work to make our patient behave,' said Beatrice. 'It is always the strongest who are the most difficult to nurse. You shall get up as soon as you are able, my lord—but I doubt you will manage it just yet.'

Justin laughed, then winced as he felt the pain of his cracked rib. 'Do not scold me, ma'am. I am not ungrateful for your care, but I have never been known for my patience.'

'I dare say you have not, but you will learn,' said Annelise firmly. 'You are married to me now, Justin—and I do not intend to let you leave this bed until you are well enough to do so without harm.'

'Indeed, madam?' A smile tugged at the corners of his mouth. 'Am I to be petticoat ruled?'

'Until you are recovered.'

'Shall you sit with me? Shall you read to me and keep me company, Annelise?'

'Of course, my husband.' Her eyes teased him wickedly. 'But only if you are good and swallow Beatrice's drops without complaint.'

Justin suffered the dose in silence, but his face reflected his horror at the taste.

'I shall not ask what is in that stuff,' he said with a look of disgust. 'But I trust that I am not being poisoned, ma'am?'

'Never fear, sir,' Beatrice replied, and smiled. 'I think you will not need it again. It was for the fever—but the healing balm to which you objected when I first came in is very necessary. We shall need to apply it for another week at least.'

Justin suspected he was being teased, but there was no mercy in Beatrice's eyes, though Annelise's expression brought a wry smile to his lips.

'I see I am to be given no quarter,' he said. 'It is a conspiracy between you. Very well, then, ladies. I warn you, you will not find me an easy victim. I shall leave this bed within four days at most!'

In fact it was five before he could stand without groaning from the pain, but by the end of a week he was able to sit in a chair with cushions at his back for an hour or so at a time.

Despite his threats, Justin was actually a very good patient. He bore the foul-smelling balm being soothed into his battered flesh with admirable restraint, swearing only two or three times, and was honest enough to admit that it eased his pain.

'Are you a witch, ma'am?' he teased Beatrice after she had taken away the bandage around his head some ten days later and pronounced the wound healed. 'I know well that men have died of such beatings. I think I have you to thank for my life.'

'My cures and your wife's prayers.'

'Yes.' Justin threw Annelise a loving look as she came into the room. 'I should not have recovered so easily without my wife's devotion. I am fortunate to have such friends.'

'You are very strong,' Beatrice said. 'Your will to survive had much to do with your recovery.'

She left then, as Justin held out his hand to Annelise. 'You gave me the will to live,' he said. 'Even when I was caught in the fever I sensed you with me. I sensed your love.'

'I told you of it over and over again.' Annelise knelt down at his side, and, looking up into his eyes, she smiled.

'I was such a fool, Justin. I loved you from the start but was afraid to let you see it.'

'And I was afraid to love you,' he said. 'Can you forgive me for all the unkind things I have said and done?'

'I think now they were said out of jealousy.' She reached up to kiss him on the lips. 'So how could I not forgive? I too was jealous and behaved badly.'

'How generous you are, my lovely wife.' He winced with pain as he drew her to him and kissed her hungrily. There was a rueful look in his eyes as he gazed down at her. 'How much longer before I can make love to you?'

'Be patient, Justin,' she said. 'You are healing well, and we have the rest of our lives to make love.'

'A hundred years would not be long enough,' he said on a sigh. 'I want you now, Annelise. And I do not think I can wait much longer…'

Chapter Thirteen

Justin was with Ralph in the long gallery when Annelise came upon them just over a week later. They were fencing. She paused to watch them, noticing the effort it cost Justin to lunge forward. His wounds had almost healed by now, but it still caused him pain to do certain things—though making love was not one of them.

He had become her tender lover once more, and these past few days had been some of the happiest she had ever known. Justin was so different from the harsh man who had been her guardian. He laughed often, teasing both her and his friends. In the evenings, they sang and danced together, entertaining their neighbours, who came often to visit now.

Annelise wanted their lives to remain peaceful and happy—but, seeing the determined efforts Justin was making to regain his skill as a swordsman, she felt as if a dark cloud had moved across their world. Justin would not try so hard so soon if he did not think it would be necessary to fight his enemy.

She stiffened her shoulders, pride forbidding her to show fear. As they noticed her approach, the men ceased their practice and she saw Justin stifle a groan of pain.

'Forgive me for disturbing you,' she said. 'I would not have done so but that a letter has come from Lady Emily…'

'Something important?' Justin raised his brows. 'It must be or you would have told me later. What is wrong?'

'Nothing is precisely wrong,' she said. 'Lady Emily has… Mama has invited us to her wedding next month.'

Justin looked stunned. 'Mama is to marry again? After all these years! I would not have thought it.'

'Come now,' offered Ralph. 'Lady Emily is a handsome woman; you cannot deny that, Justin.'

'Yes—and I believe she is sometimes lonely,' Annelise put in quickly. 'You must not mind too much, Justin.'

'Who is she to marry?'

'Sir Harold Mortimer…a cousin of Lord Montgomery.'

'That old fool!' Justin muttered contemptuously. 'He has hardly a penny to his name. If she must marry, she had done better to look higher than a baronet.'

'She says she is very fond of him and that he is a kind man,' Annelise said, frowning slightly. 'You would not begrudge her such happiness?'

'I cannot prevent her if she is set upon marrying this man,' Justin said, a harsh note in his voice. 'But I shall not give such a match my blessing. Nor shall I attend the wedding.'

'Justin!' Annelise was shocked. 'You are unkind. Your approval means so much to her.'

'Then she had better change her mind and send Mortimer packing,' he replied, unsmiling.

'That is unfair…'

'I do not wish to argue with you.' Justin turned and picked up his sword. 'Come, Ralph. We must finish our work.'

'Well, I shall go,' Annelise cried. 'I am warning you, Justin. If you will not take me, I shall go without you.'

He ignored her, intent on his fencing match with Ralph.

She was piqued that he could turn away, that he could dismiss his mother's wedding as of no account. How could he? It was unkind—unlike the man she had come to know recently.

Walking quickly from the gallery, Annelise went upstairs to put on her cloak. She was cross with Justin. She had not expected this of him. Not now that they had reached an understanding. What had made him react that way? She knew that he did care for his mother—so was it only his mother's suitor he disliked?

It was an age since Annelise had fed the swans. She collected some pieces of bread from the housekeeper, then set out towards the park and the lake. The wind was bitterly cold, but her cloak had a hood and she pulled it up over her head.

The exercise was welcome after several days cooped up in the house, and Annelise's temper cooled as she fed pieces of bread to the swans. They were so hungry, poor things! The weather had been frosty of late, and she had neglected them in her concern for Justin.

Annelise knew her husband now, and as she thought about it she realised their argument had been foolish, brought on by Justin's memories of his mother as a child. Perhaps he was afraid of losing her again? In any case, she was at fault for quarrelling with him.

She turned to return to the house, then froze in fear as she saw the figure dressed all in black, his cloak flapping about him in the wind, making him look like some monstrous bird.

'What are you doing here?' she cried. 'How dare you come here? After what you've done…'

'It seems those knaves failed to dispose of your husband,' Courtney said, a sneer on his thin lips. 'So I have come myself. First I shall kill you, madam, and then…'

Annelise screamed and started to run, her heart pounding

with fear. He was mad, evil! A wicked murderer. He was
intent on revenge and she knew herself in danger.

Courtney came after her. She could hear his feet thud-
ding behind her, the rasping of his breath as he gradually
gained on her, catching her before she had gone more than
a short distance. She struggled as he grabbed hold of her
cloak, twisting away only to be caught again, firmly this
time. She screamed out defiantly, her hands striking out at
him, nails clawing at his face, drawing blood. He let go of
her and staggered back, putting his fingers to the wound
and finding blood on his cheek.

'You witch! I'll kill you now,' he cried. 'I'll make you
pay for that, you wild cat.' Yet even as he moved pur-
posefully towards her once more the sound of shouting and
pounding hooves reached them, and, looking round, they
saw two horsemen riding hard towards them. She heard
Courtney's cry of alarm as he realised the danger. 'Damn
him!'

Before Annelise could really take in what was happening, Justin and Ralph were upon them. Justin jumped from
the saddle and came to her, his face grey with fright.

'You little fool!' he cried to her in his fear for her. 'Why
did you leave the house alone?'

'Forgive me,' she said on a sob. 'I was upset. I—I did
not think.'

'You never do!' He swung round to face Courtney, who
was being held at bay by Ralph's pistol. 'As for you, sir—
there's reckoning to be had between us. And this time you
will meet me face to face, like a man.'

'Willingly!' Courtney threw back his cloak, revealing his
sword. 'This time you die, Saintjohn!'

Pushing Annelise behind him, Justin drew his own blade.
Courtney rushed at him, forcing him to retreat behind a
flurry of wild blows that took him by surprise.

'Damn you, sir!' Ralph cried angrily. 'Fight fair. Give him time to prepare.'

'Stand back, Ralph,' Justin warned. 'Sheath your weapon. This is between Courtney and me.'

Annelise retreated to where Ralph stood, having dismounted the better to see fair play. She felt sick with fear as she watched Justin retreat yet again beneath a welter of furious blows. It was too soon! He was not well enough to fight. She had seen how much pain it had caused him to fence with his friend—and this would be a fight to the death.

'Go back to the house,' Ralph warned softly. 'It is not fitting for you to see this, Annelise.'

Her heart was racing wildly. It seemed to her that Justin was being driven back again and again, that he was finding the odds too difficult. She knew he was skilled in swordplay, but he had not long risen from his sickbed; he must be weaker than usual, and stiff from lack of practice. Surely he could not hope to win?

'I cannot,' she whispered, her throat contracting with emotion. 'If Justin…' She could not say the words, her eyes pleading with Ralph for understanding. 'Please do not…'

'You do only harm here,' her friend said in a harsh tone she had never before heard from him. 'Do as you are told, Annelise! Go back and warn the servants. If Courtney wins this fight, he shall not escape the hangman's noose. I swear it by the Holy Book.'

Annelise was subdued by this new sternness in Ralph. She went reluctantly to do his bidding, though her heart was heavy and she could hardly bear to tear herself away lest something terrible happened. Yet Ralph was right. Her presence could only hamper Justin. He would be easier if she were out of danger and saved the horror of watching this terrible fight.

She ran the last few hundred yards, rushing into the

house in near panic to warn the servants of what was happening. Holmes took charge at once, summoning all the men from the kitchens.

Within minutes, a small army of servants set out, armed to the teeth with whatever weapons had come to hand: knives, axes and a warming pan were clutched determinedly as they went marching off to defend their lord.

Had it not been so terrifying, Annelise could have found the sight amusing. She would have followed them, but Beatrice would not let her go.

'No!' she said firmly, catching her arm. 'You must stay here, my dear. Ralph was right to send you back. This is men's business. Justin would not want you to see... But do not fear his death, Annelise. Ralph will not let it happen. I am sure he would shoot rather than see Justin murdered.'

Annelise could not answer her. She was sick with fear. Why did these terrible things always happen when she argued with Justin? She ought never to have gone to the lake alone! If he died... Oh, no! She could not bear this. She must go. She must go to him now, this minute.

She would have defied Beatrice or any other to be with Justin, but just as she felt she could not bear to wait another moment she heard a commotion outside the house. Beatrice tried to stop her, but she rushed past her. She must know what was happening!

The men were coming back—carrying something. A man's limp body! She gave a scream of fear as Justin's name rose to her lips and she feared him dead. And then she saw him. He was walking slowly, Ralph's arm about him, supporting him. She could tell he was in pain, but at least he was alive...he was alive!

'Justin!' she cried, and ran towards him, tears of relief and joy streaming down her face. 'Oh, Justin. I thought...I thought he would kill you. You are not well enough to fight a duel.'

'Courtney made the mistake of assuming I would be too weak to fight,' Justin said, a little smile of satisfaction on his lips. 'He has paid the price for that in full. As for you, Annelise...'

Whatever Justin had been about to say was lost as a little moan issued from his lips and he fainted.

'It is all right, I have him,' Ralph said as her face turned ashen. 'He was too proud to be carried home, but he near swooned twice on the way.'

Annelise saw blood on Justin's shirt. She looked at Ralph anxiously. 'He has been wounded!'

'It is a mere scratch,' Ralph said. 'But I think his rib is troubling him. He may have damaged himself inside.'

Beatrice had come out to meet them. 'Carry him up to his room,' she said. 'I shall examine him. It is just as I expected. The foolish man would try to do too much too soon.'

Justin recovered his senses while she was examining him. He swore at Beatrice when she bound him tightly, but apologised almost immediately.

'It is damned sore,' he growled, then gave her a rueful smile. 'But that does not excuse my language. Forgive me, ma'am. I was wrong to abuse you. I fear I have not yet learned to curb my unfortunate temper.'

His eyes sought Annelise's, as if to convey a message. She smiled at him. 'Nor I,' she said. 'It seems we are well matched, sir.'

'So we are,' he said, 'for good or ill.'

Beatrice took Ralph's arm, leading him determinedly from the room.

Annelise moved towards the bed. She reached for Justin's hand. His fingers curled possessively about hers.

'Forgive me...'

'Forgive me, Justin. I was at fault.'

They spoke almost together and laughed.

Justin pulled a face. 'It hurts to laugh. I shall have to rest for a few days before we go up to London.'

'To London?' She stared at him in surprise. 'Does that mean you will take me to the wedding?'

'Have I any choice?' Justin pretended to scowl but she could see he was not angry, merely teasing her. 'You would go alone if I refused. Besides, Ralph took me to task after you left us. He made me go after you—and then we discovered you had gone to feed the swans.' His eyes darkened with remembered fear. 'Holmes told me a man had been seen loitering in the woods earlier. I was so terrified, Annelise. I knew if it was Courtney he would try to harm you. It was his only way of getting to me after the last attempt.'

'And he needed to fight you before you had recovered your full strength,' Annelise said, looking thoughtful. 'What a coward he was, Justin. He tried to have you killed, and when that did not work—shame on him!'

'He tried to have me killed more than once,' Justin said wryly. 'Why do you imagine I sent you here with Ralph to guard you? I always feared that he would harm you. I hoped to draw his anger by remaining in London and pursuing him and the rest of those traitors—but in the back of my mind it was you I feared for.' His eyes met hers in an intense, burning look that made her tingle all over. 'I might live on without you, my love, but my life would have no meaning. When I saw you struggling against Courtney's attempts to capture you I was sick with fear. Until that moment I had not fully understood all you mean to me.'

'Oh, Justin,' she whispered, tears in her eyes. 'It was my fault again. I disobeyed you. What a trouble I am to you!'

'You are undoubtedly,' Justin said with a gleam in his eyes, 'the most wilful, obstinate, troublesome wench I have ever met—but you are also the most amusing and charming little wretch. I do not doubt that you will cause me a great deal of trouble in the future, Annelise, but I could not bear to lose you.'

Annelise gave him a sparkling look. 'You are not gallant, sir. You were supposed to answer less truthfully but with more politeness, and assure me that whatever I do I shall be no trouble at all.'

'As your legion of admirers would, naturally.' Justin scowled at her ferociously but there was a twinkle in his eye. 'I dare say I shall have to fight a score of duels over you before I have finished, Madam Wife.'

Annelise laughed delightedly, then bent her head to kiss him briefly on the lips, her eyes bright with a wicked challenge. 'What do you suppose husbands are for, my lord?'

'Minx!' Justin murmured. 'Had I not been strictly forbidden any strenuous exercise by Beatrice, I should enjoy showing you who is master here, Annelise. As it is, I must leave that lesson for another day.'

She heard the suppressed sigh of pain and knew what it must be costing him to banter with her like this.

'You should rest,' she said, pressing his hand. 'I should leave you to sleep, my love.'

He caught her hand. 'No, don't leave me. Stay here with me, Annelise. Read some poetry to me. I like to hear your voice. I like to know you are here beside me.'

'Very well,' she said, smiling. 'But I shall sit here in this chair beside the bed and you must try to sleep.'

'La! How pretty she looks,' cried Lady Emily as Justin and Annelise were shown into the parlour where she was sitting writing letters. She got up and came to them, giving her hands to Annelise and kissing her. Then she turned to Justin, searching for something in his face. What she saw made her smile inwardly. 'And you, my son. You look tired—but you have recovered from your wounds?'

'Yes, Mama,' he agreed, gazing into her eyes. 'It has taken far too long, but I have made a full recovery. Annelise seems to be the cure for all my ills.'

She understood that he was speaking of much more than the beating he had taken and nodded.

'Thank you for coming, Justin. I was afraid you would not be inclined to wish me happy.'

He frowned, a rueful expression in his eyes. 'I am not overjoyed by your choice of a husband, Mama. I believe you might have looked higher, had you wished—but I do most sincerely wish you happy.'

'Harry is such a gentle soul,' Lady Emily said. 'You do not know him, Justin. He is very fond of me. He will be faithful and kind—and that is all I ask.'

Justin nodded. How could he deny her the happiness he had found for himself? Any anger or resentment he had harboured against her had vanished long ago; he had simply been too proud—or too unsure—to show his very real affection for her.

'And when am I to meet this paragon, Mama?'

She heard the teasing note in his voice and her tension lifted. 'Tomorrow evening,' she said. 'I have invited him to dine with us—just a small family affair.'

'Then I shall see if he is what you believe him,' Justin said. 'If he is worthy of you—then you have my blessing, Mama.' He leaned towards her, his lips brushing her cheek in the softest of kisses.

'Thank you, my son.' Her eyes were wet with tears. She turned to Annelise once more, embracing her. 'Thank you, my dearest daughter,' she whispered close to her ear. 'Thank you so very much for giving my son back to me.'

It was the following evening. Annelise was dressing for dinner and beginning to feel anxious. Where was Justin? He had gone out earlier that day, saying he had some unfinished business and promising to return in time to meet his mother's fiancé, but the guests would be arriving very soon and Justin had not returned.

Surely he would not deliberately stay away from his mother's special dinner? After he had promised to be there! He could not be so unkind.

Annelise was torn between anxiety and doubt as she went downstairs. If Justin had done this to show discourtesy to his mother's future husband she would be disappointed in him—and yet she could not believe it. He would surely have said outright if he had changed his mind about attending.

Lady Emily looked at her as she entered the large parlour. 'Justin has not yet returned?'

'Not yet, Mama. I cannot think what can be keeping him.'

'We must suppose it to be business,' Lady Emily said, putting on a smile to hide her disappointment. 'I dare say he will come soon. Now, my love, I want to present you to Sir Harold. I have told him a great deal about you, of course, and he is eager to meet you.'

The gentleman standing a little behind her came forward to greet Annelise. He was of medium height and stature, his hair almost pure white and his features unremarkable—until he smiled. There was such warmth in his eyes then that Annelise understood at once why her friend had chosen him.

'Lady Saintjohn, I am delighted to meet you,' he said. 'Lady Emily has told me much about you, and I am happy to make your acquaintance at last. I know how much you have come to mean to my dearest Emily.' He glanced lovingly at his fiancée.

'And I am very happy for you both,' replied Annelise without hesitation. 'I must ask you to forgive my husband, sir. I imagine he has been detained…'

'That is more true than you know,' said a voice from the doorway, and they all turned to look at Ralph, who was standing there. 'Justin has been arrested. He is at this moment a prisoner in the Tower.'

'Justin—a prisoner in the Tower?' Annelise's hand flew to her throat. 'Why? What has he done to anger His Majesty?'

'He was arrested for the murder of Sir Roger Courtney,' Ralph said. 'Someone laid the charge against him and the King sent his own guard to seize him.'

'But it was a duel!' Annelise cried. 'In my defence and in answer to Sir Roger's threats against his own life. How could His Majesty believe such terrible lies?'

'He is angry because Justin disobeyed him,' Ralph said. 'I asked for an audience to put Justin's side of the story but was denied.'

'I shall go to His Majesty,' Lady Emily said at once. 'He will listen to me.'

'Not this time.' Ralph's eyes were on Annelise. 'The King will see only you concerning this matter. He sent his page to tell me. He will see you at nine this evening in private. I am to escort you to the south door, where we shall be met by the royal page. He will conduct you to the King's private apartments.'

'Oh, no!' Lady Emily cried, looking at Annelise in horror. 'You see what this means? I knew His Majesty was interested in you, but I never thought he would...' She stopped, obviously in some distress.

'That he would use such a ruse to make me his mistress?' Annelise's eyes opened wide in surprise. 'Do you truly believe he would do such a thing?'

Looking at their stunned faces, Annelise could read their thoughts. All of them believed she would be required to pay a price for Justin's freedom.

'What will you do?' Lady Emily asked. 'You cannot...

I think Justin might…' Her voice caught on a sob of despair. 'This is too unkind. He was so much happier. He loves you so much, Annelise. If he ever discovered that you…' She broke off, unable to voice her thoughts. 'Forgive me. I had no right…'

'Would you have me leave him to rot in the Tower?' Annelise raised her head proudly. She knew she would do whatever was necessary for Justin's sake. 'But I think you wrong His Majesty, Mama. I do not believe he is so unkind as to demand something that cannot be freely given. I believe he will listen to my story and do what is right.'

She saw disbelief in their eyes. They all thought she would have to sacrifice her honour to save Justin's liberty— and perhaps his life.

'Of course, I am sure you are right,' Lady Emily said, and came to kiss her cheek. 'I have perfect faith in you, Annelise. You will know what you have to do. No matter what it is, I shall always respect and love you.'

But Justin would not. Annelise understood what lay unspoken. If she gave herself to the King in return for Justin's freedom, he would never forgive her. It would be the end of their new companionship; the love that was blossoming so sweetly between them would shrivel and die. Yet how could she refuse if her husband's liberty—even his life— was at stake?

'I am sure Justin will be free very soon,' she said, gazing at Lady Emily, the sparkle of tears in her eyes. 'The King will listen to reason. I am certain of it.'

Chapter Fourteen

She was not so sure an hour or so later, when the royal page conducted her to His Majesty's apartments by way of the back stairs. Her visit was clearly meant to be a secret, which seemed to indicate that Lady Emily might be right in her suspicions.

'If you will wait here, ma'am,' the page said, showing her into an elegantly appointed chamber. 'His Majesty will be with you shortly.'

As he bowed and went away, Annelise began to take notice of her surroundings. There were several fine paintings on the walls, and it was while she was studying these that the door opened softly behind her and the King entered. He had been there a moment or two before she realised, and when she turned to look she saw that he was frowning.

'You admire my pictures, madam?'

'Yes, very much,' Annelise replied, curtseying respectfully. He motioned her to rise. 'I understand Your Majesty's father was a great collector?'

'He was indeed…but many of his pictures were lost at the time of the war,' Charles said, his eyes dark with memories, some of which obviously saddened him. 'However, we begin again…'

'It must be difficult for you, Sire,' Annelise said, feeling genuine sympathy for this man, who had had such a strange life. He had gone from a life of privilege and great riches as a child to years of wandering and uncertainty, often close to capture or death, never knowing for certain where his future lay. His wanderings as an impoverished exile had at last brought him back to England and a throne—which had cost his father his life and must be an uneasy seat. 'How can you ever be certain who is to be trusted? Everyone smiles to your face—but some plot behind your back.'

Charles looked thoughtful. 'You speak of the nest of traitors your husband uncovered, Lady Saintjohn?'

'I spoke in general, Sire.'

'You will be glad to learn that the last of those particular traitors has been dealt with,' Charles told her, his dark, intelligent eyes intent on her face. 'Quietly and without scandal, for the sake of peace. You understand me?' She nodded, knowing that as ever he was trying to walk the narrow path between friend and foe. 'Have you nothing to say to me, madam? Do you not wish to plead for your husband? Do you not know he has been charged with murder?'

'My husband is innocent of that crime…' She saw a gleam in the King's eyes and paused, intuition showing her the way. 'But you know that, Sire. I do not imagine you believed the accusation for a moment. You had Justin arrested for reasons of your own.'

'How astute you are,' said Charles, a flicker of appreciation about his mouth. 'And, since you know so much, perhaps you can tell me what my reasons were?'

'I believe you acted out of friendship,' Annelise replied, meeting his intense gaze steadily. 'You thought it politic to appear to believe the charge—until all the plotters had been taken. It was your intention to prevent another attempt on Justin's life.'

'You are generous, Lady Saintjohn,' drawled Charles, clearly amused but not displeased. 'Tell me, was this my only motive? Might I not have had another…some idea that you might offer a reward for your husband's life? Remember, madam! I could have the Marquis executed if I chose, regardless of his innocence.'

'Another man might,' she acknowledged, a teasing, wicked smile about her mouth as she responded instinctively to his challenge. 'Such action might gain *that* man a reluctant mistress and lose him a true and trusted friend. Yes, another less honourable, less clever man might seek to use his power in such a way—but not *you*, Sire.'

Charles was silent for a moment, and she held her breath, then he threw back his head and gave a great shout of laughter. 'By God, madam! I vow it would be almost worth the loss of both honour and friendship to have you.'

'Justin is a better friend than I should be a mistress. Besides, Sire—have you forgot Madam Barbara's temper?'

'You are a minx,' he murmured, much amused. 'I wish your husband joy of you. And I wish he may beat you for your wilful disobedience.'

'I am an obedient wife, Sire.' Annelise smiled at him. 'And I love him very much.'

'He is indeed a fortunate man. Give me your hand, Lady Saintjohn.' She did so, and he kissed it, a look of appreciation in his eyes. She had used her wits against him and won, but in such a way that he could only admire her. 'And you may rely upon me to tell him so, when I decide to set him free. Another night or so in the Tower will do your obstinate husband no harm, madam. He is a sight too proud for his own good—but we shall forgive him. You may go home now. We shall expect you at Court tomorrow evening.'

'Thank you, Sire.' Annelise curtsied. 'You are very good.'

'And you, madam, are a sight too clever. I wish you goodnight. My page is waiting to take you back the way you came. Sir Ralph will see you home.'

Annelise smiled and thanked him again, then walked to the door. There, she paused to glance back at him. 'Forgive me, Sire.'

He waved her away, his attention seemingly drawn to the pictures she had been studying when he came in.

Annelise knew both Ralph and Lady Emily thought she had given something in return for the promise of Justin's freedom. She had not attempted to deny or justify her actions, feeling that it would seem false. She would answer only to Justin himself.

She prayed he would believe her, but if he did not there was nothing she could do. It was a question of trust. Either Justin believed in her love or he did not.

There was no word of his release when they left for the palace that evening. Annelise was not too disturbed, because she understood that the King must make his point. He was trying to discourage Justin from fighting duels, and, despite admitting the very good reasons behind Courtney's death, was determined to make his displeasure felt.

At Court, Annelise was very soon surrounded by gentlemen eager to welcome her back. Some of them clearly felt that the circumstance of Justin being in prison was an opportunity not to be missed, and Annelise was obliged to fend off more than one would-be seducer.

She did so with a smile and a jest, managing to refuse firmly but in a manner that sent them away laughing and wishing they stood in Saintjohn's place.

She was, the courtiers began to whisper to one another, that jewel beyond price: a faithful wife. She had become so popular that only a few raised their eyebrows and called her a prude. She was swiftly defended by the friends who admired her.

'She is a flawless pearl,' Montgomery declared to his companions. 'A treasure to be coveted—but from a distance.'

It was about halfway through the evening that Justin arrived. He stood for a while at the far side of the room, watching as Annelise danced with the King, his eyes narrowed in concentration, noting the way she smiled and curtsied at the end, her manner a mixture of respect and politeness, but mixed with the intimacy of friendship. For a moment longer she lingered, laughing at something Charles said, then moved away, looking every inch a queen herself.

She had not yet seen him. He waited as Montgomery laid a hand on her arm, saying something that made her laugh. She shook her head at him, clearly admonishing him, very much a woman in control of the situation. He took the rebuke well, bowing over her hand with a smile of wry amusement.

Justin made no move, merely following her progress through the room with interest. She joined a group of friends, which included Rob. He asked her to dance and she accepted.

'So, Saintjohn?' Justin swung round as he heard the slightly mocking tones of his sovereign. 'You have seen fit to obey my commands this evening?'

Justin's eyes narrowed. 'I have always sought to serve you, Sire.'

'In your own way.' Charles nodded, a flicker of something unreadable in his eyes. 'You are too proud, sir—too sure of your own judgement. I hope you have learned a lesson from your sojourn in the Tower?'

Justin inclined his head, saying nothing.

'Ah, you are silent?' There was a gleam of malicious

amusement in the royal eyes. 'Your wife had more to say when she came in answer to my summons.'

'You summoned Lady Saintjohn?' Justin asked with a frown. 'May I ask your purpose, Sire?'

'Your friends tried to defend your disobedience, sir. I wished to hear what your wife had to say on the matter.' Charles smiled ruefully as Justin raised his brows. 'Shall I tell you what took place between us? No, perhaps not. Methinks I shall leave that to the lady herself. I shall tell you only one thing, my proud friend…listen to what others say of her before you lose that infamous temper of yours in future.'

'I have no need of the opinions of others,' Justin replied, smiling as his gaze met Annelise's across the room. 'I know my wife, Sire.'

'You are very fortunate in your choice,' Charles replied, a sparkle of mischief in his eyes. 'As *she* tells me I am in having your friendship.'

Justin watched as the King sauntered away, waving a languid hand. Few in this place knew him as well as Justin, though he did not hang on his every word as others did, and he had seen more of the real man than many of these courtiers would ever glimpse.

Walking across to meet Annelise and Rob as their dance ended, Justin greeted them with a nod, giving no sign that this was anything but a normal evening at Court.

'May I have the pleasure of this next dance, madam? Or have you promised it to another?'

'I have not promised it, my lord.' Annelise felt a quiver of apprehension as Justin took her hand, his strong fingers curling about hers possessively. 'I am happy to see you back, Justin. What did His Majesty say to you just now?'

'Only that he too was glad to see me here—and that I should listen to what people were saying of you.'

For a moment, Annelise was not sure whether he was

serious or teasing her. She gazed up at him, a faint air of anxiety about her.

'What do they say of me?'

'I am not sure I should repeat it,' Justin said, a flicker of mockery in his eyes. 'Did you truly tell His Majesty that he was fortunate to have my friendship?'

He was teasing her! Annelise tipped her head to one side, giving him a naughty look. 'Your dear mama and Ralph both imagine I was asked to pay a price for your release, Justin.'

'And were you?' His tone was level, his manner calm—but she could see a little pulse flicking in his throat.

'Not in so many words.' She laughed huskily. 'But I did happen to mention that you made a better friend than I would a mistress.'

Justin controlled his desire to laugh, but his eyes appreciated her. 'Indeed, madam. And what, pray, did a certain gentleman reply to that?'

'He wished you joy of me and hoped you would beat me often for my disobedience.'

'As I shall,' Justin murmured throatily. 'Be assured, madam. You shall receive the punishment you deserve for your disrespect to His Majesty and more. Indeed, I think I should take you home at once—so that I can begin immediately to instruct you in the proper obedience due to a husband.'

'As you wish, my lord.' Annelise bestowed a demure smile on him. 'I shall always try to be a dutiful wife.'

'Ah, Annelise, my Annelise,' he replied. 'I have little hope of that—but I would not change you for the world.' He smiled lovingly at her. 'Do you wish to dance again—or will you come home?'

'Take me home, Justin,' she said. 'Please take me home.'

Annelise lay nestled close to his shoulder. If his tender, passionate loving were proof of anything, she knew she had nothing to fear from the future.

'You do believe that I did not betray you?' she asked, her long, silky hair brushing over his chest as she bent to look into his face. 'You are the only man I ever want to touch me like this, Justin. Had I been forced to plead for your life…'

'Would you have given even that?' he asked. He touched her face. 'I would rather have died.'

'I know.' She brushed her lips over his to hush him. 'Best that we both die rather than live in bitterness.'

'But you were not forced, were you?' She shook her head. 'I know Charles too well, my love. He might make his feelings known—but he would never force an unwilling lady to yield. Nor was I ever in any real danger.'

Annelise laid her head against Justin's breast, listening to the steady beating of his heart. 'What were they saying of me tonight, Justin?'

His fingers tangled in her hair as she raised her head to look at him. 'I did not listen,' he said. 'I need no one to tell me that I have found that most precious thing—a faithful wife.'

'I could not be anything else. You put your mark on me from the moment we met,' she replied, gazing deep into his eyes. 'My uncle called you Satan. He feared you—feared that you would do me harm—but I have loved you from the first.'

'Satan's mark?' Justin ran a finger down the arch of her back. 'Some have called me that, Annelise.' He frowned as she gazed at him so trustingly. 'You have a right to know about that ship…'

'I already know the order to fire it was not yours. You were sleeping when it was given. You came up on deck and saw the ship in flames—the women screaming—and you tried to get your crew to close up. You shouted to the women to jump. You would have tried to board and rescue them…but one of the crew knocked you senseless. That's why you gave them the ship. You could no longer sail with men who had betrayed you—your principles.'

'Ralph told you all this?'

'No. You forbade him—but he told Beatrice and she had made no vow of silence.'

Justin chuckled deep in his throat. 'Madam, I see you have made powerful friends. Do you know, I think our Beatrice is a witch?'

'No, you must not say it, even in jest,' Annelise said, pressing her fingers to his lips. 'Women have been burnt for such careless words. Her healing salves saved you, Justin—and I shall always be grateful to her.'

'Shall we invite Ralph and Beatrice to be married from our house?' Justin said, his hand smoothing idly over the neat mound of her bottom. 'His own house will be ready in three months from now. We could hold a lavish reception for them here—or in the country?'

'How long before we can go down to the country, Justin?'

His eyes dwelt quizzically on her face. 'As soon as my mother is married. Tell me, Annelise, shall I approve Mama's choice?'

She answered honestly. 'I met Sir Harold only for a short while—but I liked him.'

'Then I dare say he will do,' Justin replied. 'I cannot in any case forbid her.'

'You will give her your blessing?'

'Dare I do otherwise?' he asked. 'You have everyone on your side, Annelise—from His Majesty to my mother, and even my closest friends. Tell me your wish, and I shall obey.'

'Oh, Justin!' She laughed, and poked him in the arm. 'You know full well that you will do exactly as you please.'

'Yes,' he admitted, a gleam in his eyes. 'But it pleases me to please you, my Annelise. I want only to love you, and to make you happy for the rest of our lives.'

'Then take me home as soon as Mama is married,' she whispered, her lips brushing tantalisingly over his. 'Give me your sons, Justin. Spend your time with us—and do not risk your life in discovering traitors.'

'Your wish is my command,' he said huskily. He rolled her beneath him in the bed, his tongue lavishing her breasts with tender passion. 'It is also my own deepest desire, Annelise—and I think we should lose no time in the making of our first son...'

She smiled up at him invitingly. They had no more need of words. Justin had travelled a long and tortuous journey, but at last, in his lovely wife's arms, he had found his heaven.

* * * * *

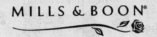

FREE
2 BOOKS
AND A SURPRISE GIFT!

We would like to take this opportunity to thank you for reading this Mills & Boon® book by offering you the chance to take TWO more specially selected titles from the Historical Romance™ series absolutely FREE! We're also making this offer to introduce you to the benefits of the Reader Service™—

- ★ FREE home delivery
- ★ FREE monthly Newsletter
- ★ FREE gifts and competitions
- ★ Exclusive Reader Service discounts
- ★ Books available before they're in the shops

Accepting these FREE books and gift places you under no obligation to buy; you may cancel at any time, even after receiving your free shipment. Simply complete your details below and return the entire page to the address below. *You don't even need a stamp!*

YES! Please send me 2 free Historical Romance books and a surprise gift. I understand that unless you hear from me, I will receive 4 superb new titles every month for just £2.99 each, postage and packing free. I am under no obligation to purchase any books and may cancel my subscription at any time. The free books and gift will be mine to keep in any case.

HOEC

Ms/Mrs/Miss/Mr ....Initials ....
BLOCK CAPITALS PLEASE

Surname ....

Address ....

....

....Postcode ....

Send this whole page to:
UK: FREEPOST CN81, Croydon, CR9 3WZ
EIRE: PO Box 4546, Kilcock, County Kildare (stamp required)